Who Done It?

Who Done It?

edited by

Alice Laurance and Isaac Asimov

Houghton Mifflin Company Boston
1980

009 307 243

Library of Congress Cataloging in Publication Data

Main entry under title:
Who done it?

   1. Detective and mystery stories, American.
2. Detective and mystery stories, English.
I. Laurance, Alice. II. Asimov, Isaac, date
PZ1.W607 [PS648.D4]   823'.0872'08   80-10657
ISBN 0-395-29166-6

Printed in the United States of America

v 10 9 8 7 6 5 4 3 2 1

DEDICATED
with respect and affection to
VIRGINIA KIDD

Foreword On Style

by Isaac Asimov

I would like to tell you why Alice and I have put together this anthology, but I insist on telling you about it in my own way.

Why not? Once I am facing the typewriter, I am an all-powerful monarch. Only I can decide which keys to hit and which words to form.

Nor is this unfair to you, Gentle Reader, since in our free society there is nothing to force you to buy this book and therefore you need not subject yourself to my arbitrariness. (But please *do* buy the book. Alice is not as well off as I am and she could use the money. Besides, my introduction will only last a couple of pages and then you will find all sorts of delightful stories following. You can even, if you are foolish, skip the introduction.)

All right, then, here goes, in my own way.

A book of mine (I forget which one) was reviewed in a fashion to which I have grown accustomed — unimpassioned praise. The reviewer, in other words, felt it was a good book and said so, but I did not detect in the course of the review any feeling of ecstasy on the reviewer's part. Instead, the reviewer seemed to be groping for something negative to say and seemed a little grumpy at my not having made it easier for him to find that something.

This particular reviewer said, "Of course, he has no style!"

This filled me with excitement. At last, I thought, here is a person who knows what style is and who can detect its absence. Here we have an intellectual bloodhound capable of snuffling out the faintest trace of style to its lair.

So I wrote a humble letter to the reviewer. "Dear Reviewer," I said, "For decades, I have tried to be as good a writer as possible, and this is a hard thing to do when no one can say, clearly, what makes writing good. For one thing, I've never known what style is and maybe that's why I don't have any. Since you have detected the absence of style, you must know what it is. I wonder, therefore, if you would be so kind as to tell me what style is so that I can sprinkle some of it over my next book and avoid displeasing you."

You cannot conceive my heartbreak when I got no answer at all.

What was there to do? I had to sit down and figure it out for myself. "What is style?" I asked myself, and after considerable thought, I came to some conclusions which I will now share with you. They are purely personal ones and there may well be Great Literary Critics who will disagree with me. It is a measure of my tolerance that I have decided to allow them to.

First, just to get the underbrush out of the way, let me tell you what style is not. It is not, of necessity, complicated and convoluted writing.

Thus, another reviewer, writing of my book *In Memory Yet Green* (the first volume of my autobiography) says, "It is astonishing that he can do so much with simple declarative sentences."

When a person says, "It is astonishing that —" it may be that what he really means to say is "I'm not very bright so I am astonished that —"

There is, after all, nothing wrong with simple declarative sentences, just as there is nothing wrong with a simple medium-done filet mignon. Some people like ketchup and I am happy for them, but how would you feel about someone who was, supposedly, an expert on food who said, "It is astonishing that filet mignon tastes as good as it does without ketchup."

So, then, what is style?

There are two chief aspects to any piece of writing: 1) what you say and 2) how you say it. The former is "content" and the latter is "style."

Everyone has his own way of writing something. It can be unbearably bad, or transcendently good. No one could possibly bear it in the first case and no one could possibly cavil at it in the second case. Very often the way of writing something falls in between, pleasing some people and displeasing others. (After all, tastes differ — which is fortunate since otherwise every man in the world would try to seduce the same woman.)

What you can't have is *no* way of writing something, unless you don't write at all.

In other words, you can have a bad style, a ridiculous style, an illiterate style, a style that is beneath contempt. But, with all due respect to the terribly intelligent reviewer who read my book, you cannot have *no* style.

For instance, you have just read the foregoing portion of this introduction (unless you have skipped it, in which case you are going to have seven years of bad luck), and you can tell something about the characteristics of its style.

In the first place, you have undoubtedly noticed that it is personal. I tend to talk about myself a lot. In fact, the first word of the introduction is *I,* which I was once told is a no-no in writing an essay.

This can easily grate on you, if you don't like presumption, if you find pushy people unbearable, if you like to choose your friends carefully, and if you never speak to strangers.

On the other hand, you can warm to a personal style if you happen to like to feel a cozy friendship with a writer, if you like to be welcomed into the printed page, if you like companionship.

Should I adopt a style that is going to grate on some people?

I don't think I have a choice. If I adopted an impersonal style, saying "It is astonishing that —" instead of "I am astonished that —" why, then, that will grate on some people, too. And if whatever style I choose is sure to grate on some people — then why not adopt one that at least pleases *me*?

I might as well not grate on myself, at least.

A personal style comes naturally to me because I tend to be aimlessly friendly; I have no inhibitions about speaking to strangers; and I like to talk about myself.

A penchant for talking about oneself is usually taken as a symptom of vanity, conceit, egomania, and a lot of other bad characteristics, and I am indeed accused of that frequently, but only by people who are not accustomed to a personal style. From people who like a personal style, I get a different set of characterizing terms, which I would quote if I *were* full of vanity, conceit, and egomania.

What else? Well, I have an informal style, which means I tend to use short words and simple sentence structure, to say nothing of occasional colloquialisms. This grates on people who like things that are poetic, weighty, complex, and, above all, obscure. On the other hand the informal style pleases people who enjoy the sensation of reading an essay without being aware that they are reading and of feeling that ideas are flowing from the writer's brain into their own without mental friction.

Third, you will notice I have a discursive style. That is, I don't follow a straight line in my exposition. I like to use parentheses, and I pause for asides.

This can drive people crazy if they are the kind who want to get from A to B in a straight line, but it can please people who like to stop on their way to the post office to watch a butterfly for a few moments.

Anything else? I have (I think) a humorous style, or even (possibly) a witty one. I say things in a way that is not meant to be entirely serious but which should manage to elicit a smile. That doesn't mean I am not serious in the *content* of what I may write, but I think I can get it across more persuasively by tickling than by jabbing.

What is my style *not?*

It isn't the opposite of anything that it is, for one thing. It isn't impersonal, formal, direct, and serious.

As an example of something I haven't mentioned, my style is not epigrammatic, either.

Some writers tend to include a frequent seasoning of clever, pointed turns of phrase. You probably have read writers whose nearly every sentence has a striking simile or metaphor. Thus: "He looked at me as though I were lemonade to which someone had forgotten to add the ade."

That would please people who enjoy novel turns of phrase, but it grates on me. I dislike useless and distracting phrases. I would have said, "He looked at me sourly." By adding all that stuff about lemonade the reader is likely to get the vague idea that the character looking at me had a drink in his hand.

Now we can move on to another question. Is there such a thing as good style or bad style?

Yes, but when it is put that briefly, the "yes" gives a false impression.

Style is not, *in itself,* either good or bad. It's not that a personal style is good while an impersonal one is bad, or vice versa. For one thing, circumstances vary. A personal style is more suitable than an impersonal one in a friendly essay; an impersonal one is more suitable than a personal one in a business report.

Beyond that, there is the quality of writing. A personal style well done is better than an impersonal style ill done, and vice versa. In fact, any writing well done is better than any writing ill done, regardless of style.

Does that mean we should forget about style and just concentrate on good writing?

Not quite. Even when we concentrate on good writing, we cannot forget style. A writer always writes better if he is using a style with which he is comfortable or a style that fits the mood he is trying to get across. In other words, while *in general,* good writing outweighs consideration of style; for a specific writer, good writing only comes if he adopts certain styles, generally the one that long custom has made his own.

Does this mean that a writer cannot change his style deliberately?

Of course he can. The more experienced he is and the more skillful, the more easily he can do it. There are even writers with a particularly sharp ear for style who can alter their styles smoothly and with ease — just as there are some people who can mimic other people's voices and mannerisms with remarkable facility.

Yet however experienced and skillful a writer may be and however gifted a mimic he may be, the matter of using a style he is not accustomed to is a matter of constant, deliberate effort. It is tiring. At any time, if his attention wavers, he will drop into his own style, so that he must be perpetually on guard.

Even if he performs perfectly through an entire piece of writing, he is bound to be glad when he is finished, glad he has a chance to rest for a while.

And I am certain that the material in an alien style does not have quite the quality of the work produced by the same author in his own accustomed style. If one is forced to concentrate on the fine details that define style, then something has to be neglected to make up for that — and what but the other fine details that define quality?

The result is that writers generally don't imitate alien styles except for purposes of humorous parody, when quality is not in question. Thus, a person who imitates James Cagney, saying, "All right, you dirty rat, you gave it to my brother and I'll give it to you," neither expects nor attempts to do a great job of acting, and neither does his audience expect it of him.

Style is important to the reader, too. A particular reader will like one writer better than another, and in my opinion this preference is much more a matter of differences in style than in content. Just as there are some actors you may find a delight to watch even in bad motion pictures, so there are some writers whose styles give you pleasure even when the content of the book is poor.

The reader may not be aware of being influenced by style, or be able to define it or to itemize the components of it if asked to do so, but that doesn't affect the pleasure that's derived from it. (You may not be able to itemize the components and proportions in various sauces, as a skilled chef might, but you like some sauces better than others even so, and knowing the components wouldn't change your decision.)

Well, then, what has all this to do with the anthology you are holding (in case you thought I had forgotten about it)? Just this —

Some forty years ago, Ellery Queen put out an anthology called *Challenge to the Reader,* an excellent collection in which stories appeared under a fictitious name for the author. Furthermore, the stories contained detectives, each characteristic of the author, and the detective's name was also changed. The reader was challenged to identify both the author and the detective.

It was fun, but you had two possible directions to go. You could try to detect items characteristic of either the author *or* the detective. Thus, if a detective spoke of "little gray cells" and you decided he was Hercule Poirot, you knew at once that the writer was Agatha Christie.

After forty years, it seems reasonable to try the gimmick again. After all, a whole new generation of mystery writers has grown up since Ellery Queen's anthology.

Furthermore, this time Alice and I thought we'd make it harder. We've asked each author to write an original story for this anthology, but one that does *not* use a characteristic detective or a characteristic background. If Agatha Christie had a story in this book (and she hasn't, of course) it would not involve either

Hercule Poirot or Miss Marple. If Dick Francis had a story in this book (and he hasn't, either) it would not involve horse-racing in any way.

Then what is left?

Style. Each writer writes in his or her own style, and it is up to you to spot that style if you can. We don't expect miracles. A list of the authors from among whom you must choose is given, in alphabetical order, on the reverse of the contents page. The name of each author is given with the story in a simple code that is explained in the back of the book.

If, then, you are impatient with guessing games, or if you haven't read enough stories of enough of the authors to feel you stand a fair chance, you don't have to play. You can look up the code, write in the names of all the authors, and then read the stories. Or you can read the stories without concerning yourself at all over who wrote them. The stories are good enough, in our opinion, to stand on their own.

If, however, you *do* like to play games and are an aficionado of the mystery, and would like to try to spot styles — why, you still have the pleasure of good stories and the added fillip of trying to solve another mystery on your own.

I hope you enjoy yourself either way — and so does Alice.

Contents

Authors (in alphabetical order)

John Ball
Robert Bloch
Dorothy Salisbury Davis
Rosemary Gatenby
Michael Gilbert
Elizabeth Gresham
Joe L. Hensley
Edward D. Hoch
R. A. Lafferty
John D. MacDonald
Florence Mayberry
Patricia Moyes
Rachael Cosgrove Payes
Bill Pronzini
Ruth Rendell
Lawrence Treat
Janwillem van de Wetering

Story introductions by Isaac Asimov

Who Done It?

Coronation Year

by JTBBDBTJNPWJNJDIBFMHJMCFSU

Nothing like a multiple mystery, and they don't come more multiple than this: See if you can guess as soon as possible (1) the year, (2) who Teddy was, and (3) the nationality, real name, and identity of the lodger. The lodger makes an unlikely hero, but actually I don't think he was ever in Britain.

Went off nice, didn't it?" said Mr. Burger, removing his billycock hat and placing it carefully on the bar counter.

"Not what you'd call a hot day, not for June," said Mr. Jopling. "All the better for that perhaps."

"You don't want a very hot day," agreed Mr. Burger. "Not with all them crowds."

"We had a fizzer when they did Teddy. Ten years ago, wasn't it?"

"Nine," said Mr. Jopling.

"Nine. That's right. Thermometer in the eighties. Women fainting. Remember?"

"Certainly I remember *that* occasion," said Mr. Burger bitterly. "A dozen of us clubbed together to hire an upstairs room in the Strand. And what happened? It got itself put off. Three pounds a head that cost us."

"I don't see you can blame Teddy for that. He couldn't help having appendicitis. Might have happened to anyone."

"So it might," agreed Mr. Burger. "All I'm saying is, I wasn't risking anything like that this time. Went down early and found myself a place on the pavement in Piccadilly. Got a good view of them driving back from the Abbey. Very nice they looked, too."

"A handsome pair," agreed Mr. Stoop. "Now, wottle-it-be?" The invitation included Mr. Jopling.

"The usual, thank you, Charlie," said Mr. Burger. Mr. Jopling nodded his agreement.

"Three pints of old and mild, Jack," said Mr. Stoop, "and have one for yourself." He slammed down his shilling on the bar. It rang on the mahogany, a bright new shilling minted to celebrate a bright new reign.

"Some year, taken all round," said Mr. Burger. "Coronation, Naval Review. Kids' tea party at the Crystal Palace. Now this march past. Someone has to pay for it all, I suppose." He glanced out of the window at the sanded street, and the crowd that had already started to gather on the pavement.

"Year started well, too," said Mr. Stoop. "Clapham Common and Sidney Street."

This remark was felt to be in doubtful taste.

"I venture to think," said Mr. Jopling, who was tall and serious, and a student of affairs, "that there are other things than two sordid outbreaks of crime for which this year of grace will be held memorable. In my view it will go down in history as the year in which the legislative power of the Upper House was first seriously challenged. If the debate goes the wrong way, we shall feel the effects of *that* for many a long year, mark my words."

"I read in the papers," said Mr. Burger, "that some Italians in Tripoli dropped a bomb out of an airplane."

"What in the world did they do that for?" said Mr. Stoop.

"I suppose they were aiming to kill someone."

"Crazy," said Mr. Stoop. "My nephew, he was out in South

Africa for two years with the C.I.V., he told me it was difficult enough to hit a man with a bomb when you and him was both standing still. What chance would you have in an airplane?"

"True enough," said Mr. Burger. "Look at that business in Madrid four years ago. All that chap had got to do was lob one out of an hotel window into a ruddy great coach and four. And then he went and missed."

"Five," said Mr. Jopling.

Mr. Stoop counted up on his fingers. "That's right. Five years ago. Come to think of it, that was quite a year, too. Funny, isn't it, how some years everything seems to happen. Frisco earthquake. Typhoon in Hong Kong. Olympic Games."

"Asquith's first budget," said Mr. Jopling, patiently raising the tone of the conversation.

"Hackenschmidt and Madrali at Olympia," said Mr. Stoop, lowering it again. "Then take the year after. Dull as ditchwater."

"Ah," said Mr. Burger. He finished his pint and placed his glass on the counter.

"South African cricketers. They were over that year."

"Colonial Conference," said Mr. Jopling.

Neither was felt to be a matter of memorable importance.

"Ah," said Mr. Burger again. "Some might think it a dull year. Not me though. It's a year I shan't forget in a hurry."

"Cut your first tooth?" suggested Mr. Stoop facetiously.

"That was the year I had lodger trouble."

Silence descended on the trio. Mr. Burger had spoken a word of power. He had the attention of the company.

"That was the year *that* happened, was it?" said Mr. Stoop thoughtfully. "So it was. I'd forgotten."

"Very unfortunate business," said Mr. Jopling. A sense of the importance of world events seemed to be struggling with human curiosity. "I never did hear what happened, really. Plenty of rumors."

"After it was all over," said Mr. Burger, "I promised my old lady I wouldn't talk about it. Now she's gone" — he touched the faded black band on his left sleeve — "and now that all that time's gone by, it really would be a sort of relief to talk about it."

Mr. Jopling motioned quietly to the landlord, who refilled their glasses, and then leaned his elbows on the bar so as not to miss a word. From outside, the shouts of the crowd came distantly and indistinctly.

"Lodgers," said Mr. Burger, "are what I never really could get used to. They brought in money, but they brought in trouble, too. Trouble and hard work."

Here Mr. Burger knew, and Mr. Burger's listeners knew, he did himself rather more than justice. His flat-fronted North London house had not been run by him. It had been run by his wife, Alice. In spite of her small size and meek look, Alice had been a running woman. She had run the house, the maid, and the lodgers, and she had also run Mr. Burger, whose contribution to the common purse had consisted of important but unspecified work in the Caledonian Market. Yet despite all her running, she had contrived to remain an essentially feminine woman. This was one of the crosses that Mr. Burger had had to bear.

The other cross was their maid, Tania.

"Speak no ill," he said, "but she was a difficult girl. Moody. Keep her busy and she was all right. Let her stop for a moment, and she fell into the dumps. Sit for half an hour at a time, in a chair, with her hands folded, thinking about God knows what."

"I expect she was thinking about the foreign parts she came from," said Mr. Jopling.

"Or boys," suggested Mr. Stoop. "Mostly when girls seem to be thinking about nothing they're thinking about boys."

"Pretty?" asked the landlord.

"In a way." Mr. Burger spoke as a man to whom mere material prettiness meant nothing. "The word I'd have used would be — susceptible. And with Barker in the house it didn't do to have a susceptible girl around. I can see that now. He was a holy terror with girls, old Barker was. We called him old Barker, not that he was all that old, come to think of it. But he was getting to an age when a man begins to doubt his powers, and has to prove himself wrong every girl he meets."

"Traveler, wasn't he?" said Mr. Jopling.

"Soap. Traveled in soap. 'I spend my life cleaning up the world,' he used to say. Wouldn't have done any harm if he'd cleaned himself up a bit. Morally, I mean. He could do what he liked when he was on the road, but in my house he had to behave himself. I had to warn him more than once. Him and Alice. Duets. I soon put a stop to *that,* I can tell you."

"I wonder you tolerated him in the house," said Mr. Jopling.

"So do I," said Mr. Burger. "But it's easy to be wise after the event, isn't it? If I'd known what was going to happen I'd have got rid of him, of course. But a lodger who paid his bill regular was a thing you thought twice about losing. Even a man like Barker. And it wasn't only him carrying on with every bit of skirt he set eyes on. He'd a nasty tongue, too."

"He liked an argument," agreed Mr. Stoop. "I heard him in here more than once."

"Argue?" said Mr. Burger. "He'd no more idea of arguing than my dog Toby. Just shout the other man down. The lodgers didn't like it above half. A quiet debate, that was one thing. But not a slanging match. We lost more than one lodger on account of Barker. In fact, at the time I'm talking about, we'd only two others with us. There was Mr. Crocker, who was deaf and hardly ever came out of his room. And this young chap. A sort of foreigner, white face, black hair sticking up like a mop, and a small pointed beard, that made him look even younger than he was, somehow. Middle twenties, I'd have said. Came from somewhere over there." Mr. Burger waved his hand expansively in the direction of the Eastern hemisphere — "I called him Joe. His real name I never could get my tongue round."

"Pole," suggested Mr. Jopling.

"Very likely. I can tell you one thing. He wasn't French. I

tried him in French once, and he never understood a word I said. I did think, at one time, he might have come from the same parts as Tania. I heard them once, jabber-jabbering together in some foreign lingo. Not that he ever paid much attention to her. He was a serious sort of youngster. When he did say anything it was mostly economics and politics and such."

Mr. Jopling approved of that. "I'd have liked to have met him," he said.

"You'd have made a pair. He was over in England for a conference. Summer school, or something, at the Brotherhood Church Hall. Out he'd go after breakfast, and back after tea. Talk all day to his compatriots, I don't doubt, but we never had a lot out of him when he got home."

"He could talk English then," said Mr. Stoop.

"When he first arrived, it was just a few words. But he picked it up wonderful quick. I tell you, he'd a good head on him. By the time he'd been with us a month or so he was stringing sentences together. Quite interesting to listen to, some of his ideas. Then, in the middle of it, old Barker would blow in, half cut, and start taking the micky out of him. 'Some people,' he'd say, 'never done a hand's turn of real work in their lives. Nothing but talk. That's all you and your friends ever do, isn't it? You produce enough gas between you to fill a gas works.' Or it might be, 'My advice to you, Joe, is cut the cackle. And whilst you're about it, get your hair cut, too.' "

"Tsk, tsk," said Mr. Jopling. "That wasn't very polite. What did Joe say?"

"Nothing," said Mr. Burger. "Nothing at all. I did wonder, sometimes, if he understood him. From what happened later, I think he must have done. Well, as I was telling you, it was about that time we had our trouble. It would have been — let me think — one night toward the end of May, I woke up, smelling gas. Alice said, 'You're always smelling things. Go to sleep.' I said, 'I think I'll just make sure.' So I went down. Nothing downstairs. Then I came up again, and it was stronger. 'Must be up in the attic,' I thought. Only Tania slept up there. I went up, and found her door was locked. I thought, 'She's gone to sleep and left her fire on, silly girl.' As for locking the door, I didn't think anything of that. If I'd been a girl I'd have locked *my* door with Barker sleeping in the room below. I banged on the door. Nothing doing. Then I remembered you could get at the window from the roof. Sort of catwalk with a parapet to stop you slipping off. I hopped out and went along. The window was tight shut, but I broke that and got in and turned the gas fire out. Wasn't any use. I might just as well have stayed in bed for any good I could do. She was dead. Nearly passed out myself. I tried to get out of the door, but the key wasn't in the lock. Then I got back to the window, and, tell you the truth, I was sick. Then we got the police."

Mr. Burger took a pull of his beer to revive himself.

"Very nice, the police was. We had a Sergeant come round from the local station. His first idea was accident. Was she a careful sort of girl? Well, we had to say 'No' to that. If anyone left a light on, or a tap running, it was pretty certain to be Tania. 'Then perhaps,' said the Sergeant, 'she went to sleep with the fire on, and the draft blew it out.'

" 'Where comes the draft if the door was locked and the window shut?' says Joe, who'd been listening to me and the Sergeant.

"Well, that was a bit of a poser, but we didn't stick on it, because the next thing we got was the doctor's report, and that was that."

"She was —?"

"Yes," said Mr. Burger. "She was. Five months gone. Well, of course, that put a different complexion on things. A girl in that condition will do anything. And the more you looked at it, the more it did look like suicide. The window tight shut and latched, although it was a warm night. The door locked. There was only one key, as far as we knew, and that was under her pillow. What's more, there was a bottle of sleeping pills on the

table by her bed. It was a new bottle, five or six gone. Not
enough to hurt her, see, but enough to make her sleepy. Then
she turns the gas on, gets into bed, and dozes off —"

"Sad," said Mr. Stoop. "Sad. But a judgment really."

"Ah," said Mr. Burger, "but it didn't end there. Not by half.
The next thing was we lost the cruets."

"Cruets?"

"A week later. All the cruets out of the sideboard cupboard.
Wedding presents, most of them. Solid silver. Alice was very
put out. So we had the police in once more. It was the same
Sergeant. 'Well,' he said, 'troubles never come singly. What's
happened this time?' We were all there that evening, in the dining room. Even old Mr. Crocker, not that he understood much
of what was going on.

" 'Anyone might have walked in and picked them up, I suppose,' says Alice. 'The front door's on the latch all day.'

"The Sergeant looked as if he couldn't quite swallow this. It
wasn't as if the house was left empty. It'd be pretty cool for a
stranger to walk in and empty the sideboard.

" 'Me, I think,' says Joe, 'it would be more natural to suspect
one of us, yes?'

"Well, so did I, but no one had quite liked to say it.

" 'Since I am a stranger, I should be most suspect. I insist
that my room and luggage are searched.'

"This cheered the Sergeant up a lot. It's what he'd wanted to
do anyway. Then we explained it all to Mr. Crocker, who
nearly busted himself laughing, and said, come along, they
could search his luggage, and him too if they wanted to. Old
Barker looked very put out, but of course he had to go along
with the others. After all, it would have looked pretty funny if
he hadn't, wouldn't it?"

"And did he find the cruets?" said Mr. Stoop.

"No," said Mr. Burger, pausing to take a couple of inches off
his drink. "He didn't find the cruets. But he found a key, at the
bottom of old Barker's suitcase, tucked away under a pile of
shirts, a bright, new, shiny duplicate of the key to Tania's bed-

room. It didn't take the Sergeant long to work *that* out. Not that he did anything at once. He just borrowed the key, and pushed off to make a few enquiries, whilst old Barker spent the evening swearing blind *he* didn't know how the key had got there, *he'd* never seen it before, and so on and so forth.

"The more we thought about it the less we liked it. But there was worse to come. Two days later the police were back. They hadn't traced the key, but they'd been making enquiries about those sleeping tablets. And what do you think? They didn't belong to Tania at all. They were Barker's."

Mr. Stoop said, "Well, what do you know?" and Mr. Jopling said, "Yes, I see," in the tones of a hanging judge.

"They fairly put Barker through it then. After a bit he admitted buying the tablets. He couldn't deny it, really. They brought along the man who'd sold them to him, to identify him. So why hadn't he said something before?"

"He said he'd been scared to say anything about it.

"How had the girl got hold of them? She must have pinched them from his room. What was she doing in his room, anyway? He got deeper and deeper into it. In the end he more or less admitted he'd been intimate with Tania. Of course, he said she led him on. Which, knowing Tania, was nonsense. However, the one thing he was absolutely firm about was that key. He couldn't think where it had come from. He'd never seen it before."

"Cold blooded," said Mr. Stoop. "Make love to her, I take it, then give her a tablet or two to help her off to sleep. Hold her hand until she was well away, turn the gas on, shut the window, and lock the door behind him. He ought to have thrown away the key, though."

"Strong enough evidence to charge him, I should have thought," said Mr. Jopling. "I take it they arrested him."

"Not then and there, they didn't. I think they were still hoping to find the man who'd cut the key for him, and that would have clinched it. But I imagine they left someone watching, to see he didn't get away."

"Did he try to get away?" said Mr. Stoop.

"You might say, in a manner of speaking," said Mr. Burger, "that he succeeded. Cut his throat, two nights later, in the bathroom."

In the distance a drum rolled.

The crowd outside raised a cheer.

"Pity they didn't arrest him sooner," said Mr. Jopling.

"A man like that," said Mr. Stoop. "Hanging would've been too good, in my opinion."

"In a way, yes," said Mr. Burger. "In a way, no. Because even that wasn't quite the end of the story. It was about a fortnight later. Joe's last day with us. He was already packed up to go home. We were sitting in the front room waiting for the cab, just him and me. When he pulled out his note case to pay the reckoning a paper came out with it and fell on the floor. I picked it up, and saw it was a receipt for five pounds, in queer sort of writing, with a foreign name on it.

" 'Hullo,' I say, 'what've you been paying out fivers for?'

"He takes it back, looks at it for a moment with a sort of smile on his face, then drops it on the fire.

" 'It's not important now,' he says, 'some money I pay to a comrade. He cut a key for me.'

" 'He — what?' I say. You know, taking it in slowly. 'A key? Are you meaning to tell me —'

" 'Nothing,' says Joe, 'I tell you nothing. Mr. Barker, he was responsible for that girl's death. He got her with child. She took her own life.'

"I started to say something, but he cut me off pretty sharp.

" 'She felt it bad. I think she try twice. Once with the tablets she stole. Not quick enough, perhaps. So she turns the gas on. Don't worry about Mr. Barker. He got off lightly.

" 'And by the way,' he adds, 'you'll find all your silver. It's under the coal, in the cellar.'

"I was past saying anything by now, and was glad when I heard the cab coming along. Joe gets up and says, very solemn,

'If you wish to punish a man, do it with the Law, not against the Law. If you can use the Law for your own ends you can rule the world.'

"By this time I'd come to the conclusion that he was either pulling my leg, or he was mad. I said, 'Rule the world, eh? Well, just in case you manage to pull it off, Joe, I'd better make a proper note of your name.'

"To tell the truth, I'd never seen it written down, and I'd never got my tongue round it since he'd been there.

" 'It is no matter,' he says, very solemn. 'In my country, when a man comes to power, he is born again. He leaves his father's name behind him, and takes a new one from the people.'

"I said, to humor him, 'I expect you've thought out a nice one for yourself.' And so he had."

The others waited patiently, whilst the noise outside grew.

"Well," said Mr. Jopling, at last. "What *was* he going to call himself?"

"To tell you the truth," said Mr. Burger. "It's just slipped my memory. Except that it was a bird. Sparrow, I think. I remember, as he got into the cab, I was pulling his leg about it. 'If you and all your friends get into power,' I said, 'it'll be a regular Parliament of Birds.' He didn't seem to think it funny."

"Foreigners haven't got much sense of humor," said Mr. Jopling.

"Drink up," said Mr. Stoop. "Here they come."

The head of the column was swinging round the corner into their street. A roll of side drums and the shrill squeal of the fifes. Some talk of Alexander, and some of Hercules. Of Hector and Lysander —

They flung open the door. The noise came in like a tidal wave.

Over it Mr. Burger was trying to say something.

"Got it," he shouted.

"Got what?" said Mr. Jopling.

"Starling," said Mr. Burger. "Not sparrow, starling."

"What's the odds?" Mr. Stoop shouted back. "Sparrow, starling. It isn't cranks like that who are going to rule the world. And they're not going to bother *us,* neither."

Outside, the army of the greatest imperial power in the world came marching proudly along the sanded street; marching to usher in a reign of peace and plenty.

Appointment with the Governor

by B M J D F M B V S B O D F B M J D F K P I O C B M M

We make so many casual assumptions. We don't realize this because the assumptions are *so* casual we're not even aware they exist. If I warn you in advance that something you will take for granted will turn out not to be so, will you be placed on the *qui vive* and guess? Somehow, I don't think so.

It never would have happened at all if Maggie MacDonald had been at her desk as usual. Through four administrations Maggie had presided over the governor's appointments, and no one could recall that she had ever made a mistake. Because of her unerring ability to keep everything sorted out in proper order, and the acute sixth sense that she sometimes displayed in knowing who should get in and who should be kept away, no one had brought up the matter of her age. There was no one her equal to replace her and if perchance she were technically over the age limit for her job, no one was going to be rude enough to even think about it.

But Maggie had an appointment for her annual physical ex-

13

amination and the person who had been designated to fill in for her was unaccountably late. Which is why Mrs. Willis M. Roberts and Mrs. Chester R. Burke were shown into the same waiting room when every effort should have been made to be sure that they never met. By the time the replacement for Maggie was at her desk the damage had been done. She realized it at once, but there was nothing she could do about it except pray that the two women did not fall into conversation. If that happened . . .

Meanwhile, the governor's clemency secretary was standing beside the desk of the state's chief executive. He was a thoroughly conscientious man, perhaps the single best appointment that the governor had made. He gave his recommendations very carefully and never without a full consideration of the evidence available. If a further investigation was indicated, he was tireless in seeing that it was done properly. He was also a very tough man to lobby. He had the full respect of his associates, the press, and the members of the bar.

As he spoke the governor listened carefully and silently. It was the most important case to come up since the election, and it involved the newly reinstated death penalty. If the execution did go forward as scheduled, it would be the first one under the new law. There was a great deal of public emotion on both sides of the question, but the voters had been decisive in the referendum that restored capital punishment. That was a mandate, and the governor knew it, but it was not going to be allowed to decide the issue.

"I want to know something," the governor said. "Is there the least possibility that Roberts might be innocent? Could he have been framed? I know such things are done. Could he simply have been in the wrong place at the wrong time?"

The clemency secretary shook his head. "Governor, I can give you my assurance there is no possibility of innocence. After the trial and sentencing, Roberts admitted that he was guilty. That fact was not publicized, but I checked it out and it's true. Also, he supplied some additional details that the sheriff himself didn't know."

"That's bad," the governor said.

The clemency secretary nodded, regretfully. "It is," he agreed. "And now you want my recommendation."

The governor took a breath and held it for a moment, knowing that a man's life was at stake.

The clemency secretary spoke calmly and quietly. "I am recommending that clemency be denied. In my own conscience I don't believe in capital punishment, but it is part of the law and if anyone has ever deserved it, Roberts is the man. I can't find a single mitigating condition: He wasn't drunk, under the influence of any drug, or otherwise incapacitated. He killed the little girl in cold blood, knowing what he was doing, and the penalty for his crime. He has a long history of violent offenses, many of them sexual in nature. Like Chessman, one of his victims is in a mental hospital, probably permanently. Another, a girl of sixteen, can never have children."

The governor sat a little straighter. "We aren't passing judgment here on those offenses. Or the fact that he was on parole at the time he committed the murder. I have to decide this solely on the grounds of the crime for which he was sentenced — to die."

The clemency secretary fingered a folder that he held, but which he had not opened. "I certainly agree with that," he said. "I beg your pardon — I should not have brought up the matter of his record. Please ignore it if you can."

The governor relaxed visibly, reached for a cigarette, and then pushed the pack away. "How about life imprisonment, without possibility of parole? Then he would have to look forward to the rest of his natural life behind bars. Taking away all hope is pretty severe punishment."

The clemency secretary allowed a moment to pass before he responded to that. When he did, he was quite factual. "I considered that alternative very carefully, governor, before I made my recommendation. We may say 'without possibility of parole' now, but ten or fifteen years hence, under a different administration, he might very well be let go. It has happened, you know."

For almost a full minute it was stone quiet in the big office. Then the governor asked one more question. "Is there anything else that you haven't told me — anything you think I should know?"

Again the clemency secretary fingered the folder. "Yes," he answered. "I have some photographs here. They're pretty awful. They show something that has been kept completely under cover. One reporter knows it, but he has given his word to keep it to himself. Frankly, they are largely responsible for my recommendation."

The governor was not one to duck a responsibility, even an extremely unpleasant one. "Let me see the pictures."

Reluctantly, the clemency secretary handed them over.

The governor looked at them carefully. It was a grisly job, one that brought home for the first time the magnitude of the crime.

"Was the victim tortured?" the governor asked.

"Yes."

"Badly?"

"Very badly."

"And she had done nothing to this man to incite him to this kind of horror?"

"Nothing whatever. She was completely innocent. She hadn't even been taught the basics of human sexuality, only to guard and protect herself."

"So there's nothing there."

"I'm afraid not."

The governor looked again at the pictures, because the decision to be made was so important. The clemency secretary waited. He had spoken his piece, and he knew enough to remain silent.

"Part of one leg is missing," the governor noted.

"That's — the vital point."

His tone, cautious and careful, was nevertheless decisive. The governor looked up. "Can that mean what I'm thinking?"

The clemency secretary nodded. "Yes, it does. He confessed to that too."

"Did he say anything — anything at all — to indicate remorse?"

He hated to do it, but the clemency secretary delivered the knockout blow. It was his duty and he would not shun it. "He said she was delicious."

Ten seconds ticked away. "Clemency refused," the governor said. "Now show his mother in. I'll tell her myself."

The girl sitting in Maggie's chair could not help it; she had to go to the bathroom. She rose silently from her place and went out quickly with the air of someone who would be back momentarily. When the door had closed behind her the two women who had been waiting were left alone, looking at each other. It was Mrs. Roberts who spoke first. "Are you here about — the Roberts case?" she asked.

Mrs. Burke nodded, quietly and firmly. "Yes, I am. I'm waiting to see the governor." This was self-evident, but it gave her something to say and she was in need of it.

"Are you a social worker?"

"No, I'm not." Realizing that that was a trifle brusque, she added, "I work in a computer plant."

"But you are here about clemency."

Mrs. Burke's eyes were suddenly wet. "Yes. I didn't want to come, but now I know that I must."

"That's so good of you." Mrs. Roberts spoke from her heart; she had had no hope of an ally.

Mrs. Burke was the first to realize. "May I ask . . ." she began.

The other woman nodded. "I'm Mrs. Roberts," she said very simply. "It's my son who . . ."

Mrs. Burke's first thought was to wonder why they had ever been brought together. She was revolted by the very name "Roberts." Now to meet like this . . .

Then she swallowed and remembered the sermon she had heard the day before in church. At the time she had had no idea that it had been prepared with her in mind, to offer some comfort at the most terrible time of her life. The words of the minister came back to her — that the greatest comfort lay in forgiveness. She could never forgive, she doubted if Christ himself could totally forgive if He were placed in her position. But the woman sitting across from her had a heavy cross to bear too. She had spawned a fiend, but the crime itself had not been hers.

She looked at the other woman again and saw comprehension in her eyes. The question came quite simply. "Are you Mrs. Burke?"

"Yes. I am."

The silence was suddenly intensely thick and heavy; it was broken when Mrs. Roberts reached for a handkerchief. Her tears were open then, and she could do nothing to stop them.

In a way it was a good thing, because Mrs. Burke saw them and through them had some insight into the agonies that the innocent woman opposite her was going through. When the secretary came back to her desk, neither of the women noticed it.

It was Mrs. Roberts who spoke. "I'm . . . terribly sorry about your little girl. I would give anything . . . everything I have . . ."

"Thank you," Mrs. Burke said. Then she added, "I know what you must be going through. I'm sorry . . . for you."

Again it was quiet, and the secretary fervently hoped that the conversation was over. But it wasn't.

Mrs. Roberts spoke, choosing her words like steppingstones. "I came to ask the governor to commute the sentence. I know what my son did, and that he can never be allowed to walk the streets again." She shook her head. "I don't want him to. I almost killed myself when I found out . . ."

Mrs. Burke was touched despite herself. She shook her head. "Don't do anything desperate," she said. "It won't help a thing, and it won't bring my daughter back." Again she realized how her words sounded. She remembered the sermon and did what her Savior expected of her. "It wasn't possibly your fault."

Mrs. Roberts put her thoughts into words to steady herself. "I came here to ask for mercy. You came here to ask that the law . . . take its course."

Mrs. Burke would not deny that. "Yes, I came to ask the governor to . . . not to interfere. I've always been opposed . . ."

Mrs. Roberts understood. "I don't think that the governor will see one of us and not the other," she offered.

Mrs. Burke understood what an effort those words had cost. That sermon kept pounding back into her head. Normally she did not listen much to sermons, but on that day of all days, she had hung on every word. And the message had been unmistakable. "Perhaps the governor," she began. She could not bring herself to withdraw, but she had a firm division by then in her mind between the monster on death row and the desperately unhappy woman who, like her, was waiting to see the governor.

Before she knew what she was doing, Mrs. Burke stood up and crossed the room. "I want you to know," she said, "that I understand, a little at least, how you feel." She sat down.

Mrs. Roberts looked at her. "You must be a wonderful Christian," she said. She had been thinking a lot about religion, and it had come much closer to the surface for her. Then she added, "If you're some other faith, you know what I mean."

Mrs. Burke was genuinely touched. For a bare moment she considered the idea of quietly leaving and letting compassion help the poor woman beside her. Then she remembered, and she could not be that generous. She wanted to, but she couldn't.

Mrs. Roberts folded her hands in her lap and looked at

them. "There's something I very much want to know," she said. "I have no right to ask. I'm sorry, forget what I said."

Mrs. Burke had steeled herself a few moments before. She understood what the question might be, and what the answer might mean to the woman who had the courage to ask it. "What do you want to know?" She put it calmly and factually.

Mrs. Roberts made a supreme effort. "I know that my son is a murderer," she said, forcing the loathsome words from her lips. Then she dropped her head quite suddenly. "I want to know if he is anything else."

Mrs. Burke knew it would bring pain, but it vindicated her position and the temptation was too strong. Slowly she nodded. "Yes," she said.

Mrs. Roberts looked her directly in the face for the first time. "If that is so," she said, "then perhaps we should see the governor together. And we will both ask . . ." She broke down into tears totally beyond her control.

The clemency secretary came into the room. Mrs. Burke saw him and knew who he was. "I think the decision has already been made," she said, "but, yes, let's go in together." Because her God wanted her to, she held out her hand and laid it on Mrs. Roberts's arm.

By their wish, they went in together. As they entered the room the governor rose. Seeing the two women together was a nasty shock; too late the clemency secretary tried to signal a warning.

"Please sit down," the governor said. "Which of you is Mrs. Roberts?"

The lady named lifted her hand just enough to be seen.

"You have met this other lady?"

"Yes, I have. We have been talking, and we decided to come together."

For a moment or two the governor did not know how to go on; there was no precedent for the situation. If only Maggie. . . !

The clemency secretary was about to speak when Mrs. Roberts anticipated him by a second or two. "Governor," she said, "I know you have the power to spare my son. You can commute his sentence to life in prison. Before I ask you to do that, I have a question."

"Please," the governor said.

She found the courage to look up. "I happened to meet Mrs. Burke. I learned that she is a very wonderful woman. I know we can never be friends, but . . . I think you understand."

"Indeed I do," the governor confirmed.

"My question is this: Did my son do . . . terrible things . . . besides the murder?" She turned quickly to Mrs. Burke. "Please forgive me," she added.

Mrs. Burke only nodded, waiting for the governor to speak.

"Yes, Mrs. Roberts, I'm very much afraid he did." That made it a little easier to announce the decision.

"Then," Mrs. Roberts said, "I won't ask you for mercy. I know now that I bore a monster, and it's best if I never see him again. If I never have to worry that some day . . ."

The governor looked at the other woman. "Mrs. Burke?"

The mother of the slain girl composed herself. "I came to ask you — not to intervene. Instead I would like to ask you to do what you think best."

The governor turned back to Mrs. Roberts. "Then you are not asking me to commute?"

Very slowly, and with great effort, Mrs. Roberts shook her head. "I can't now," she said.

The clemency secretary was about to speak, but the governor silenced him with a slightly raised hand. "Then let it be as you wish."

Mrs. Roberts looked up, tearfully. "Yes," she barely whispered. "God is all merciful, so let Him . . ."

The governor got up and came around the desk. It was not an easy time, but at least there was no need to tell this utterly miserable, but completely courageous, woman that her appeal for clemency had been denied. Neither of the women would ever know what the terrible pictures in the folder showed. It had been safely removed before the women had been admitted to the office.

The governor stood before both of the women and spoke with complete sincerity. "Thank you for coming. I'm very glad that you did. And, believe me, I understand and admire both of you. As you know, I'm a mother myself."

The clemency secretary showed them out.

The Locked-Room Cipher

by BTJNPWJTBBDBTJNFEXBSEEIPDI

John Dickson Carr, in one of his novels, went through an exhaustive listing of every possible gimmick that could be used in a locked-room murder. Working from memory, I don't think he included the one in his story. Ah, the end-less ingenuity of the mystery writer.

New York is a city where nightclubs and discos have been known to open and close in the same week, so when the instant success of Sequin City proved to be more than a passing fad it became a matter of special interest to me. I'm Ross Calendar, and if you read the entertainment section of New York's largest newspaper you'll see my column there every day.

The pundits had many explanations for the success of Sequin City right from the beginning. Its Midtown–East Side location was ideal, and it was specifically designed to appeal to the reverse snobbery of Manhattan's wealthy night people. The very name, and the flashy glitter of the decor, made visitors to Sequin City feel just a bit as if they were slumming in Holly-wood or Las Vegas.

But the real reason for its instant success was Terry Box, the guiding force behind Sequin City from the beginning. It was

Terry who took his profits from various Manhattan real estate deals and pumped them into the enterprise, turning a former theater and television studio into the hottest new disco restaurant since Studio 54. Terry Box was not only the founder and owner of Sequin City but its manager as well, dealing with a hundred different daily chores to insure the success of his investment.

There were two things that struck me as odd about Sequin City, even before the murder. One was Terry's absolute unwillingness to take in other investors. And the other was the elaborate security system he'd installed in Sequin City. Every corner of the place, from the massive disco on the ground floor to the exclusive dining rooms above, was covered by closed-circuit television. And the mirrored panels set into the ceiling over the dance floor were really one-way glass, enabling viewers on the catwalk above to watch the action without being seen.

It was something more suitable to a bank or gambling casino than a New York disco, and I told Terry Box that when he was showing me around. "Well, we're trying to copy Las Vegas, you know," he said by way of explanation, but it took me several more months to grasp the full meaning of his words.

Terry was a tall, handsome fellow who'd been married twice before deciding he was better suited to the single life. At forty-three he still looked good enough to attract the attention of even the youngest female patrons — and some of the males, too. His hair was dark and his eyes were a deep shade of green like a cat's. He had the mind of a computer, and he always seemed to have just finished reading tomorrow's newspaper.

Terry Box had worked in Washington in his younger days, doing something with codes and computers for the Justice Department. He still knew a good many people from those days, and I suppose it was natural for him to invite a few of them up one weekend to sample the success of Sequin City. The place had been open about six months when he called me in to tell me about it.

"You should get a column out of it, Ross," he suggested amiably.

"And you'll get more publicity for this place. Not that you need it!"

"Come on, I'm doing you a favor! The idea of the four of us, who used to spend our time with computers and ciphers, holding a reunion in a New York disco is certainly bizarre enough to interest even your jaded readers."

"It's not a bad idea. When are they coming?"

"Friday afternoon. I'm putting them up at the Plaza for the weekend. Two men and a quite attractive woman. You'll want to use a photograph."

"I might but I doubt if my editor will." I took out my notebook. "I'm hooked. Give me their names."

"Rufus Kinkaid, a man in his late fifties now, and looking every bit the elder statesman. He was my mentor at Justice, though now he's a computer expert in private industry. Dora Polk, only in her midthirties and a lovely woman. You'll like her. You might even fall in love with her. Some men have."

"You, for one?"

"She was married when I worked with her, but she's divorced now." I couldn't help noticing how he avoided a direct answer to my question.

"She still with Justice?"

"Yes, and so is Steve Schwartz, the third of my guests. He's my age. We spent a good many nights together in Washington bars after working hours. I used to tell him some day I'd have a nightclub of my own, but he never believed it."

I closed my notebook and stood up. "Then I'll see you Friday?"

"Come around seven. You can dine with us in one of the upstairs rooms."

"Just the five of us?"

"Oh, I suppose Milly will be there to make it six."

Milly Nostrum was Terry's current girl, a sad-eyed blonde

who had her own problems. Every time I saw her I felt sorry for her, mostly because of the way Terry treated her.

"OK," I said. "I'll see you Friday at seven."

Downstairs, the day crew was polishing the dance floor of Sequin City. With sunlight streaming in the big side windows it just wasn't the same place. I glanced up at the TV camera as I went out the door, waving in case Terry was watching.

◆ ◆ ◆

Terry Box was right about one thing. Dora Polk was a lovely woman, and quite a charming one too. If I'd been ten years younger I just *might* have fallen in love with her myself. She was tall and slim, with long perfect legs that she knew how to show off to their best advantage. The thought of her cooped up in a Washington office all day was enough to make me weep.

"I was only a girl when Terry worked with us," she confided to me. "Really, I was quite surprised to get this invitation. I doubted that he even remembered me."

"How could he forget you?" I was rewarded with a smile and I pressed on. "Do you think of yourself as something of a spy, working with codes and things?"

Her laughter was a pleasant, engaging sound. "Hardly! The work is really quite boring, and the codes are usually the commercial sort. I'm a mathematician, maybe, but not a spy."

"What's this about spies?" Steve Schwartz asked, interrupting our cozy chatter. He might have been Terry Box's age, but he hadn't worn nearly as well. His thinning hair was flecked with gray and his stomach was starting to bulge out.

"Just pumping her for information," I admitted with a smile.

"Our jobs are the dullest things in the world," he insisted. "I've got Terry's old position, checking transfers from bank accounts. Just columns of numbers, all day long. Rufus was smart to get out. Now he's got a cushy job at twice the pay."

Rufus Kinkaid, looking very much the white-haired father figure, had been chatting with Terry at the other end of the private upstairs dining room ever since my arrival. Except for a brief introduction I'd had no conversation with him. I left Dora and Steve together and was moving toward Terry and the older man when Milly Nostrum intercepted me. She didn't look good. Her nose seemed just a bit misshapen and I wondered if Terry had hit her.

"I saw you talking to Terry's latest conquest," she said quietly.

"You mean Dora Polk? A charming woman."

"Terry arranged this whole charade so he could get her into bed."

"Did he tell you that?"

"He didn't have to. I know him well enough."

"What's the matter with your nose?" I asked.

"God, is it that noticeable?"

"Only to me. What's the trouble?"

"The doctor says I need an operation. The cartilage between my nostrils has a hole in it, and if I don't have the operation he says my whole nose could collapse."

I'd heard of similar troubles. "That comes from snorting cocaine too much."

"Yes," she agreed quietly. "Every night with Terry. He got me doing it and now that my nose is falling apart he won't even pay for the operation." She was speaking frankly, knowing it wasn't the sort of thing I'd ever use in my column.

"Is there anything I can do to help?" I asked. "Would it do any good if I talked to him?"

"You've known each other a long time, haven't you?"

"Not so long, but I've spent a lot of time in Sequin City since it opened."

Her quiet anger was getting the better of her. She watched Terry leave Rufus Kinkaid and cross over to where Dora was sitting with a cocktail. "Did he ever tell you the real reason for this place?"

"Reason?"

"It's only a matter of time before New York State has legalized casino gambling. The politicians can't stand to see all that money going to Atlantic City. This place is constructed so it could be turned into a casino almost overnight."

Comprehension suddenly burst upon my tired brain. "The TV cameras and the one-way glass in the ceiling of the disco!"

"Of course. The entire disco floor could be filled with black-jack and crap tables in a day's time. He'd only wait long enough to put down a carpet. While the others are chasing around try-ing to renovate hotel lobbies he'll be in business."

"Interesting," I admitted. It was damned interesting, but I tried to keep my excitement under wraps. "What if the state decides to operate the casinos itself, though?"

She shrugged. "He's still got the perfect location, all set to go. He'd lease it to the state and probably stay on as manager. Ei-ther way he'll make a fortune."

I downed the rest of my cocktail. "You don't much like Terry anymore, do you?"

"I guess not."

At dinner I sat next to Rufus Kinkaid, listening to his enter-taining accounts of life in Washington when Terry and Dora and Steve Schwartz had been young. For the moment, at least, Milly served as the perfect hostess, pinning a white carnation on each of the men and presenting Dora Polk with a small cor-sage. I hoped it wasn't poisoned.

"It's so good to have you all here," Terry said at the end of the meal. "If you're a bit too old for disco dancing I hope you'll at least watch it for a while, and look over the rest of our club. I like to think of Sequin City as an adult playground — though I'll grant you some of our disco customers are just barely adult."

"Well, I'm not too old for dancing," Kinkaid announced. "And I'm looking forward to a spin around the floor with these two charming ladies."

"Watch out you don't have a heart attack," Dora cautioned.

The older man snorted. "Listen here — Terry'll tell you

about the time we had a race down the main corridor of the Pentagon. I beat him by fifty feet."

"That was ten years ago," Terry reminded him, not unkindly. "We were always doing crazy things together in those days."

"Well," Schwartz said, getting to his feet, "I'm for a little dancing, whatever you people do." He led a general exodus from the room, leaving it in the hands of the waiters and busboys.

I started for the elevator, telling Terry it was time to get back to the paper. "Nonsense! Stay around awhile, Ross. Look, I have to check out some things downstairs. Go up to my office and I'll meet you there."

"I don't —"

"Just give me a few minutes, will you? There's something I want to talk over, off the record."

"All right." You can always snag a newsman's curiosity.

I went up to his office, through the unlocked reception room where his secretary had long since departed, and settled down in the oversized swivel chair behind his big oak desk. Against the side wall was a bank of television monitors with a row of buttons under each one, giving him a view through any of the several dozen cameras scattered around the club. I played with them a bit as Terry might have, pressing a button under one screen to bring in a view of the dance floor. The black-and-white image wasn't too sharp, but I didn't see anyone I knew.

"Fun, isn't it?" Terry Box said, entering the office while I was playing with the monitors.

"Do you have cameras in the rest rooms too?"

He laughed. "Not quite. Though maybe it would cut down on some of the pot selling."

I yielded the chair to him. "Are drugs much of a problem?"

"Not really. Now and then we have an incident."

"They've become a problem with Milly, though."

He looked at me, a bit startled by my words. "Oh, you mean

her nose? The damn fool — how could she have let that happen?"

"She thinks you're trying to seduce Dora Polk."

Terry Box snorted. He leaned over and pushed some of the monitor buttons at random. "If she told you I'm sure she was far more graphic than that. Milly never used a word like 'seduce' in her life."

"Is it true?"

"I wouldn't —" He stopped, his finger on one of the buttons. "There's Rufus back in the room where we dined. He must have forgotten something."

I stared at the screen with interest. The white of his face and shirt front were the only breaks in the dark-suited image that was entering the private dining room, but even with the fuzzy picture it was clearly Rufus Kinkaid.

And then he did an odd thing. He closed the door after him and turned the bolt, locking it. The dining table was bare now and he walked around it, toward the camera, his eyes fixed on something below the camera, out of range.

"Well?" Kinkaid asked. "Now what do you want?"

There was a sharp crack and we saw him stagger backward.

"My God!" Terry gasped, on his feet now. "Come on!"

We didn't wait for the elevator but ran down the carpeted stairs to the floor below. I was the first to reach the door. It was still locked and I pounded on it with my hand. Terry ran up and shouted, "Rufus! What happened in there?" Waiters were coming now too, attracted by our yelling.

When there was no response, Terry reached a quick decision. "We'll break it down," he said. Terry and one of the waiters hit the middle paneling with their shoulders. It cracked on the first blow, and smashed inward after two more tries. They pushed the wood out of the way and we entered the room.

Rufus Kinkaid lay on the other side of the bare dining table, where we'd seen him fall. He'd been shot once in the chest and the blood had stained the front of his shirt and the white carnation.

There was no one else in the room.

◆ ◆ ◆

The room in which Rufus Kinkaid had been murdered, and in which we'd eaten dinner earlier, was some thirty feet long by fifteen feet wide. Other than the table and chairs, and a side serving table, it was virtually devoid of furnishings. There were no windows, and the few pastel paintings on the walls might have been chosen for the express purpose of passing unnoticed. Otherwise there was only a buzzer for summoning the waiter, and the small black television camera mounted in the far right corner of the room.

There was no place the murderer could have hidden, and no way he — or she — could have left the room.

It was an impossible crime, the kind you read about in books.

As the police quickly brought out in their questioning, no one could have left the room after shooting Kinkaid and still managed to have the door bolted from the inside. In books they're always turning the bolts with loops of string pulled under the door, but in this case Terry and I had been on the scene in less than a minute. No killer could have gotten out and fiddled with the bolt in that length of time.

"What was the purpose of the inside bolt?" a detective lieutenant named Buckley asked.

Terry Box put on his most winning smile. The stark tragedy of Kinkaid's death had been weighed in his mind against the future of Sequin City. "Nothing sinister, Lieutenant. These are private dining rooms, often used for business meetings. Sometimes it might be inopportune for a waiter to walk in and overhear something. The bolt may be operated only from inside the room. There's a separate key lock on the outside, of course, for locking the room when it's not in use."

Lieutenant Buckley, a New York detective of the old school,

was staring up at the television camera. "All your private dining rooms are like this?"

"Yes. We have six this size, plus our larger public dining area."

"If they're so private, what's the TV doing up there — and with a sound mike, too!"

"Both picture and sound may be disconnected on request, if my customers wish privacy. But generally we leave them on as a security measure."

"Damn funny you got a murder, with all the security measures in this place!" He walked to the table and started going through the contents of the dead man's pocket. "You say this Kinkaid was in intelligence work?"

"Years ago," Terry explained. "More recently he was a computer specialist."

"Looks as if he was carrying some sort of code in his pocket."

"Code?" We both moved to his side to examine the find.

"It's a computer print-out," Terry said, looking over the folded sheet of paper. "A cipher, with the message split into five-letter groups."

"Yeah? What's it say?" the detective asked.

"How should I know?"

I glanced over Buckley's shoulder and read: "QETMD UNHFV ZGPJB OIKSX AWRCY LQURE ZSDWI MTFXV GCKNH OJBAL PY."

"Fifty-two letters in the message," I commented. "One for each week of the year."

"That means nothing," Terry said. "The real message could be shorter or longer, depending upon the cipher used."

"Could you break it if you worked on it?" I asked him.

"I've been away from the business too long. Ask Dora or Steve."

"They could be suspects," Buckley pointed out. "But you seem to be in the clear, with Calendar here giving you an alibi."

"He was with me all the time," I verified. "We saw the murder on the monitor together."

I said it, but I didn't completely believe in Terry's alibi myself. It was just too neat, and I'd read a few books where a person was killed in a locked room with some sort of mechanical device. While Buckley questioned the others, I prowled around the corner where the camera was. Kinkaid had been shot in the chest, from a point directly under the camera, so that's where I looked.

I found nothing but the corner where two walls came together. No niches, no wood paneling that could be slid away. Nothing but solid wall.

Next I turned my attention to the television camera itself. It was a little Japanese model of the sort often used to provide security in apartment and hotel elevators. It was a sound model, with a tiny microphone beneath it, but there was no hidden gun — not even a slender tube capable of firing a bullet by electricity.

The killer had been in the room with Kinkaid, and now he was gone — through a locked door in a matter of less than a minute.

It was as simple as that.

Suddenly I remembered I worked for a newspaper and I was sitting on a hot news story. I found a telephone and called the city desk.

◆   ◆   ◆

It was Steve Schwartz who came to me a bit later, after the police had finished questioning him. He ran a nervous hand through his thinning hairline and said, "You look like someone I could talk to. That damned Buckley would as soon lock me up as look at me!"

"What's there to talk about?"

"That computer print-out they found in Rufus's pocket."

"The cipher?"

"That's the point. It's not a cipher. At least not in the usual sense."

"Then what is it?"

"Computers can be programmed to deliver randomly generated letters or numbers. It's useful for all sorts of things, from game playing to experiments in extrasensory perception, and even to the production of one-time pads for use in ciphers. If you remember that print-out of fifty-two letters, no letter was repeated until the entire alphabet had been used up. Then the machine started over again on a second alphabet. It's virtually impossible for any cipher message to come out that way by chance."

"So what are you telling me?" I asked.

"It's not a cipher in itself, but a computer print-out of two randomly generated alphabets."

"Arranged in five-letter groupings?"

Schwartz shrugged. "For easy reading."

"Have you ever seen any like it before?"

He hesitated. "As I told you, it's used for many things."

"What, in your department? Or in Kinkaid's position with his company?"

"Well, computerized storage of records has come a long way in recent years. Sometimes when highly classified information is stored in a computer, an elaborate routine must be followed to retrieve it."

I got what he was driving at. "You think the two scrambled alphabets might be a key to the computer storage bank, enabling Rufus Kinkaid to retrieve one particular item?"

"It's a possibility."

"Would it be a computer in Washington or at Kinkaid's office?"

"At his office, I'd say. That particular type of print-out paper wasn't used by our bureau when Rufus worked with us."

"How could I gain access to it?"

Steve Schwartz frowned. "Look — I'm as anxious as you are to find the person who killed Rufus, but I don't think I want to break any laws to do it."

"You're not breaking the law. You're helping to catch a killer."

Still he hesitated, and I wondered if it was because he feared that Dora Polk might be implicated. "All right," he said at last. "The computer at Rufus's place is available for time sharing. That means anyone can buy an hour or more of time on it and use it as he wishes. Rufus needed the key to protect his information against accidental discovery. But you or anyone else could rent time on the computer, type in this access code and retrieve his information."

"What do you think it'll say?"

"I haven't any idea."

I left him, thinking that computers and ciphers and locked rooms all needed keys of one sort or another. And perhaps, just as the apparent cipher was really a key to the computer, the information I found there would be a key to Rufus Kinkaid's locked room.

◆   ◆   ◆

When I returned to Sequin City late the following day, I went directly to Terry Box's office. His secretary was nowhere in sight, and I walked right in, figuring he'd seen me already on one of the TV monitors.

I was wrong. He was seated on the couch with Dora Polk, sipping a glass of champagne, and the murderous look he gave me indicated I'd interrupted the early stages of a classic seduction scene. Maybe Milly Nostrum's jealousy had been well founded after all.

Dora leaped to her feet, looking vaguely guilty. "What —? You're a reporter, aren't you?"

"Columnist," I corrected. "I like the sound of it better."

"What do you want, Ross?" Terry asked. "I don't enjoy people barging into my private office."

"I know who killed Rufus Kinkaid and how it was done. I just thought you might be interested."

"You know?" Dora exclaimed, startled by my words. "How could you know?"

"Just a little detective work. A computer print-out this afternoon supplied me with the motive, but I didn't need that to tell me how the locked-room trick was worked."

"Computer?" Terry Box asked with a scowl. "What computer?"

"Rufus Kinkaid stored some information in his computer years ago, when he left government service and took the job in private industry. Don't ask me why he did it. Maybe it was insurance of a sort. He carried with him the access code to this information — two randomly generated alphabets. I bought time on that computer this afternoon and typed out those fifty-two letters in their proper order. The computer responded with the print-out of a confidential file on one of Kinkaid's co-workers in Washington, indicating this person had been indiscreet in the handling of classified information. No formal criminal charges were ever brought, but the evidence was there. It involved connections with organized crime, and furnishing them with information regarding government monitoring of fund transfers from certain large Las Vegas bank accounts."

Dora Polk gasped. "Steve works on that sort of thing."

"But only since Terry's departure," I said. "The print-out concerned you, Terry."

He strode angrily to his desk. "Are you saying I killed Rufus?"

"Yes."

"That's ridiculous! You were with me at the time! We saw it happen together."

"What we saw was a videotape of a performance Rufus Kinkaid staged at your urging some hours earlier before we all sat down to dinner. You told us yourself that you and Kinkaid were always doing crazy things together. A phony murder staged for the closed-circuit cameras could have seemed like a practical joke."

"But I was still with you," Terry insisted.

"Not for the whole period. You went to check out something downstairs, you told me, though I didn't see you on any of the video screens while I waited in your office. You met Kinkaid in the private dining room, shot him with a silenced pistol, and locked the door from the outside with your key. After you returned to your office it was a simple operation to flick the switch that would start the videotape playing. I saw Kinkaid bolt the door and apparently take a shot in the chest from an unseen gunman. You led me out of the office before I could see the tape come to an end. Downstairs we smashed down the locked door without realizing it was the key lock and not the bolt that was fastened. It was easy for you to close the bolt on the splintered door before anyone examined it too closely."

"Do you think Rufus would take part in a joke like that if he knew I meant to kill him?"

"That's just it — he didn't know. Perhaps he even brought that computer key along to give you as a gift, to bury the past once and for all. He never dreamed that Sequin City was the first step toward a legalized gambling casino in Manhattan — a goal that would be ruined forever if word got out of your past underworld ties. You invited them up here for exactly that reason — not to seduce Dora but to silence Rufus Kinkaid forever."

The door opened behind me and I turned to see Milly Nostrum come in. That was my mistake. When I glanced back at Terry he was holding a revolver in his hand, pointed at my chest.

"Terry!" Dora gasped. "You can't be serious!"

"I'm serious," he barked. "Damn you, Ross, you've ruined everything for me!"

"I've already told it all to Lieutenant Buckley. That gun won't get you anywhere."

"It'll get me out of here." He motioned to a spellbound Milly. "Cover them while I get some money from the safe."

I could hardly believe my eyes when he handed her the gun. He really had no idea what he'd done to her.

She was sobbing when she shot him.

◆   ◆   ◆

Lieutenant Buckley wasn't happy about any of it. "You just stood there and let her shoot him?"

"Everything happened so fast!" It was the only excuse I had. "Will he live?"

"His condition is critical, but they think he'll make it." He finished making some notes on his report. "Now before you scoot off back to your newspaper I want to know a few things."

"I've told you everything there is to know. Terry Box killed Kinkaid to keep secret his past underworld ties. He knew Kinkaid could ruin his chances for a gambling license in New York State, if the casino law passes. And I told you about the locked room."

He fixed me with an icy gaze. "But you didn't tell me how you *knew* about the locked room!"

"I remembered something on that television monitor. When Rufus Kinkaid appeared on the screen the only spots of white were his face and shirtfront. Yet I saw Milly pin a white carnation on him at dinner, and he was still wearing it when we reached the body. I asked myself how that carnation could disappear and then appear again. The answer was, it hadn't. I was seeing Kinkaid as he looked earlier, before dinner. The image on the screen was a videotape. And once I knew that, only Terry Box could have arranged the whole thing — including the murder."

Buckley sighed and finished his notes. "All right. But we'll still want a full statement from you."

"Just buy a morning paper, Lieutenant. It'll all be in tomorrow's column."

The Cow and the Jackrabbit

by MBVSKBOXJMMFNWBOEFXFUFSJOH

I suppose it does us good to look at the other side of the coin now and then. Sherlock Holmes taught us all to believe in the keen and indefatigable fitter-together of tiny bits of evidence with an inexorable chain of logic leading to an ineluctable conclusion. But who says that every detective has to be a Sherlock Holmes?

A detective-superintendent once stated, at the end of his retirement speech, and while being certain that most of us were no longer sober, *that police officers are not known for their intelligence.* Which was fine, he continued. Not to worry. We don't have to be intelligent, as long as we are forever present. The scene of the crime is all around us and it harbors the criminals. If we keep close to the criminal he will stumble into us, and if he does we can't help grabbing him.

The audience roared and applauded. We all thought the old chief was a brilliant wit. This impression was further confirmed by a little story that he told us to explain his hypothesis.

"A jackrabbit ran through a field without paying attention. He ran into a post, hurt his head, and staggered about blindly. A cow happened to be on the field, too. The jackrabbit stumbled between her legs and collapsed. 'Look,' the cow said, 'I've caught a jackrabbit.'

"You see?" the detective-superintendent asked.

We slapped each other on the back and held our sides. Then we went home and forgot. I didn't forget the story altogether, I guess, for when I solved the Johnson case it popped up in my mind again. Here is why.

One afternoon a Mr. Johnson called on me, at police head-quarters. He wished to report the disappearance of his wife Geraldine, who wasn't home when he returned from work the previous day, and hadn't come home since. Presuming that the complainant wanted to be reassured, I endeavored to do so. I mentioned that many wives disappear for short periods. They usually visit their mothers, and there is no need for excessive alarm, as they nearly always return in good health.

Mr. Johnson said that he wasn't worried. He was sure his wife was well and comfortable, at some unknown address. She had left him of her own free will and would now want a divorce. He was expecting a letter from her lawyer. He was only informing the police because Geraldine had left in an irregular manner.

"Irregular?" I asked. Had she perhaps flown away?

She had not. But she hadn't left a note.

I still wasn't impressed.

And she had taken the contents of their apartment, Trevor Johnson added, leaving nothing. When he came home he encountered no furniture. There were no pots and pans in the kitchen. There wasn't even any paper in the bathroom. She had removed all their possessions, hers, and his. He was missing his books, clothes, and toiletries. Not that he was charging his wife with theft. He informed us because others might come to see us too, neighbors perhaps, or relatives, or friends. It would be better if he, the husband, came first.

I thereupon accompanied Mr. Johnson to his home, but mostly to humor him. My attitude changed when his report proved to be correct. The apartment consisted of five rooms on the top floor of a luxurious building overlooking Willow Park and, all rooms being empty, that was all it consisted of. We listened to our own hollow footsteps and observed the light that reflected from the parquet floors. The evidence — or rather, the total lack of everything that constituted the evidence — convinced me. I instigated an official investigation.

A missing-person routine, based on copies of a photograph that Mr. Johnson had in his wallet, produced no results. The photograph was a clear portrait and it was printed on the front page of all local newspapers. There was also a reward. But there were no responses.

There was the removal of the furniture, and I worked from that side. I found a witness, an old lady living next door to the Johnson apartment. Unfortunately she was in her dotage and didn't remember much. She had seen several men and a large truck. The men emptied the apartment and filled up the truck. She couldn't remember if there had been any lettering on the truck. But she did remember that the men had worked without the supervision of either Mrs. or Mr. Johnson.

I contacted all moving and trucking firms in the city. Again, nothing.

I tried another approach again and collected information from Mr. Johnson, using him and some of the couple's relatives and friends as sources. Soon I learned the following: Trevor Johnson was forty-eight years old, his wife was ten years younger, and they had been married fifteen years. No children. Financially they were well off. Mr. Johnson taught history at the city's college; Mrs. Johnson kept the house. They had both inherited money, so there was no need for him to work.

The complainant was handsome; tall, wide-shouldered, strong-jawed, and he still had all his hair. He didn't have an outgoing personality; on the contrary, it seemed that he liked to be by himself. He was a recluse, given to study and walks in the park with his dog. When I heard about the dog I prodded a little further. There was no dog in the apartment, so what happened to it? Mr. Johnson told me it had disappeared about a week before the disappearance of his wife. Another disappearance.

By chance I found the dog's body. I was talking to the old neighbor, and she complained about the seagulls and the crows and their raucous cries that disturbed her afternoon naps. The birds had been particularly noisy some days ago, she added, stamping about on the roof and fighting amongst themselves. I remembered that both gulls and crows are carrion birds, and searched the roof. The dog's corpse was a bag of skin filled with bones. The police laboratory took a look at it and came up with the startling conclusion that it had been killed with a hammer. Its skull was crushed.

Encouraged, I continued. I found out that although Mr. Johnson liked to be by himself, Mrs. Johnson didn't. Geraldine's socializing was hampered, of course, by her husband's lonely habits. The lack of transportation wasn't helpful either. Mr. Johnson had never bothered to learn to drive and Geraldine kept failing her driving tests. She didn't like having to rely on friends to take her to parties, movies, and so forth. She was said to nag and complain and to suffer from psychosomatic illnesses — itches, headaches, cramps, and so forth. I could find no trace of lovers.

Whenever I called on Mr. Johnson I found him to be calm and in good spirits. He would take his time before he answered a question. He would also smile, mostly when I could see no cause for amusement at all. I asked him to explain his over-calm and over-slow reactions and was told that he suffered from a heart condition. His doctors urged him to be careful and to avoid all emotional stress. A heart attack had almost killed him some years back; another heart attack would kill him altogether. Being aware of his near-terminal position he constantly disciplined himself until his detachment had become habitual.

Once I asked him to explain his apparent happiness. He told me about feeling relieved. He had always thought that he depended on his wife, on his home, on the continuous relationship with the wife in the home. But the recent experience had proved, overwhelmingly, that he needed neither wife nor home. This discovery made him feel as if heavy chains had suddenly been removed. A very light feeling, so to speak. Hence the smiles.

I smiled too, to cover up my thoughts. Mr. Johnson didn't know that I had called on his spinster sister that day. She had told me a strange tale. It seemed that as a child Trevor Johnson had been a weird little fellow. I deduced this fact from several instances the spinster sister related, but it was mainly confirmed by the feat of the buried toys. Little Trevor had ("to punish our poor parents," the spinster sister said), one bleak and dark night, sneaked out of the house and dug a grave for his toys. The grave was discovered and opened. "And not only had he buried all his lovely things," my informant said, "he had also smashed them. And he had cut the head off his teddy bear."

I left my suspect and returned to my desk to dream. This was pure Poe indeed. What a pity Geraldine Johnson had to disappear from a modern apartment. I imagined the correct setting: a stately Victorian mansion against a forest of dark pines. Trevor Johnson, the local squire, is visited by the chief-constable of the county. I visit him to enquire about the mysterious disappearance of his wife. The butler ushers me into a vast room where my host stumbles about, one leg swollen by gout. We sit down, opposite crackling logs in a gigantic brick fireplace. Wine glows in crystal tumblers. The smoke of fine cigars crinkles to a high ceiling. The squire tells me his wife is probably in London, engaged in a dalliance. He assures me he doesn't care, as long as she is happy. He then tells an amusing story and laughs boisterously. And then, after his "Ho! Ho!" has died away, a bloodcurdling shriek, wrenching itself from the thick wall behind us. I jump up, shouting for the butler. We find crowbars and picks. We tear at the wall. And the corpse of the squire's wife faces us, grinning from rotting lips. A scarecrow of a cat stands on her decaying head and yells again, before it jumps down and scrambles away.

I sighed. No cat this time, but a dog. I had already found the dog. But where was Geraldine's body? Not, for sure, in the flimsy walls of a modern apartment. Where had he hidden it? He didn't have a car, so he couldn't have taken it very far. And he wouldn't have left it for the moving men to find. The body had to be close to the apartment. Most likely I would locate it in the park.

I visualized the scene of death. I didn't think the crime had been premeditated. It had been an evening like many others, with Trevor trying to read his history book and Geraldine nagging. She was whining to be taken out, to a movie, or a party. The nagging increased in volume, perhaps in venom as well.

I had been told that Trevor Johnson didn't like to play as a child. He would not want to play as a grownup either. As a child he killed his toys, as an adult he killed his dog and his wife. All killings had been for the same reason, and on the spur of the moment. Having killed his wife in anger he couldn't have been careful. Blood had splattered on the furniture, the carpets. He knew about police tests, knew that the smallest particle of blood can be found and identified. He would have to remove both corpse and furniture. The idea to remove *all* the furniture was a good bizarre touch, likely to confuse the police.

I groaned. Proof, I needed proof. I studied a map. Willow Park consists of many acres. I could call in draglines and bulldozers, and arm a hundred constables with spades. It would be the end of the park, and the end of me, even if we did find the corpse.

Then I conceived a more modest plan. I would disguise myself and attach myself to the suspect, like a burr on his clothes. He would lead me to his doom, to either grave or storage.

My final attempt started that afternoon. It dragged itself out, and I named it the Willow Park Wake. I watched my suspect from afar, followed him to the college and back to the park, then watched him go home again. He had told me that he was camping in the apartment, sleeping on an air mattress, cooking on a little stove, reading books he borrowed from the college library. A happy man. Each day he would spend an hour or so in the park enjoying the spring weather, ambling about. He was delighted by the baby birds splashing about in the ponds. He gazed at the insects buzzing above bright bushes. He looked at everything except at the other Willow Park habitués. He didn't see the ladies, wistfully observing his elegant six-foot-five frame, topped by golden locks, or the gays, doing the same.

Becoming bored with the birds and the bees, I began to observe the ladies and the gays paying attention to my suspect. After a while I concentrated on one lady and one gay. The lady I selected was quietly stunning, with a sleek maturity enhanced by her tweed jacket and matching skirt and a silk blouse that hadn't been buttoned well. The clothes seemed demure, but weren't. Her mouth wasn't either. The full softly curling lips were lascivious. Her long eyelashes hid a wicked twinkle. The tiny wriggle in her slim hips made me feel the full and terrible impact of the season.

The gay I studied with less enthusiasm. He was slender, attractive, well dressed in a three-piece linen summer suit and a felt hat with a wide rim. The hat's rim hid his eyes, but I could feel, from the direction and the tension of his body, that his vibrations were constantly directed at Mr. Johnson.

When Mr. Johnson continued not to notice the lady she became impatient. He watched the goslings, she stood next to him. She placed herself in such a way that he would have to bump her when he would turn away from the pond. He did, she staggered, overacted, tripped on a pebble. She even hurt herself and showed all of her legs.

Mr. Johnson's reaction followed the pattern programmed by the lady. He apologized, fussed, helped her up, dabbed at the scratch on her knee with his handkerchief. She smiled and leaned on his arm. He walked her home. I followed. I saw the gay watching the couple from a distance. I felt sorry for him.

The lady lived close by. She didn't ask Mr. Johnson in; perhaps she was married. They were holding hands and mumbling and I felt sure that their next meeting would be soon.

I had to wait until sunset. I saw Mr. Johnson come out of his building, and head for the park. There were still quite a few people in the park for the evening was warm. I spotted the gay, standing next to an azalea bush.

Mr. Johnson waited near the pond, in the exact spot where the lady had fallen earlier. She joined him a few minutes later, the tiny wriggle in her hips more noticeable now. They walked off to the azaleas together. Then she stopped and held up her lovely lips. The gay turned toward them and held up a gun. I held up a forbidding hand, dropped it, and tackled Johnson. He went down nicely. The shot went wild. I freed myself from the tangle, yelled, and grabbed the gun. Johnson was up again, too. The gay's hat had fallen off. Johnson peered into his face.

"Geraldine!"

I arrested Geraldine Johnson for the attempted manslaughter of her husband.

◆ ◆ ◆

I didn't let on. No one ever knew I spent a large number of hours in a park because I expected a killer to lead me to a grave. My report doesn't even try to explain what I was doing there. But it does mention the arrest.

Geraldine confessed, lengthily. I wrote down only the last part, where she admits that she fired a shot at her husband because he was about to embrace another woman. The earlier attempts, both of them attempted murders, are ignored completely. I don't think they would hold in court. Our public prosecutor is sufficiently confused *as is,* there is no need to add to his suffering.

Geraldine, crying in her cell, would pause every now and then to tell me about *her* suffering. Trevor never noticed her, never. And he wouldn't retire. They had enough money to buy a beautiful house, with a large garden. They could have parties, all sorts of parties. She loved parties. She loved life, but it was slipping away, and she was almost forty. So she had become desperate. If he wouldn't listen to her, if he would continue to ignore her forever, she would make him into a helpless invalid. The doctors warned that he was not allowed to be shocked. Very well. So she killed the dog, his darling, and made it disappear. She cried a little more. I waited.

"And then, when he didn't react to my taking Chérie away I took myself away, and everything else too. He always said he loved me, loved the apartment, the way I had it arranged. He liked the antiques we had collected, the oriental rugs. And he *loved* me, he always said so."

I waited again, but there wasn't much more to come. Just that she had bought the gun, in desperation, but hadn't had the courage to use it, that she was planning to return to him, and then there had been that horrible woman and Trevor about to kiss the horrible woman.

"And then *you* were there too, a police officer."

Quite. And I caught her. I was around, like the cow was on the field and the jackrabbit came and collapsed between her legs.

"Look," the cow said, "I've caught a jackrabbit. And the other cows were impressed."

Connoisseur

by JTBBDBTJNPWJTBCJMMQSPOAJOJ

I think we should always be grateful if a murder tale, in addition to entertaining us and providing us with the task of trying to outguess the author, also provides us with an edifying moral. Oh, dear reader, beware the demon rum or, in this case, the devil claret, for see how it leads to sin and violence!

Norman Tolliver was a connoisseur of many things: art, music, literature, gourmet cuisine, sports cars, beautiful women. But above all else, he was a connoisseur of fine wine.

Nothing gave him quite so much pleasure as the bouquet and delicate taste of a claret from the Médoc region of Bordeaux — a 1924 Mouton-Rothschild, perhaps, or a 1929 Haut-Brion; or of a brilliant Burgundy such as a Clos de Vougeot 1915. His memory was still vivid of the night in Paris when an acquaintance of his father's had presented him with a glass of the *impériale* claret, the 1878 Latour Pauillac. It was Norman's opinion that a man could experience no greater moment of ecstasy than his first sip of that venerable Latour.

He resided in an elegant penthouse in New York that commanded a view of the city best described as lordly. That is, he resided there for six months of the year; the remaining six months were divided among Europe and the pleasure islands of the Caribbean and the Mediterranean. During his travels he expended an appreciable amount of time and money in seeking out new varieties and rare vintages of wine, most of which he arranged to have shipped to New York for placement in his private cellar.

It was his custom every Friday evening, no matter where he might happen to be, to sample an exceptional bottle of claret or Burgundy. (He enjoyed fine whites, of course — the French Sauterne, the German Moselle — but his palate and his temperament were more suited to the classic reds.) These weekly indulgences were always of a solitary nature; as a connoisseur he found the communion between man and great wine too intimate to share with anyone, too poignant to be blunted by even polite conversation.

On this particular Friday Norman happened to be in New York and the wine he happened to select was a reputedly splendid claret: the Château Margaux 1900. It had been given to him by a man named Roger Hume, whom Norman rather detested. Whereas he himself was the fourth-generation progeny in a family of wealth and breeding, Hume was *nouveau-riche* — a large graceless individual who had compiled an overnight fortune in textiles or some such and who had retired at the age of 40 to, as he put it in his vulgar way, "see how the upper crust lives."

Norman found the man to be boorish, dull-witted, and incredibly ignorant concerning any number of matters, including an understanding and appreciation of wine. Nevertheless, Hume *had* presented him with the Margaux — on the day after a small social gathering that they had both attended and at which Norman chanced to mention that he had never had the pleasure of tasting that difficult-to-obtain vintage. The man's generosity was crassly motivated, to be sure, designed only to impress; but that could be overlooked and even forgiven. A bottle of Margaux 1900 was too fine a prize to be received with any feelings other than gratitude.

At three o'clock Norman drew his study drapes against the afternoon sun and placed one of Chopin's nocturnes on his quadrophonic record changer. Then, with a keen sense of anticipation, he carefully removed the Margaux's cork and prepared to decant the wine so that it could breathe. It was his considered judgment that an aged claret should be allowed no less than five hours of contact with new air and no more than six. A healthy, living wine must be given time to breathe in order for it to express its character, release its bouquet, become *more* alive; but too much breathing causes a dulling of its subtle edge.

He lighted the candle that he had set on the Duncan Phyfe table, waited until the flame was steady, and began to slowly pour the Margaux, holding the shoulder of the bottle just above the light so that he could observe the flow of the wine as it passed through the neck. There was very little age-crust or sediment. The color, however, did not look quite right; it had a faint cloudiness, a pale brown tinge, as wine does when it has grown old too quickly.

Norman felt a sharp twinge of apprehension. He raised the decanter and sniffed the bouquet. Not good, not good at all. He swirled the wine lightly to let air mix with it and sniffed again. Oh Lord — a definite taint of sourness.

He poured a small amount into a crystal glass, prepared himself, and took a sip. Let the wine flood over and under his tongue, around his gums.

And then spat the mouthful back into the glass.

The Margaux was dead.

Sour, unpalatable — *dead.*

White-faced, Norman sank onto a chair. His first feelings were of sorrow and despair, but these soon gave way to a sense of outrage focused on Roger Hume. It was Hume who had given him not a living, breathing 1900 Margaux but a dessicated *corpse;* it was Hume who had tantalized him and then left him unfulfilled, Hume who had caused him this pain and anguish, Hume who might even have been responsible for the death of the Margaux through careless mishandling. Damn the man. Damn him!

The more Norman thought about Roger Hume, the more enraged he became. Heat rose in his cheeks until they flamed scarlet. Minutes passed before he remembered his high blood pressure and his doctor's warning about undue stress; he made a conscious effort to calm himself.

When he had his emotions under control he stood, went to the telephone, found a listing for Hume in the New York City directory, and dialed the number. Hume's loud coarse voice answered on the third ring.

"This is Norman Tolliver, Hume," Norman said.

"Well, Norm, it's been awhile. What's the good word?"

Norm. A muscle fluttered on Norman's cheek. "If you plan to be in this afternoon, I would like a word with you."

"Oh? Something up?"

"I prefer not to discuss it on the telephone."

"Suit yourself," Hume said. "Sure, come on over. Give me a chance to show off my digs to you." He paused. "You shoot pool, by any chance?"

"No, I do not 'shoot pool.' "

"Too bad. Got a new table and I've been practicing. Hell of a good game, Norm, you should try it."

The man was a bloody Philistine. Norman said, "I'll be by directly," and cradled the handset with considerable force.

He recorked the bottle of dead Margaux and wrapped it in a towel. After which he blew out the candle, switched off his quadrophonic unit, and took the penthouse elevator to the street. Fifteen minutes later a taxi delivered him to the East Side block on which Hume's town house was situated.

Hume admitted him, allowed as how it was good to see him again, swatted him on the back (Norman shuddered and ground his teeth), and ushered him into a spacious living room. There were shelves filled with rare first editions, walls adorned with originals by Degas and Monet and Sisley, fine Kerman orientals on the floor. But all of these works of art, Norman thought, could mean nothing to Hume; they would merely be possessions, visible evidence of his wealth. He had certainly never read any of the books or spent a moment appreciating any of the paintings. And there were cigarette burns (Norman ground his teeth again) in one of the Kerman carpets.

Hume himself was fifty pounds overweight and such a plebeian type that he looked out of place in these genteel surroundings. He wore expensive but ill-fitting clothes, much too heavy for the season because of a professed hypersensitivity to cold; his glasses were rimmed in gold-and-onyx and quite thick because of a professed astigmatism in one eye; he carried an English walking stick because of a slight limp that was the professed result of a sports car accident. He pretended to be an eccentric, but did not have the breeding, intelligence, or flair to manage even the *pose* of eccentricity. Looking at him now, Norman revised his previous estimate: The man was not a Philistine; he was a Neanderthal.

"How about a drink, Norman?"

"This is not a social call," Norman said.

"No?" Hume peered at him. "So what can I do you for?"

Norman unwrapped the bottle of Margaux and extended it accusingly. "*This* is what you can do me for, as you put it."

"I don't get it," Hume said.

"You gave me this Margaux last month. I trust you remember the occasion."

"Sure, I remember. But I still don't see the point —"

"The point, Hume, is that it's dead."

"Huh?"

"The wine is undrinkable. It's *dead,* Hume."

Hume threw back his head and made a sound like the braying of a jackass. "You hand me a laugh sometimes, Norm," he said, "you really do. The way you talk about wine, like it was alive or human or something."

Norman's hands had begun to tremble. "The Margaux *was* alive. Now it is nothing but 79-year-old vinegar!"

"So what?" Hume said.

"So what?" A reddish haze seemed to be forming behind Norman's eyes. "So what! You insensitive idiot, don't you have any conception of what a tragedy this is?"

"Hey," Hume said, "who you calling an idiot?"

"You, you idiot. If you have another Margaux 1900, I demand it in replacement. I demand a *living* wine."

"I don't give a damn what you demand," Hume said. He was miffed too, now. "You got no right to call me an idiot, Norm; I won't stand for it. Suppose you just get on out of my house. And take your lousy bottle of wine with you."

"*My* lousy bottle of wine?" Norman said through the reddish haze. "Oh no, Hume, it's *your* lousy bottle of wine and I'm going to let you have it!"

Then he did exactly that: He let Hume have it. On top of the head with all his strength.

There were several confused moments that Norman could not recall afterward. When the reddish haze dissipated he discovered that all of his anger had drained away, leaving him flushed and shaken. He also discovered Hume lying quite messily dead on the cigarette-scarred Kerman, the unbroken bottle of Margaux beside him.

It was not in Norman's nature to panic in a crisis. He marshaled his emotions instead and forced himself to approach the problem at hand with cold logic.

Hume was as dead as the Margaux; there was nothing to be done about that. He could, of course, telephone the police and claim self-defense. But there was no guarantee that he would be believed, considering that this was Hume's house, and in any case he had an old-fashioned gentleman's abhorrence of adverse and sensational publicity. No, reporting Hume's demise was out of the question.

Which left the reasonable alternative of removing all traces of his presence and stealing away as if he had never come. It was unlikely that anyone had seen him entering; if he was careful his departure would be unobserved as well. And even if someone *did* happen to notice him in a casual way, he was not known in this neighborhood and there was nothing about his physical appearance that would remain fixed in a person's memory. An added point in his favor was that Hume had few friends and by self-admission preferred his own company. The body, therefore, might well go undiscovered for several days.

Norman used the towel to wipe the unbloodied surfaces of the Margaux bottle — a distasteful but necessary task — and left the bottle where it lay beside the body. Had he touched anything in the house that might also retain a fingerprint? He was certain he had not. He *had* pressed the doorbell button on the porch outside, but it would be simple enough to brush that clean before leaving. Was there anything else, anything he might have overlooked? He concluded that there wasn't.

With the towel folded inside his coat pocket, he went down the hallway to the front door. There was a magnifying-glass peephole in the center of it; he put his eye to the glass and peered out. Damn. Two women were standing on the street in front, conversing in the amiable and animated fashion of neighbors. They might decide to part company in ten seconds, but they might also decide to remain there for ten minutes.

Norman debated the advisability of exiting through the rear. But a man slipping out the back door of someone's house was much more likely to be seen and remembered than a man who departed the front. And there was still the matter of the doorbell button to be dealt with. His only intelligent choice was to wait for the street in front to become clear.

As he stood there he found himself thinking again of the tragedy of the Margaux 1900 (a far greater tragedy to his connoisseur's mind than the unlamented death of Roger Hume). It was considered by many experts to be one of the most superlative vintages in history; and the fact remained that he had yet to taste it. To have come so close and then to be denied as he had was intolerable.

It occurred to him again that perhaps Hume *did* have another bottle on the premises. While presenting the first bottle last month Hume had boasted that he maintained a "pretty well-stocked" wine cellar, though he confided that he had never had "much of a taste for the grape" and seldom availed himself of its contents. Neanderthal, indeed. But a Neanderthal with a good deal of money who had managed, through luck or wise advice, to obtain at least one bottle of an uncommon and classic wine —

Was there another Margaux 1900 in his blasted cellar?

Norman debated a second time. On the one hand it would behoove him to make as rapid an escape as possible from the scene of his impulsive crime; but on the other hand the 1900 Margaux was virtually impossible to find today, and if he passed up this opportunity to secure a bottle for himself he might never taste it. It would be a decision he might well rue for the rest of his days.

He looked once more through the peephole; the two women were still talking together outside. Which only served to cement a decision already made. He was, first and foremost, a connoisseur: he simply *had* to know if Hume had another bottle of the Margaux.

Norman located the wine cellar without difficulty. It was off the kitchen, with access through a door and down a short flight of steps. It was also adequate, he noticed in a distracted way as he descended — a smallish single room, walled and floored in concrete, containing several storage bins filled with at least two hundred bottles of wine.

But no, not just wine; remarkably *fine* wine. Reds from Châteaux Lafite, Haut-Brion, Lascombes, Cos D'Estournel, Mouton-D'Armailhacq, La Tâche, Romanée Saint-Vivant; whites from the Bommes and Barsac communes of France, from the Rhine Hessen of Germany, from Alsace and Italy and the Napa Valley of California. Norman resisted the impulse to stop and more closely examine each of the labels. He had no time to search out anything except the Margaux 1900.

He found two different Château Margaux clarets in the last row of bins, but neither of them was the 1900 vintage. Then, when he was about to abandon hope, he knelt in front of the final section of bins and there they were, a pair of dusty bottles whose labels matched that on the spoiled bottle upstairs.

Norman expelled a breath and removed one of them with care. Should he take the second as well? Yes: If he left it here there was no telling into whose unappreciative hands it might fall. There would doubtless be a paper sack in the kitchen in which to carry both. He withdrew the second bottle, straightened, and started across to the stairs.

The door at the top was closed. Blinking, Norman paused. He could not recall having shut the door; in fact he was quite certain he had left it standing wide open. He frowned, went up the steps, set the two living Margaux 1900s down carefully at his feet, and rotated the knob.

It was locked.

It took a moment of futile shaking and rattling before he realized that the top of the door was outfitted with one of those silent pneumatic door closers. He stared at it in disbelief. Only an idiot would put such a device on the door to a wine cellar! But that was, of course, what Hume had been. For whatever incredible reason he had had the thing installed — and it seemed obvious now that he carried on his person the key to the door latch.

There was no other way out of the cellar, no second door and no window; Norman determined that with a single sweep of his gaze. And the door looked to be fashioned of heavy solid wood, which made the task of forcing it or battering it down an insurmountable one.

He was trapped.

The irony was as bitter as the taste of the dead Margaux: trapped in Roger Hume's wine cellar with the man's murdered corpse in the living room upstairs. He had been a fool to come down here, a fool to have listened to the connoisseur in him. He could have been on his way home to his penthouse by now. Instead, here he was, locked away awaiting the eventual arrival of the police . . .

As he had done earlier, Norman made an effort to gather his

wits. Perhaps all was *not* lost, despite the circumstances. He could claim to have been visiting Hume when two burly masked men entered the house; and he could claim that these men had locked him in the cellar and taken Hume away to an unknown fate. Yes, that was plausible. After all, he was a respected and influential man. Why shouldn't he be believed?

Norman began to feel a bit better. There remained the problem of survival until Hume's body was found; but as long as that did not take more than a week — an unlikely prospect — the problem was not really a serious one. He was surrounded by scores of bottles of vintage wine, and there *was* a certain amount of nourishment to be had from the product of the vintner's art. At least enough to keep him alive and in passable health.

Meanwhile, he would have to find ways to keep himself and his mind occupied. He could begin, he thought, by examining and making a mental catalogue of Hume's collection of vintages and varieties.

He turned from the door and surveyed the cellar again. And for the first time, something struck him as vaguely wrong about it. He had not noticed it before in his haste and purpose, but now that he was locked in here with nothing to distract him —

A faint sound reached his ears and made him scowl. He could not quite identify it or its source at first; he descended the stairs again and stood at the bottom, listening. It seemed to be coming from both sides of the cellar. Norman moved to his left — and when the sound became clearer the hackles rose on the back of his neck.

What it was was a soft hissing . . .

◆   ◆   ◆

Roger Hume's body was discovered three days later by his twice-weekly cleaning lady. But when the police arrived at her summons, it was not Hume's death which interested them quite so much as that of the *second* man, whose corpse was found during a routine search of the premises.

This second "victim" lay on the floor of the wine cellar, amid a rather astonishing carnage of broken wine bottles and spilled wine. His wallet identified him as Norman Tolliver, whose name and standing were recognized by the cleaning lady, if not by the homicide detectives. The assistant medical examiner determined probable cause of death to be an apoplectic seizure, a fact which only added to the consternation of the police. Why was Tolliver locked inside Roger Hume's wine cellar? Why had he evidently smashed dozens of bottles of expensive wine? Why was he dead of natural causes and Hume dead as a result of foul play?

They were, in a word, baffled.

One other puzzling aspect came to their attention. A plainclothes officer noticed the faint hissing sound and verified it as forced air coming through a pair of wall ducts; he mentioned this to his lieutenant, saying that it seemed odd for a wine cellar to have heater vents like the rest of the rooms in the house. Neither detective bothered to pursue the matter, however. It struck them as unrelated to the deaths of the two men.

But it was, of course, the exact opposite: It was the key to everything. Along with several facts of which they were not yet aware: Norman's passion for wine and his high blood pressure, Roger Hume's ignorance in the finer arts and *his* hypersensitivity to cold — and the tragic effect on certain wines caused by constant exposure to temperatures above 60 degrees Fahrenheit.

No wonder Norman, poor fellow, suffered an apoplectic seizure. Can there be any greater horror for the true connoisseur than to find himself trapped in a cellar full of rare, aged, and irreplaceable wines that have been stupidly reduced to vinegar?

The Lily Pond

by B M J D F M B S B D I F M D P T H S P W F Q B Z F T

We all know fiction is fiction. When I was merely a writer, I used to feel sometimes (just sometimes) that editors were villains. Now, however, that I fulfill editorial functions occasionally, and after a fashion, my eyes are opened, and I know that editors are sweet, delightful, and rigidly, rigidly ethical. So I emphasize — the following is fiction.

The scruffy young man had worked as a yard man for Duncan Mallory for nearly a month before he approached him with the tattered notebook. Mallory was sitting on the terrace, a tall cool drink at his elbow, as he read through manuscripts, most of them so abysmally poor that they gave him a headache.

"Uh — sir — Mr. Mallory — "

Interrupted, Mallory was rather short with the man.

"Yes, Chris, what is it? I'm busy."

"Uh — well, Mr. Mallory, I have these poems . . ."

Oh, God, not another budding writer. Mallory sighed. "You wrote them?" The young man nodded, his expression an odd mixture of diffidence and confidence that Mallory found particularly repellent. Obviously in hiring Chris he'd taken a viper unto his bosom.

"Have you tried to market them?"

"N-no, sir. I don't know if they're good enough."

Mallory tried hardening his heart. "You'll never know if you don't try. Go to the public library, find a copy of *The Writer* with the poetry markets, and start sending them out."

Chris's face fell. There was something so confoundedly abject about him, from his shaggy hair and scruffy beard to his ragged but clean jeans and barefoot sandals, that Mallory found himself saying, against his better judgment, just as he'd done when Chris approached him for a job weeks ago, "Well, give them here. Let me have a look."

The poems were scribbled in an execrable longhand that nearly finished the interview on the spot. "You have to submit typed manuscript for publication, Chris."

"Yes, sir, I know that; but I don't type very well. And I haven't a typewriter."

"Oh, very well, when I have time I'll glance at them."

Ostentatiously he picked up another manuscript and began reading it. As it, too, was a dud, along with all the others he tried that morning, in desperation Mallory finally picked up the dog-eared notebook and read the first poem. It was a gem, its words facets on the jewel of truth. Tears came to Mallory's eyes as he absorbed the powerful poem. All his life he had longed to be a poet; but all of his efforts produced only doggerel. Mallory was a good enough editor to recognize his own inadequacies in the field of writing — but it didn't prevent his longings. If only he could have written these words! He read the next poem, and the next, expecting that the first was a fluke, probably the only true thought that Chris had ever had. He was wrong. All of the poems in the slender copybook were beautiful, powerful, worthy of great acceptance. If he published these, even though the market for poetry was limited, his success as an editor would be established forever.

It wasn't enough. Holding these marvels of the written word in his hands, Mallory wanted it all. That was the moment when, subconsciously, he began plotting murder.

"There may be some promise in a few of your little verses," he said later to an eager Chris, his voice deprecatory. "I'll have a few typed up, let our poetry editor look at them. But don't get your hopes up."

Later he said casually, after they'd discussed digging a lily pond for a spot in the garden, "Need a bit of biographical information about you. The usual thing. For the editor."

"Why should who I am influence an editor's decision?" The fellow's eyes were suspicious.

"Now, now, don't get so uptight. You young people!" Mallory shook his head and smiled. "It's just that sometimes there are things in your past which give clues to an editor as to your ability to produce more work later."

Slightly mollified, Chris gave bare bones of autobiography. He'd parted company with his family, changed his name, was a loner. No ties. No current girl friends. No companions in this area.

A bit sheepishly he admitted, "I asked for a job here on purpose, Mr. Mallory. Came here deliberately. Because of my scribblings."

"Yes."

Chris signed his own death warrant that day. The backhoe came to dig out the hole for the lily pond. After the workman had gone, Mallory ordered Chris into the hole "just to make sure it's level enough for the concrete liner. The man's coming tomorrow to do the forms."

Once Chris was in the excavation, Mallory bashed him over the head with a large, dirty stone from the pile of dirt the backhoe had carefully deposited beside the hole. Then Mallory worked feverishly with a spade to dig a grave below the level of the proposed lily pond. He unceremoniously rolled in the young man's body, filled in the hasty grave, got out of the excavation, threw in some shovelfuls of loose dirt as a camouflage, and went into the house to clean up after his unusual labors.

The concrete liner of the pond was poured without problems. The lily pond was floored with a base of rich earth, then planted with bulbs, and filled with water.

Mallory copied the poems, typing them himself. After all were transcribed, he burned the notebook, taking care that every bit of paper was demolished to ash. As an additional precaution, he flushed this ash down the toilet and scrubbed the fireplace. He had no live-in help, so it was a simple enough task for Mallory to steal the poems and remove all evidence of Chris's stay. The young man had slept in a room over the garage. Mallory bundled up his extra jeans, and the few bits and pieces of civilization Chris had allowed himself, and dropped them into a Goodwill box miles from his home. Then he painstakingly went over the room, the garage, and the gardening shed, wiping every possible surface for fingerprints.

As a final precaution, he hired another drifter to do his yard work, so that another's presence overlaid Chris's brief stay in this place.

The following year the slender volume of poems was published by his firm, to gratifying critical acclaim. Much was made of the fact that Mallory, an editor, had never tried his hand at writing before this.

"I've been scribbling all my life," Mallory would tell interviewers. "I finally got up the courage to show my stuff to our poetry editor."

The water lilies bloomed in the pond. His book of poems was reviewed widely.

On the fatal day, Mallory went into the office of the publishing company, unaware that his whole future was about to disintegrate. There was a memo on his desk to see Stanton, editor-in-chief. Assuming it might have something to do with the critical success of his poems, Mallory went into the office, all smiles. They soon disappeared.

"A most peculiar thing has happened, Mallory." Stanton's voice was cold, his manner aloof. "Our legal department says we're being sued for plagiarism by a Mrs. Della Tremaine, who claims she wrote every poem in your book. Seems she's belonged to some local poetry club where she lives for years. They do a little mimeoed poetry magazine for their members — have back issues to the Year One. The members, recognizing her ability, have tried for ages to get her to submit her work to a publisher; but she thought her poems amateurish and satisfied her ego with publication in their private journal. She thought her notebook of poems had been stolen by her no-good grandson, Christopher, who seems to be missing; so she didn't pursue the matter. But when the poems came out under *your* name, she got a lawyer and sued. I'm afraid there will be an investigation. I do hope you have some explanation, Mallory." It was obvious that Stanton didn't think he did.

Mallory saw his stolen success falling down in rubble around him, for the investigation would surely try to trace Chris and would find his connection with Mallory. It wouldn't be plagiarism he'd be charged with — it would be murder. Now he desperately regretted his little conceit, his private in-joke, in titling the slim volume of verse. He had facetiously, nay, arrogantly, called it *The Lily Pond.*

Past Tense

by BTJNPWJTBBFMJABCFUIHSFTIBN

The world before 1900 was full of mother idealization. Grown men were not ashamed to sing "I want a girl just like the girl who married dear old Dad." Half the popular songs were populated by gray-haired old ladies with toil-worn features. Freud, by the simple invention of the Oedipus complex, converted love of mother from a fragrant tender thing into a horrible perversion and freed us from the unbearable sentiment that gave us all emotional diabetes. For that alone he should be toasted on every Mother's Day. Of course, the disease crops up now and then, even today.

A Miss Gretchen Bevis to see you, sir."

Adam Dillard looked up from the infuriating report he was reading and blinked his eyes to change focus.

"Who?"

"A Miss Gretchen Bevis," the pale girl in the doorway repeated patiently. "She knows she has no appointment, but she — she's anxious to see you. She told me — she asked me to mention Timothy Lauder's name."

"Ah!" Adam laid down his red pencil and took off his glasses. "She is alone?"

64

"Yes, sir."

"Very well. Show her in, please."

Adam rose and stood watching the door, keeping his mind open to receive a second impression of this young woman that he had disliked so unaccountably the other day.

There she was: tall and dark, with naturally high color and glinting black eyes.

"So good of you to see me," she said, grasping his hand. "I felt I must come to you."

She sat in the chair he held for her and looked around her rather deliberately.

"How wonderfully warm and colorful," she remarked with a flash of a smile. "It doesn't look at all like one's picture of an orphanage."

This attempt at diplomatic relations amused Adam. He knew what she wanted and how she had found him, and he still felt the strong urge to disoblige her. But common sense required that he hear her out.

So, he smiled, not helping her.

She abandoned diplomacy. "I got the impression at the gallery that you were on Timothy's side and determined not to tell me any more about his — background than he will, himself."

A sarcastic rejoiner occurred to Adam, but he said merely, "It's a good many years since I've seen Tim."

She sat forward; tense, eager, and handsome. "I used no tact — no finesse with you. I was so thankful, when I saw you greet Timothy, to find someone at last who'd obviously known him and meant a lot to him that I just jumped in with both feet. It is my way."

She cocked her head at him and tried the smile again. He waited.

"Mr. Dillard, I need your help badly — and so does Timothy. And you're the first person I've found who can give it to us."

He still waited.

"I'm in love with Timothy, and I'm sure he loves me — as much as he's able. But he's only half alive, Mr. Dillard. There's something tight in him, like a cork in a bottle, sealing off his past and himself — something that hurts and shrinks him and keeps him from being a full man."

Adam looked for some reaction of sympathy with her in himself, but found that he was still antagonistic. After a pause in which, half-puzzled, she searched his face, she went on:

"I've tried to make him go to a psychiatrist. Finally, he laughed at me. He told me he didn't need one; that he knew all about what was wrong with him. But he won't tell me."

This headlong confession was making Adam more uncomfortable by the minute. The time to stop it had come.

"I can't help you, Miss Bevis. I don't know how to. As I said, it is so long since I knew anything of Tim Lauder that my wife had to drag me to the gallery to see if the man of that name who was exhibiting could be the boy I'd known."

For the moment, her face lighted. "He is good, isn't he? He has really *arrived*. But he won't try portrait photography and I feel he should, but if . . ."

The light faded and she rose from her perch and began to pace in front of Adam's desk.

"The whole thing is getting to be too much for us, Mr. Dillard. Timothy wants to marry me, but he won't. He never will until he throws off this — this albatross, whatever it is. If I knew more, I could help him. I could *make* him do something about it."

Adam shrugged. She was beginning to exhaust him. She was going on and he suddenly felt a great sympathy for psychiatrists.

"I don't know why I fell for Timothy, Mr. Dillard. I think it's because there's something *in* him, trying for release, that I want. Do you understand that?"

"Ah — yes." Adam had the urge to kick himself into some kind of action, but he couldn't make up his mind what course to take. He wanted to repulse her but he didn't want to do anything to injure Tim.

She was still talking. "I've managed to pry a few things out of him. After you left the other day, he admitted he'd been an orphan here, but that's all he'd say. I knew, before that, he was very poor, but his mother had had money and lost it somehow. He worships his mother . . ."

Gretchen Bevis stopped completely, run down and silent. Adam moved to rise from his chair and Gretchen repeated, "He worships her, as if she were alive. He says I look like her — although she was small — and sometimes I'm afraid that's all he loves about me."

It seemed to Adam that it wasn't fear she felt but bafflement.

Suddenly, she leaned on his desk with clenched fists. "Mr. Dillard, you've got to tell me all you know. Please . . ."

Adam cleared his throat, longing for his father's advice. Gretchen Bevis was determined to have the facts. If he refused, she'd keep on, now that she'd located the orphanage, and she'd find others who were here when Tim was. Their "facts" would be different from Adam's and much more dangerous to Tim Lauder.

"Please sit down again, Miss Bevis . . . I'd be glad to tell you all that I — or anyone here at the Home — knows. I — I think you and I could easily do more harm than good, but there are reasons why I want to help Tim as much as you do. I believe he deserves help. But . . ."

As he paused, Gretchen almost jumped from her chair again. "But — *what*, Mr. Dillard?"

"If I am to tell you anything, I want Tim to know about it."

"He'll refuse to let you. Surely you gathered that, at the gallery?"

"Perhaps not, if he realizes that you'll persist until you find a — less reliable source of information," Adam said impulsively.

Gretchen's response was complicated. Anger and amazement were finally overcome by puzzled hurt.

"Do you really think I'm such a relentless harpy?" she asked at last.

He avoided a direct answer. "I think you believe you love

him and see this as a way to 'free' him, as you put it. But, neither of us knows what we're getting into. Tim might never forgive you. You might never forgive yourself."

"You mean — is it as bad as that?" Her eyes filled with alarm. "He was only a child."

"Nothing I know is 'bad' enough to bother you." Adam was angry at himself — and her. "I've told you I like Tim and believe he deserves any break you can give him. But I saw the other day how he feels about your interest in his past. Can't you see that I must have him give his consent to my confiding in you?"

To Adam's surprise, she gave in at once. "Yes," she said calmly, "you're probably right. When can you see him with me?"

So, he was trapped. For better or worse, he'd let himself into meddling with Tim Lauder's tormented life . . .

It was — how long? — seventeen years since he'd first seen Tim Lauder. Adam had been a senior at college and was home for Christmas vacation. "Home" was Endicott House, a refuge of many years' standing for orphans and children of shattered families. Adam's father was the superintendent at that time.

Adam and his father had been together in the super's office when the matron brought in a small, white-faced boy. Adam heard the matron's uncompromising voice saying, "Timothy has been accused of stealing again. Steve's new lunch pail is gone from his locker. It can't be found and . . ."

Then she noticed Adam and apologized for interrupting. Adam's father made an appointment for later and the sad little figure was led away.

After they had gone, Adam's father told him the whole story. The Lauder boys had been brought to the Home that autumn: Timothy and his older brother, Edward. The father had been killed in a bar brawl; and the mother, in poor health anyway, had worked herself to death, being too proud, apparently, to seek welfare aid.

Superintendent Dillard shook his head sadly. "The two boys

puzzle me a good deal," he said. "Ed is twelve and Tim — the boy you just saw — is ten. It's hard to believe that they're brothers. Ed is tall and husky for his age. He's a tough, self-reliant street boy. And you've seen Tim."

"He looks like a lost, starved dog," Adam said.

"Yes, but when you've seen more of him, he has the look of breeding. And his speech is cultured while Ed's is pure street arab. But, they're full brothers — that's certain."

"What about this stealing — 'again'?" Adam asked.

"Almost as soon as they got here, little things that belonged to other boys began to disappear, and Timothy was caught stashing some of them."

When he didn't continue, Adam looked at him, surprised. "What did you do, Dad? What's troubling you?"

"The brother — Ed — he fights and argues constantly for Tim's innocence but — he's a bully. I think he has some hold over Tim and forces him to do these things for his own sadistic amusement."

"Good lord. Are you sure?"

"Of course not. But, left to himself, Tim's a good child. He's studious, obedient, considerate. But he's scared to death of something real and actual, and it can only be Ed."

"How are you handling it?"

The elder Dillard sighed. "Badly, so far, I'm afraid. Tim is not only a thief. He comes in here sometimes, in agony, and tells tales on other boys and girls. I've tried to question him, but, after he has sung his song, he has nothing more to say. It becomes like kicking a wounded animal to push him any further . . . I have to let the matron punish him, but, so far, I've resisted the Board's efforts to have him sent to reform school — and Ed Lauder has seconded me valiantly."

Adam wondered if his usually level-headed father could perhaps be romanticizing in this case because of the surface differences in the brothers. After all, sneaks and petty thieves were often meek and generally well-behaved . . .

As time passed, Adam was seldom at Endicott House, but he

kept up his interest in the Lauder boys, as well as the others. He was taking graduate work to prepare himself for a job like his father's.

At one point, Superintendent Dillard was driven to decide to send Tim to a correctional school. Ed, in a passion of pleading, promised there would be no more thieving. And there was no more that could be traced to Timothy Lauder.

Neither boy ever showed any sign of profiting from the sale of stolen things. Ed wore a flat object, like a locket, wrapped in red cloth, on a chain about his neck, but he'd had this on the day he came to the orphanage and was never without it. He told everyone it was a lucky piece and to show it would spoil the luck.

Seven years went by. In all that time, Tim was blamed for practically everything that went wrong. No one who could avoid it spoke to him; no one but Ed, a few zealous members of the staff, and Adam and his father.

But Ed stood by, so Tim was never injured in body. His shoes often had no laces in the morning. His bed often held worms and other objects. His themes were drenched in ink, his books torn, his food peppered, but no one confronted him or knocked him down.

When Ed was nineteen and Tim seventeen, they both finished their schooling. Adam's father had died that year and Adam had been appointed to replace him, so it was Adam's responsibility to find jobs for the brothers.

Ed begged that they be placed somewhere together. Adam could still see the magnificent almost-man Ed Lauder had become standing by his desk and saying earnestly that Tim could never get along without him.

Ed loved sports and he'd never shunned work. He'd toned down his surface toughness and smoothed out his speech. His record was good enough, but Adam didn't trust him. Adam knew he was clever and ruthless and suspected he was bad for Tim. So, although he didn't altogether share his father's belief about Tim, Adam felt the urge to give him a break, and he pretended that he couldn't place them together and sent Ed to a shoe factory in Connecticut and Tim to a tree nursery in New Jersey.

Tim had grown nearly as tall as his brother, but he was thin as a flagpole and stooped. It always struck Adam as strange that Tim didn't need glasses. Glasses seemed to go with his ducked head and constantly lowered eyes.

They went off together. Endicott House gave Ed an enthusiastic sendoff and nodded to Tim for Ed's sake. A few months later, Adam learned that Tim was at the shoe factory with Ed. He was sorry, but there was nothing he could do. He had no authority, and presumably, Tim was his own master.

But the thought of Tim Lauder nagged at Adam. He wondered sometimes if he had let his father down — if he was allowing a life of mysterious slavery to his brother for that strange, sad boy.

After a while, Adam received a routine report that Tim had been sent to a state sanitarium for treatment for tuberculosis. Later still, he learned in the same way that Ed had been made a foreman at his factory.

Adam often thought of visiting Tim, but his job filled his days and then he fell in love and got married, and little by little, Tim Lauder left the surface of his mind. But he had spoken of Tim often to Catherine, his wife, who was interested in all that concerned him, and, last week she had shown him an invitation to the opening of an exhibition of photographs by a Timothy Lauder at a distinguished gallery.

It had seemed impossible, and yet . . . Looking at the sensitive pictures that came in the folder with the invitation and reading the generous praise of the critics, Adam wondered and hoped that this could be the Tim his father had believed in.

So, Adam had gone to find out. The gallery was well filled with people sipping wine and coffee and commenting on the photographs with approval. All the pictures were imaginative, but Adam was particularly struck by the compassion shown in those of the poor.

He scanned the crowd in the three rooms with growing excitement, and at last he saw Tim standing in a corner with a tall brunette who was pretty obviously acting as a watchdog.

Tim hadn't changed beyond recognition but he was certainly much improved. He stood straight and his hair gleamed with grooming. In fact, his whole person showed care, but he was clearly allowing his companion to handle almost everyone who stopped to speak to him.

Adam wondered what kind of welcome he would get.

"He looks shy," Catherine said softly. "You go to him alone. I'll join you later, if it works out that way."

"Do you know the woman with him?"

"Yes, it's Gretchen Bevis. She makes a thing of patronizing the arts. She's a dynamo and some people resent her, but she gets things done."

"Do you know her well enough to cut her loose from him for a few minutes?"

"I think so, yes."

Catherine managed this skillfully and Adam found himself alone beside Tim Lauder.

He smiled at Adam and took both his hands. "This is wonderful, Mr. Adam," he said softly. "I — I've often thought I'd come to see you, but I — I never made it."

"I should have come to see you at the sanitarium," Adam told him ruefully. "Please tell me what I should know. Your photographs are marvelous. How did you get started?"

"Dini came to the sanitarium to take pictures. He — he got interested in some snapshots I'd taken and, when I got well, he took me in."

Adam was impressed by the name of the great photographer, and Tim talked about him warmly for a few minutes but had nothing further to say about himself.

Adam was getting ready to beckon Catherine and feeling sad that there was no meeting ground between Tim and himself, such as Tim would have had with Adam's father, when Gretchen Bevis came up to them.

She said, "Timothy, may I know your friend?"

Two small surprises came together. Adam couldn't see why Catherine hadn't told Gretchen Bevis who he was, and he was startled by Tim's reaction.

They had each accepted a glass of wine from a passing waitress and Tim's glass was nearly full. As Gretchen Bevis spoke, the glass tilted and Gretchen righted it neatly before much was spilled. The escaping drops went on her dress.

"That's what I get," she said, laughing, "for being an interfering woman."

She waved away Tim's anxiously offered handkerchief and stood waiting for the introduction.

Tim seemed genuinely tongue-tied. Puzzled, Adam said, "I'm Adam Dillard. I knew Tim years ago, and it's good to see him again."

"Oh, do tell me about Timothy as a boy," she almost demanded.

"No!" Tim's voice was strangled. "Please, Gretchen. I've begged you."

She smiled at him fondly. "Timothy insists on being mysterious about his early days, Mr. Dillard. His biography begins and ends with Dini."

She looked eagerly at Adam. "Please tell me. Where did you know him?"

Adam was irritated. Surely this girl could see that Tim didn't want him to answer. He looked around for Catherine to rescue him, but she was across the room, chatting with a stranger to Adam.

"At my home, Miss Bevis," he answered shortly.

This should be enough, but she persisted. "And where was that, Mr. Dillard?"

Adam smiled at her. "If Tim wants a mystery, he should have it, don't you think? They tell me mystery is good for artists' careers."

Adam caught Tim's eye and was astonished at his expression. It was the gratitude of a starving creature who had been given food.

Catherine turned and Adam signaled her. She joined them, and after some minutes of awkward platitudes, Adam was able to escape.

When he had described the encounter to Catherine she said, "Several people interrupted us before Gretchen could ask me anything, but she saw me talking to George Shattuck and I'm afraid she'll ask him about you."

"It can't be helped and I don't understand Tim's violent objection. After all, look where he is now; at what he has overcome. I'd think he would be proud to have the girl know about it."

"Your father thought Tim was in thrall to his brother," Catherine suggested gently. "Perhaps he doesn't want her to find out anything about that."

"But," Adam objected, "Ed Lauder could turn up any time, now that Tim is news. Incidentally, he's become an officer of that shoe firm, the last I heard."

"It's a puzzlement," Catherine agreed. "But, maybe it's something different. Perhaps Tim just hates to have Gretchen learn about his shabby boyhood, poor fellow."

"Well, she won't learn it from me," Adam declared . . .

But now, he heard Gretchen Bevis saying, "Could you make it tomorrow night? I'm having dinner with Timothy, and we could meet at his studio afterward?"

Thinking that he might as well get it over with, and quickly, Adam agreed.

Adam went to Timothy's studio, planning to "play it by ear." He intended to be guided entirely by what he learned there.

Gretchen stood beside Tim at the door. He took Adam's hand and smiled as he had at the gallery.

"Thank you for everything, Mr. Adam," were his first words, as he crushed Adam's fingers.

So, she had prepared him, Adam thought, and was grateful.

Tim ushered Adam into a modest but very attractive room. Its outstanding feature was the display of photographs on walls and easels. There weren't many, but each one was singular and striking.

For a few moments, Adam exclaimed over them. He could almost feel Gretchen's constraint. The pictures were all very fine, but she wanted to get on with the business of the evening.

At last, she seated herself in one of the three chairs that had, for Adam, the look of having been carefully arranged for this seance.

Tim watched her and Adam saw his shoulders rise and fall slowly in a gesture of resignation.

"I see that I must tell Gretchen my — my story," he said, "and I want you to hear it, too. Afterwards, perhaps you will say — what you can, for me."

"Most certainly," Adam said, as he took the chair between them.

Tim Lauder wasted no time. He launched into his bitter, aching tale at once, and the strangest part of it was the telling.

He sat straight, hands pressed down on the arms of his chair, eyes lowered. He spoke rapidly, without expression, and he spoke in the third person and the present tense. The effect was that of a subject of hypnotism unburdening himself.

"There is a family," he began, "a man and woman and their two sons. The father is a rough man, strong and ugly-tempered. The older son is like him. The mother is all perfection. All that woman was meant to be — she is."

At that point, Tim raised his eyes to look briefly at Gretchen. Adam found his expression disquieting. It was worshipful, but impersonal and sorrowful.

Tim's lids covered his eyes again. "The younger son tries to be like her, always. But, of course he can't. He tries to protect her, but he can't do that either.

"This family has only two things that matter: the mother's love for her little son and a — a miniature of herself, in a locket."

The sigh that escaped Tim stopped Adam's heartbeat. He was sure this was the first time Tim Lauder had ever spoken aloud of this treasure.

"A famous artist painted it for the man the mother should have married. It is set in matched pearls and is very beautiful and valuable.

"But that man died before the marriage and the locket is both a comfort and a curse to the mother. The father and his son want to sell it. There are many quarrels and the little boy tries to take his mother's part, but he is always beaten.

"Finally, the father beats the mother and takes the locket from her. But, when he tries to sell it, he is suspected of theft and only the mother can save him. The judge awards the miniature to her and she hides it and will not tell where it is — no matter what the father and his son do to her.

"At last, the father dies. Times are really bad now, and no one the mother asks can buy the locket, so she pawns it and can never afford to redeem it. When she dies, her gift to her younger son is the pawn ticket."

Tim paused, immobile, staring at the floor. Adam glanced at Gretchen. She was frowning and her black eyes showed nothing.

Tim drew a deep breath and resumed his mesmerized tale. "The first thing the brother does is take the pawn ticket from him. He gets the money from an older boy and they redeem the locket together, for the older boy knows where to sell it. But, before this can be done, the brothers are picked up by welfare workers and taken to an orphanage.

"As long as they are there, and as long as the younger boy does all he wants, the older brother agrees to keep the locket. It's fun for him — fun that lasts for many years. But, at the shoe factory, the boy who put the money up finds the brother and the fun is over. The locket is sold at last."

With startling suddenness, Tim moved, crossed his legs, and spoke to Adam normally. "I got away from Ed then, Mr. Adam. I went to the sanitarium and I've never seen him since.

But — he has the locket again. He got it back, just a month ago."

Adam was breathless. "How do you know?" he managed to ask.

"I knew who had it. I asked how much it would cost to buy it back and was told. Last month, I'd earned enough to get it — but Ed had been there just before me. He has the locket now."

Adam had the helpless, nauseating feeling of "if-I-had-only-known." His father — and he — might have saved Tim all these years of hell. But — could they have? Ed was fearless, sadistic, and crooked, and the miniature meant as much to him, in his way, as it did to Tim.

What were the bully's plans now?

Thinking of this made Adam remember Gretchen Bevis. He looked at her. She raised her eyebrows at him. Fury filled Adam as he realized that she was waiting for corroboration of this — to her — fantastic story.

Then he reminded himself that she didn't know, yet, that Ed had made Tim lie and cheat and steal.

"My father," he said to Tim, "always believed that Ed was responsible for your actions — for the things he made you do."

Tim nodded. "Without your father, I'd have gone to reform school. But it was my weakness — I know. I should have called Ed's bluff."

Now, at last, Tim looked at Gretchen. Adam wished he'd done so before because now she was convinced and she was crying.

Tim sprang up to go to her and Adam rose. "I must go," he said, wanting nothing more.

"Wait," Gretchen cried. "Don't you agree, Mr. Dillard, that Timothy must go to his brother and demand the locket?"

Tears had dried. She was all practicality. "I know an excellent lawyer," she went on.

"It's for you two to decide." Adam didn't care how pompous he sounded. But he *was* anxious to know how Tim felt about the locket now. Could Ed still use it as a lever? If so — it might be disastrous for Tim.

Gretchen got this answered for him. "Suppose," she said, your brother sold the locket again — or gave it away?"

"He won't do that — not now."

Tim's bleached face told Adam that he had looked at the possible future.

"You must have it back. He might destroy it."

Tim shuddered. He whispered, "He must never do that."

Adam found himself agreeing with Gretchen, little as he liked to. To be happy — even safe — Tim should find a way to get the precious locket, which his mother had meant for him.

"I agree with Miss Bevis, and I'll help you in any way I can," he said quietly. "Why not start with the Endicott House lawyer?"

"No!" Tim said violently. "*You* should understand, sir. Gretchen can't, of course. But you knew Ed."

He spoke of evil incarnate — terrible beyond description.

Adam reached for common sense. "Think, Tim. Remember, Ed is vulnerable now. He's rich and respectable. Our lawyer, with our stories — yours and mine — ought to be able to throw enough of a scare into him to allow you to buy . . ."

"*You* think, Mr. Adam," Tim interrupted harshly. "Who alive, but you, from the orphanage, would believe my story? Think of all the friends Ed could summon to tell *his* side, if I pushed any!"

He put his hands over his face and turned away. "I didn't want fame. I wanted money to buy my locket . . . That door never opens now but I think it may be Ed coming back. All I want is invisibility. Invisibility!" He was almost praying.

"Timothy!" Gretchen's clear, calm voice had an edge of reprimand and contempt. "You'll never have an hour's peace till you face Ed and see he is nothing but a bully."

"I know that, Gretchen, but I'm the coward every bully needs. Ed made me, and I know he made me too well — too long — ever to change."

Adam didn't agree. He saw dignity and wisdom in Tim that Tim didn't recognize. Perhaps courage was there, too.

But Gretchen wasn't thinking as Adam was. She asked slowly, "You mean you're resigned to taking it from your brother, always? You'd rather make us both miserable forever than stand up to him just once?"

"It isn't a question of 'rather,' Gretchen," Tim answered. He was aloof, almost disembodied, with concentration; looking squarely at his own self and soul. "I went through nearly twenty years of inquisition. I didn't weather it. I have no choices where my master is concerned."

Gretchen shuddered. She had touched dead flesh in the dark and her bright color faded. For a second or two, she saw beyond her horizon. Then she rallied.

"It's inconceivable to me how you can resign yourself to destruction when one breath could blow it away."

Adam was amazed to hear Tim laugh — a real laugh, full of genuine amusement. *"Your* breath, dear, perhaps — not mine."

Gretchen was curious, not affronted. "Do you mean that you'd let me go to your brother and ask him to return your locket?"

"No. I'd let you go if I was sure he wouldn't harm you."

Timothy seemed bent on speaking the whole truth, no matter how it affected Gretchen's feelings for him. He continued doggedly: "But he would. He'd guess that we cared for each other, because you had gone to him and because — you look like my mother."

Adam felt the pain all this was giving Tim and was overcome at the courage it was requiring. Tim must really love this strong, insensitive girl very much or — was it possible that he was disoriented enough really to see her as an extension of his mother?

"You must be mad," Gretchen said, echoing part of Adam's thought. "No man is such a villain as that."

"How can you understand?" Tim said gently. "It's a feud,

Gretchen: his father — my mother — our parents. I can see his point of view. I've always seen it."

He wandered over to the wall where one of his most striking pictures hung. It showed, in black and white, a brutish, ragged man staring down at a tiny boy who was sailing a matchbox boat in the gutter. The man's unconscious face was ugly with the thought of his next action. Adam could almost see him lean down to grab the child.

Tim said, "Ed hates weakness. He hates sentiment. But my mother's magnificent endurance keeps shaming him. She escapes his contempt. I am — and always will be — his only answer to that. In me, she fails and he wins."

Gretchen looked at him for a long moment. At last, she spoke, without heat. "I'm *not* your mother, however much you've tried to make me so. I can't love a man who can't fight his own battles. I'm going."

When Tim neither moved nor spoke, her eyes narrowed until they looked like splinters of jet.

"By the way," she said, going to the door, "you'd better start speaking of your mother in the past tense, Timothy. She's been dead a long time."

She went out, leaving the door wide. She didn't see the white anger that galvanized Tim. He took a few steps to the door, but then, with a sound both groan and sob, he ran to what Adam supposed was his bedroom.

Adam left, carefully closing the door with a shaking hand.

For the next few days, Adam neglected everything else in order to see as much of Timothy as Timothy's schedule would permit. Catherine was of great help in this, and they were both pleased that Tim seemed to take an interest in everything they did together. During that time, Catherine learned that Gretchen had left town — destination unknown.

Gretchen wasn't mentioned by the three of them, and Adam couldn't bring himself to broach the subject.

The following month, Adam asked Tim to come to Endicott House to take pictures of the boys and girls for a folder the

Board wanted to circulate. Adam had wondered if Tim would refuse, but he agreed and took pictures that subsequently raised a good deal of money for the orphanage.

As Tim was putting away his cameras that day, one of Adam's boys handed him the evening paper.

"There's a story about the Home on page seven, Mr. Dillard," the boy said, grinning. "Some boy who used to be here has sure made good. Same name as yours, Mr. Lauder."

Tim looked over Adam's shoulder while he folded the paper to a page devoted to social items. The biggest thing on it was a picture of Edward M. Lauder, Vice-President of Consul Shoes, and his fiancée, Miss Gretchen Bevis.

The item beneath the picture stated that Mr. Lauder was visiting Miss Bevis' home in New York City for a few days and that the wedding would be in May and also that Miss Bevis was wearing her fiancé's gift, "an exquisite miniature of Mr. Lauder's mother, set in flawless pearls."

Without a word, Tim walked out of the room and to the front door, leaving his cameras behind him. Adam followed anxiously.

A cab was passing and Tim hailed it. Adam almost didn't make it to join him. He gave the driver a Park Avenue address that Adam knew was Gretchen's.

For a few minutes, they rode in silence. Tim was rigid and staring straight ahead.

"What are you planning to do, Tim?" Adam ventured, at last. After a moment with no answer, Adam tried again. "Confrontation right now won't work, you know. Let's put it up to our lawyer and . . ."

"Adam," Tim said, omitting the *Mister,* "either shut up or get out."

Adam felt constrained to obey. He sat, wondering if Gretchen had engineered all this to force Tim into action. Doubtless Tim thought so, but Adam wasn't so sure.

Gretchen had never heard the details of Tim's treatment by Ed Lauder. Adam guessed that her overpowering curiosity had driven her to see Ed and hear his story and that Ed's smooth brain and intense masculinity had done the rest. But, of course, there was the chance that she had acted, and was still acting, on Tim's behalf.

If so, it was a dangerous game, the rules of which were unknown to her.

And, Adam thought helplessly, this foray of Tim's could only end in disaster. He would be hurt — even jailed — and nothing would be changed.

"Gretchen Bevis can take care of herself," Adam muttered, not conscious of voicing his thought.

Tim looked at him for the first time since they'd entered the taxi. "Just give me another minute, Adam," he said. He had recommanded himself as Adam had seen him do at the studio.

Adam sat, considering: Tim had been weak and cowardly in the long slavery to his brother — to a mother fixation and its symbol, the miniature. But his mother's gallantry had certainly been in him that day at the studio and it was in him now, and Adam was fearful of what might happen to it.

"I'd rather do this alone, Adam," Tim was saying, "but you can come along if you'll keep out of it."

They were in the sixties now, nearing Gretchen's apartment house. "They won't be there," Adam objected hopefully.

"I think they will. Gretchen knows I look at the pictures in the paper every afternoon. They'll be waiting to see if I come. They'll be laughing and betting I won't."

He was right. Adam heard the laughter as the maid ushered them in — Gretchen's and Ed Lauder's, too.

They stood together near a window in a large room that was furnished in a faintly Moorish style. It had a handsome tiled floor, lavishly strewn with rugs. At any other time, Adam would have been happy to enjoy their beauty.

Gretchen was wearing the locket. Her eyes were watchful and eager as an aficionada's at a bull fight. Ed was much heavier than he had been, but he was roughly handsome and virile.

Adam had the incongruous thought that it was convenient for Gretchen that Ed had never married.

Then he saw the miniature clearly, as the pair came forward. It hung on a thin gold chain. Even though Adam had been partly prepared, he was struck by the resemblance in coloring and features to the living face above it.

Gretchen smiled at him. "I was startled myself," she said. "It could be *my* . . ."

Her speech was cut by Tim's action. With terrific speed, he grasped the locket, broke the chain, and ground the ivory under his heel on the tiled floor. Even when Ed sprang at him, he ducked and continued to stamp on the locket.

Ed's hands closed on Tim's throat. Gretchen screamed, and Adam hit Ed on the jaw. Adam boxed constantly with his older boys. He didn't need to hit Ed again. The bully's hands relaxed and he slid to the floor.

Tim paid no attention to this. He finished demolishing the miniature and its encircling pearls while Gretchen looked from him to his fallen brother in goggling stupefaction. Then he picked up the shattered remains and put them in his pocket.

"It's mine, you know," he said mildly. "It always has been mine."

Ed groaned and Gretchen knelt by him. Tim smiled at Adam. "Glad I brought you along," he said, "but I know karate now, and I was getting into position."

He winked at Adam and smiled at Gretchen. "I must offer my congratulations," he told her. "You and my brother should get along famously."

"Ed will prosecute you for this," she snapped at him. "He'll make you pay."

"I doubt it." He took Adam's arm and started for the door. Then he turned and spoke softly:

"By the way, you were quite right, Gretchen. My mother *is* dead."

A Dark Blue Perfume

by MBVSBODFBMJDFMBSVUISFOEFMM

There is something open about good, honest hate. It gets lots of exercise and use, and what with scowling and snarling and sneering and an occasional Bronx cheer, there are many ways and occasions for bleeding off its intensity. But you take the kind of hate that is mixed with love and therefore cannot express itself and cool down — and *then* you have trouble.

It would be true to say that not a day had passed without his thinking of her. Except for the middle years. There had been other women then to distract him, though no one he cared for enough to make his second wife. But once he was in his fifties, the memory of her returned with all its old vividness. He would see other men settling down into middle age, looking toward old age, with loving wives beside them, and he would say to himself, "Catherine, Catherine . . ."

He had never, since she left him, worked and lived in his native land. He was employed by a company that sent him all over the world. For years he had lived in South America, Africa, the West Indies, coming home only on leave and not always then. He meant to come home when he retired, though, and to this end, on one of those leaves, he had bought himself a house. It was in the city where he and she had been born, but he had chosen a district as far as possible from the one in which she had gone to live with her new husband and a long way from where they had once lived together, for the time when he had bought it was the time when he had begun daily to think of her again.

He retired when he was sixty-five and came home. He flew home and sent the possessions he had accumulated by sea. They included the gun he had acquired forty years before and with which he had intended to shoot himself when things became unendurable. But they had never been quite unendurable even then. Anger against her and hatred for her had sustained him, and he had never got so far as even loading the small unused automatic.

It was winter when he got home, bleak and wet and far colder than he remembered. When the snow came he stayed indoors, keeping warm, seeing no one. There was no one to see, anyway; they had gone away or died.

When his possessions arrived in three trunks — that was all he had amassed in forty years, three trunkfuls of bric-a-brac — he unpacked wonderingly. Only the gun had been put in by him; his servant had packed the rest. Things came to light he had long forgotten he owned, books, curios, and in an envelope he thought he had destroyed in those early days, all his photographs of her.

He sat looking at them one evening in early spring. The woman who came to clean for him had brought him a bowl of blue hyacinths, and the air was heavy and languorous with the sweet scent of them. "Catherine, Catherine," he said as he looked at the picture of her in their garden, the picture of her at the seaside, her hair blowing. How different his life would have been if she had stayed with him! If he had been a complaisant husband and borne it all and taken it all and forgiven her. But how could he have borne that? How could he have kept her when she was pregnant with another man's child?

The hyacinths made him feel almost faint. He pushed the

photographs back into the envelope, but he seemed to see her face still through the thick, opaque, brown paper. She had been a bit older than he; she would be nearly seventy now. She would be old, ugly, fat perhaps, arthritic perhaps, those firm cheeks fallen into jowls, those eyes sunk in folds of skin, that white column of a neck become a bundle of strings, that glossy chestnut hair a bush of gray. No man would want her now.

He got up and looked in the mirror over the mantelpiece. He hadn't aged much, hadn't changed much. Everyone said so. Of course it was true that he hadn't lived much, and it was living that aged you. He wasn't bald, he was thinner than he had been at twenty-five, his eyes were still bright and wistful and full of hope. Those four years' seniority she had over him, they would show now if they stood side by side.

She might be dead. He had heard nothing; there had been no news since the granting of the divorce and her marriage to that man. Aldred Sydney. Aldred Sydney might be dead, she might be a widow. He thought of what that name, in any context, had meant to him, how emotive it had been.

"I want you to meet the new general manager, Sydney Robinson."

"Yes, we're being sent to Australia, Sydney, actually."

"Cameron and Sydney, Surveyors and Valuers. Can I help you?"

For a long time he had trembled when he heard her surname pronounced. He had wondered how it could come so unconcernedly off another's tongue. Aldred Sydney would be no more than seventy, there was no reason to suppose him dead.

"Do you know Aldred and Catherine Sydney? They live at Number Twenty-two. An elderly couple, yes, that's right. They're so devoted to each other, it's rather sweet . . ."

She wouldn't still live there, not after forty years. He went into the hall and fetched the telephone directory. For a moment or two he sat still, breathing deeply because his heart was beating so fast, the book lying in his lap. Then he opened the directory and turned to the S's. Aldred was such an uncommon name, there was probably only one Aldred Sydney in the country. He couldn't find him there, though there were many A. Sydneys living at addresses that had no meaning for him, no significance. He wondered afterward why he had bothered to look lower, to let his eyes travel down through the B's and find her name, unmistakably, incontrovertibly, hers. Sydney, Catherine, 22 Aurora Road . . .

She was still there, she still lived there, and the phone was in her name. Aldred Sydney must be dead. He wished he hadn't looked in the phone book. Why had he? He could hardly sleep at all that night, and when he awoke from a doze early in the morning, it was with her name on his lips: "Catherine, Catherine."

He imagined phoning her.

"Catherine?"

"Yes, speaking. Who's that?"

"Don't you know? Guess. It's a long time ago, Catherine."

It was possible in fantasy, not in fact. He wouldn't know her voice now; if he met her in the street he wouldn't know her. At ten o'clock he got his car out and drove northward, across the river and up through the northern suburbs. Forty years ago the place where she lived had been well outside the great metropolis, separated from it by fields and woods.

He drove through new streets, whole new districts. Without his new map he would have had no idea where he was. The countryside had been pushed away in those four decades. It hovered shyly on the outskirts of the little town that had become a suburb. And here was Aurora Road. He had never been to it before, never seen her house, though on any map he was aware of precisely where the street was, as if its name were printed in red to burn his eyes.

The sight of it at last, actually being there and seeing the house, made his head swim. He closed his eyes and sat there with his head bent over the wheel. Then he turned and looked at the neat, small house. Its paint was new and smart and the fifty-year-old front door had been replaced by a paneled oak one and the square bay by a bow window. But it was a poor, poky house for all that. He sneered a little at dead Aldred Sydney who had done no better than this for his wife.

Suppose he were to go up to the door and ring the bell? But he wouldn't do that, the shock would be too much for her. He, after all, had prepared himself. She had no preparation for confronting that husband, so little changed, of long ago. Once, how he would have savored the cruelty of it, the revenge! The handsome man, still looking middle-aged, a tropical tan on his cheeks, his body flat and straight, and the broken old woman, squat now, gray, withered. He sighed. All desire for a cruel vengeance had left him. He wanted instead to be merciful, to be kind. Wouldn't the kindest thing be to leave her in peace? Leave her to her little house and the simple pursuits of old age?

He started the car again and drove a little way. It surprised him to find that Aurora Road was right on the edge of that retreating countryside, that its tarmac and gray paving stones led into fields. When she was younger she had possibly walked there sometimes, under the trees, along that footpath. He got out of the car and walked along it himself. After a time he saw a train in the distance, appearing and disappearing between green meadows, clumps of trees, clusters of red roofs, and then he came upon a signpost pointing to the railway station. Perhaps she had walked here to meet Aldred Sydney after his day's work.

He sat down on a rustic seat that had been placed at the edge of the path. It was a very pretty place, not spoiled at all, you could hardly see a single house. The grass was a pure, clean green, the hedgerows shimmering white with the tiny flowers of wild plum blossom, which had a drier, sharper scent than the hyacinths. For the time of year it was warm and the sun was shining. A bumblebee, relict of the past summer, drifted by. He put his head back on the wooden bar of the seat and fell asleep.

It was an unpleasant dream he had, of those young days of

his when he had been little more than a boy but she very much a grown woman. She came to him, as she had come then, and told him baldly, without shame or diffidence, that the child she carried wasn't his. In the dream she laughed at him, though he couldn't remember that she had done that in life, surely not. He jerked awake and for a moment he didn't know where he was. People talking, walking along the path, had roused him. He left the seat and the path and drove home.

All that week he meant to phone her. He longed fiercely to meet her. It was as if he were in love again, so full was he of obsessional yearnings and unsuspected fears and strange whims. One afternoon, he told himself he would phone her at exactly four, when it got to four he would count ten and dial her number. But when four came and he had counted ten his arm refused to function and lift the receiver, it was as if his arm were paralyzed. What was the matter with him that he couldn't make a phone call to an old woman he had once known?

The next day he drove back to Aurora Road in the late afternoon. There were three elderly women walking along, walking abreast, but not going in the direction of her house, coming away from it. Was one of them she?

In the three faces, one pale and lined, one red and firm, the third waxen, sagging, he looked for the features of his Catherine. He looked for some vestige of her step in the way each walked. One of the women wore a burgundy-colored coat, and pulled down over her gray hair, a burgundy felt hat, a shapeless pudding of a hat. Catherine had been fond of wine-red. She had worn it to be married in, married to him and perhaps also to Aldred Sydney. But this woman wasn't she, for as they passed him she turned and peered into the car, and her eyes met his without a sign of recognition.

After a little while he drove down the street and, leaving the car, walked along the footpath. The petals of the plum blossom lay scattered on the grass and the may was coming into green bud. The sun shone faintly from a white, curdy sky. This time he didn't sit down on the seat but left the path to walk under the trees, for today the grass was dry and springy. In the distance he heard a train.

For so many people coming this way from the station he was unprepared. There must have been a dozen pass in the space of two minutes. He pretended to be walking purposefully, walking for his health perhaps, for what would they think he was doing, there under the trees without a companion, a sketching block, or even a dog? The last went by — or he supposed it was the last. And then he heard soft footfalls, the sound light shoes make on a dry, sandy floor.

Afterward he was to tell himself that he knew her tread. At the time, honestly, he wasn't quite sure, he didn't dare be, he couldn't trust his own memory. And when she appeared it was quite suddenly from where the path emerged from a tunnel of trees. She was walking toward Aurora Road, and as she passed she was no more than ten yards from him.

He stood perfectly still, frozen and dumb. He felt that if he moved he might fall down dead. She didn't walk fast but lightly and springily as she had always done, and the years lay on her as lightly and gently as those footfalls of hers lay on the sand. Her hair was gray and her slenderness a little thickened. There was a hint of a double chin and a faint coarsening of those delicate features — but no more than that. If he had remained young, so had she. It was as if youth had been preserved in each of them for this moment.

He wanted to see her eyes, the blue of those hyacinths, but she kept them fixed straight ahead of her, and she had quickly gone out of his sight, lost round a curve in the path. He crept to the seat and sat down. The wonder of it, the astonishment! He had imagined her old and found her young, but she had always surprised him. Her variety, her capacity to astound, were infinite.

She had come off the train with the others. Did she go out to work? At her age? Many did. Why not she? Sydney was dead and had left her, no doubt, ill-provided for. Sydney was dead . . . He thought of courting her again, loving her, forgiving her, wooing her.

"Will you marry me, Catherine?"

"Do you still want me — after everything?"

"Everything was only a rather long bad dream . . ."

She would come and live in his house and sit opposite him in the evenings, she would go on holiday with him, she would be his wife. They would have little jokes for their friends.

"How long have you two been married?"

"It was our second wedding anniversary last week and it will be our forty-fifth next month."

He wouldn't phone, though. He would sit on this seat at the same time tomorrow and wait for her to pass by and recognize him.

Before he left home he studied the old photographs of himself that were with the old photographs of her. He had been fuller in the face then and he hadn't worn glasses. He put his hand to his high, sloping forehead and wondered why it looked so low in the pictures. Men's fashions didn't change much. The sports jacket he had on today was much like the sports jacket he had worn on his honeymoon.

As he was leaving the house he was assailed by the scent of the hyacinths, past their prime now and giving off a sickly, cloying odor. Dark blue flowers with a dark blue perfume . . . On an impulse he snapped off their heads and threw them into the wastepaper basket.

The day was bright, and he slid back the sunshine roof on his car. When he got to Aurora Road, the field, and the footpath, he took off his glasses and slipped them into his pocket. He couldn't see very well without them and he stumbled a little as he walked along.

There was no one on the seat. He sat down in the center of it. He heard the train. Then he saw it, rattling along between the tufty trees and the little choppy red roofs and the squares of green. It was bringing him, he thought, his whole life's happiness. Suppose she didn't always catch that train, though? Or suppose yesterday's appearance had been an isolated happening, not a return from work but from some occasional visit?

He had hardly time to think about it before the commuters began to come, one and one and then two together. It looked as if there wouldn't be as many as there had been yesterday. He waited, holding his hands clasped together, and when she came he scarcely heard her, she walked so softly.

His sight was so poor without his glasses that she appeared to him as in a haze, almost like a spirit woman, a ghost. But it was she, her vigorous movements, her strong athletic walk, unchanged from her girlhood, and unchanged too, the atmosphere of her that he would have known if he had been not shortsighted but totally blind and deaf, too.

The trembling that had come upon him again ceased as she approached, and he fixed his eyes on her, half-rising from the seat. And now she looked at him also. She was very near and her face flashed suddenly into focus, a face on which he saw blankness, wariness, then slight alarm. But he was sure she recognized him. He tried to speak and his voice croaked out:

"Don't you know me?"

She began walking fast away, she broke into a run. Disbelieving, he stared after her. There was someone else coming along from the station now, a man who walked out of the tree tunnel and caught up with her. They both looked back, whispering. It was then that he heard her voice, only a little older, a little harsher, than when they had first met. He got off the seat and walked about among the trees, holding his head in his hands. She had looked at him, she had seemed to know him — and then she hadn't wished to.

When he reached home again he understood what he had never quite faced up to when he first retired, that he had nothing to live for. For the past week he had lived for her and in the hope of having her again. He found his gun, the small unused automatic, and loaded it and put on the safety catch and looked at it. He would write to her and tell her what he had done — by the time she got his letter he would have done it — or, better still, he would see her once, force her to see him, and then he would do it.

The next afternoon he drove to her house in Aurora Road. It was nearly half-past five, she would be along at any moment. He sat in the car, feeling the hard bulge of the gun in his pocket. Presently the man who had caught up with her the day before came along, but now he was alone, walking the length of Aurora Road and turning down a side street.

She was late. He left the car where it was and set off to find her, for he could no longer bear to sit there, the pain of it, the sick suspense. He kept seeing her face as she had looked at him, with distaste and then with fear.

Another train was jogging between the tree tufts and the little red chevrons, he heard it enter the station. Had the green, the many, varied greens, been as bright as this yesterday? The green of the grass and the new beech leaves and the may buds hurt his eyes. He passed the seat and went on, further than he had ever been before, coming into a darkish grove where the trees arched over the path. Her feet on the sand whispered like doves. He stood still, he waited for her.

She slowed down when she saw him and came on hesitantly, raising one hand to her face. He took a step toward her, saying, "Please. Please don't go. I want to talk to you so much . . ."

Today he was wearing his glasses, there was no chance of his eyes being deceived. He couldn't be mistaken as to the meaning of her expression. It was compounded of hatred and terror. But this time she couldn't walk on without walking into his arms. She turned to hasten back the way she had come, and as she turned he shot her.

With the first shot he brought her down. He ran up to where she had fallen but he couldn't look at her, he could only see her as very small and very distant through a red haze of revenge. He shot her again and again, and at last the white ringless hand which had come feebly up to shield her face, fell in death.

The gun was empty. There was blood on him that had flown

from her. He didn't care about that, he didn't care who saw or knew, so long as he could get home and reload the gun for himself. It surprised him that he could walk, but he could and quite normally as far as he could tell. He was without feeling now, without pain or fear; and his breathing settled, though his heart still jumped. He gave the body on the ground one last vague look and walked away from it, out of the tree tunnel, on to the path. The sun made bright sheets of light on the grass and long, tapering shadows. He walked along Aurora Road toward the car outside her house.

Her front door opened as he was unlocking the car. An old woman came out. He recognized her as one of those he had seen on his second visit, the one who had been wearing the dark red coat and hat. She came to the gate and looked over it, looked up toward the left a little anxiously, then backed and smiled at him. Something in his stare must have made her speak, show politeness to this stranger.

"I was looking for my daughter," she said. "She's a bit late today, she's usually on that first train."

He put his cold hands on the bar of the gate. Her smile faded.

"Catherine," he said, "Catherine . . ."

She lifted to him enquiring eyes, blue as the hyacinths he had thrown away.

The Arabella Plot

by JTBBDBTJNPWJTMBXSFODFUSFBU

The difficulty writers labor under is that their carefully knit stories must be tight and self-consistent and free of obvious flaws. One can't help but envy the freedom of reality, which can be as inconsistent and flawed and confused as it wishes — without bringing upon itself caustic editorial comments. But what if one inexplicable event in real life is so widely known that it can be used as an excuse to have a similar event invade a story? How fortunate that would be for the harried writer.

Slattery, attached to the criminal division of the state police, got home around eight that evening, kissed his wife, and then stowed his gun on the top shelf of the bedroom closet.

"Pam," he said, "how did things go today?"

"Fine. And you?"

"Well," Slattery said, "it's a little complicated, so maybe I'd better begin at the beginning."

Pamela repressed a sigh of impatience. "About Arabella Ware?" she said. "Are you handling the case?"

"I am, and it's a toughie, it's a humdinger and a lollapalooza. Three suspects, same motive, same opportunity, and I got to guess which. Draw lots or something. But first off, maybe I'd better explain Ara-

bella." Slattery paused, as if weighing the far-reaching significance of his words. Then, after due consideration, he qualified the remark. "If possible," he said.

Pamela gave him a mild verbal prod. "She was terribly wealthy, wasn't she?"

Slattery agreed, and settled down to his story.

She had money, *he said.* Dough, bread, lettuce. Moolah or spondulicks or whatever you want to call it, Arabella had it. The Ware fortune had been made over the bodies of a few hundred thousand victims, and Arabella's conscience made her suffer the pangs of the damned. It was blood money. She felt guilty and ashamed, but she still hugged her fortune to one of the flattest bosoms I've ever happened to notice.

I never saw her in life, but from her pictures and from what they said about her, she was a kind of sorry little *fraulein,* thin as a ball pen, scared of dogs, people, and anything that either moved or didn't move. One look at that small, pathetic face of hers, and you wanted to get hold of whoever killed her and take them apart inch by inch, to see whether they were really human inside.

From what everybody told me today, her mission in life was to save money, and she spent her life looking for bargains. Tell her about a real one, and she'd order her chauffeur to bring the Rolls around and to drive fast, so she could get there ahead of everybody else.

She went in for dolls in a big way, and she sewed clothes for them, hours at a time. She had a talent for the tiny and the trivial and the useless, and she ran away from anything that would involve her with other people. Sewing for dolls was the perfect answer for her, and I'm told she had a couple hundred of them tucked away in the attic, until somebody suggested giving them away as Christmas presents for needy children. Which she did. It was her hobby, and her one contribution to society.

She lived in the Ware mansion, which had ten upstairs guest rooms, as empty of people as a department store on a Sunday morning. She ate in the formal dining room and used the famous Ware silverware and china, but all she ever ate was scraps of meat and day-old bread because it was cheaper. And every night she tape-recorded what she'd spent that day and how much money she'd saved.

Skinflint? Miser? Sure. She half-starved herself, wore cheap clothes, and never gave parties — they were too expensive; but her help lived off the fat of the land and got paid top wages. Whatever they asked for, they got. I guess you could call her the goose with the papa that laid the golden eggs.

Beginning to get the picture? She hated herself, devoted her life to trying to punish herself and make up to the world for the sins of her ancestry. Which is where the unholy trio came in. They were willing to further her atonement.

Number One Boy was Edie Aimee, private secretary, a sophisticated graduate of one of the best finishing schools, and married three times before she got her long green nails into Arabella.

"Dear Miss Ware," she said to me. "She was so sweet, she leaves a yawning gap in my life."

Some gap! The gap is the dough Edie's been stealing. After you embezzle for a few years, you get to thinking you have a right to the spoils.

Number Two Boy was Jasper. Jasper K. Oates, with a mouth like a goosefish, wide open and swallowing up cash, bills, checks, bonds, stock certificates. Anything negotiable was his meat and his caviar. He's an accountant, talked himself into getting a job as Arabella's live-in business manager. He had a suite of rooms all to himself, near Edie's, and they both had private entrances. No shenanigans between those two characters, though, not much in common except their love of money. Edie's beautifully crooked mind concocted most of the ideas for gypping Arabella, while Jasper tended to the fine art of calculating. He loves decimal points, interest rates, and tax schedules. And that's about all he's made of.

Number Three Boy is David Manch, attorney at law. He talks like a congressman making a Fourth of July speech on Kosciusko day. His style is striped pants and frock coat, and his function was to sit down with Edie and Jasper and tell them whether their latest brain child would land them in jail or not. From the look of that unholy three and from what I get of Arabella's character, Manch was the one who usually convinced her that Edie's idea and Jasper's figures were honest, practical, idealistic, and in the best interests both of Arabella and of all humanity, including the hundreds of thousands of widows and fatherless children who had suffered and bled in the course of the accumulation of the Ware fortune.

Pam, after I interrogated those three and sat down with the captain and the commissioner and tried to map out the investigation, I was blank. And so were the captain and the commissioner. Every once in a while I wonder why they're big brass and I'm the one that carries the case, and the answer I usually get is that I'm a naïve, modest guy who loves his work and doesn't get mixed up in departmental politics.

I know what you're going to say, Pam. That I'm too direct, I'm not practical, I shoot off my mouth too much, but let's not argue about that. The point is I wouldn't want to do anything else in the world except police work.

There are parts of it I hate, of course. Like seeing Arabella this morning. She was sitting up in bed, with that bloody knife alongside her. She had a light blue dressing gown over her nightgown, lots of fancy lace on both, and she looked like a rag doll that somebody had spilled ketchup over. The TV was on, low volume, the remote control switch was still on her bed, hadn't even fallen off. Everything was neat and in place, with the blanket hardly rumpled. But a meek little ninety-five pounder who felt she had no right to be alive in the first place — she couldn't have put up much of a fight, could she?

When the commissioner asked me for details, I had nothing much to offer except that tape recorder that was in the wrong place. It was lying on the bureau instead of on the night table, where I'd been told it usually was. And it was empty. So what happened to the cassette? Where was it and who had it and why?

Well, I told the commissioner that Arabella had been stabbed with the knife that was usually on her escritoire. I had to tell him what the word meant, and I said the knife was really an antique dagger that she used for opening letters and things like that. I said the M.E. had decided she'd been killed around one A.M., that the lab men were checking on the physical evidence, and that the photography boys would show him the scene a lot better than I could describe it. All I had at the beginning was a homicide by knife in a house that had the best burglar alarm system going, which was in working order as of now. Which meant an inside job.

I had a look at a copy of her will, too. Substantial bequests to some distant relatives. Bequests of ten thousand apiece to her cook, her chauffeur, her maids, and, respectively, to her devoted secretary named Edith Aimee, to her business manager named Jasper Kenneth Oates and to her attorney named David Manch, with the remainder to the Ware Foundation, of which the unholy three were to be directors for the rest of their lives. And that amounted to a nice little sinecure, but no improvement over their present rackets. If anything, they were better off with Arabella alive, and there was no reason for one of them to kill her, although one of them did.

Why do I say that? I don't know. I could kind of smell it. I felt it, I knew it. My problem was, which one of the three had done it, because they were all there in the house that night and they all claimed they'd slept nice and sound, until the maid went in and found her, and started screaming.

Believe me, Pam — the commissioner and the captain were no help. They told me to make a thorough investigation, to leave no stone unturned. They said they'd back me up and that this was a big case. In other words, they chickened out.

But at least I had a clue — that tape recorder without a cassette. It was common knowledge that she kept the recorder on

the night table next to her bed and dictated to herself before
she went to sleep, and maybe during the night if she happened
to wake up and remember a few cents that she'd maybe spent
on a piece of ribbon or a candy bar.

"A woman like Arabella," Pam remarked, *"doesn't eat candy bars."*

Slattery, with a fine disregard for the picayune, continued his narra-
tive with hardly a break in his stride.

Next morning, *he observed,* she always transcribed the tape
and put it all down in a ledger book. You study that book and
you know pretty well everything she's been doing on any particular day, and believe me, I went through that book as if I
was studying for an exam. And I learned nothing that I didn't
know before, so how do I locate a missing cassette about the
size of a pack of playing cards?

I was stumped, bewildered and bebaffled and belicked.
They'd been stealing from her for years, so why did they have
to do something to her now? I couldn't figure out why, I was
up against a wall and waiting for somebody to come along and
give me an answer, and the somebody turned out to be an
I.R.S. man, name of Sara Walters.

I know I have my genders mixed up, but do you want me to
say an I.R.S. person, or what? So Sara is an I.R.S. man, just as
Edie is the Number One Boy of my unholy trio.

Sara has a nice voice. She may turn out to be bald and
scrawny and messed up with acne, but she has a lovely voice. I
could fall in love with a voice. Lots of people have. Would I
rather look at a lovely face or listen to a lovely voice? Well, I
don't have to make the choice, Pam, because here you are with
both.

Anyhow, Sara not only had a lovely voice, but she said sweet
things with it. She said she'd been going over the Arabella
Ware tax returns and found an overpayment of a hundred
thousand dollars.

"It seemed to me," Sara said, "that nobody can make a mistake of that magnitude, and in particular no professional accountant can. Maybe my job makes me unusually suspicious, as

it probably should, or maybe I've been reading too many mystery stories, but I felt that there was something queer behind this, so I called Miss Ware's home and spoke to her secretary. A Miss Aimee."

"That's Edie," I said. "What did she say?"

"That she had complete confidence in the I.R.S., and if I said there's been an overpayment she'd take my word for it and please refund, and make the check payable to the Arabella Ware Special Account."

Sounded screwy, Pam. From what Sara said, I figured that this was a pretty slick scheme. Overpay from one account, and refund to another one that Edie and Jasper and Manch controlled. Then they could divide up a hundred grand. Thirty-three apiece, and all done legally.

I told Sara I'd look into the matter, and she popped back with, "I already have."

"What did you find out?" I said.

"I went to see Miss Ware, and I told her what had happened and what my suspicions were. She was terribly upset and said I was accusing her most trusted friends of betraying her and that I was unworthy of being a public servant. She said that, far from taking action against them, she'd take their advice on what to do about me, whether to report me or what.

"It was rather pathetic, because here was a woman with all the power of ten or fifteen million dollars, and she was apparently in the hands of some unscrupulous advisors who were using their power over her for their own ends. But I'd gone too far to back out, so I told Miss Ware that if she loved and trusted them, she ought to take steps to defend them against the federal charges that I'd guarantee would be preferred by the United States district attorney. That scared her, and she burst out crying and asked me what to do, and I said she'd better consult a lawyer, somebody objective, with whom she'd had no previous contact."

"Sara," I said, "you're a gem, and if you ever leave the I.R.S., come around and see me, because you're a born investigator."

"Thanks," she said, "but I think I'll stay where I am. Still, I love cops, and any time you want to take me out for a drink, just let me know."

Pam, think I should?

"I think," Pamela said, "that you should assume Arabella did get in touch with an attorney, and that you should find out who he is."

"A sound idea," Slattery said. "Of course, what the unholy three did was no crime, although they probably intended one, and Sara gave me a nice lead in my homicide."

"As to why she was murdered now?" Pamela said. "Maybe, but it doesn't tell you which of the three did it."

"You got me there," Slattery said, yawning. "But it's been a long day, and I'm getting up early in the morning. Maybe I can figure things out when my mind is fresh, but right now I'm pooped."

Pam was asleep when he left the house the following morning, and she didn't see him until evening when, as usual, he sat down and discussed his day's work.

You were right about her consulting an attorney, *Slattery said.* Arabella had an appointment for later on this week with one of the big law firms. Hammond, Mayer, Considine, and Higgins. I spoke to Mayer, and he told me she hadn't mentioned the subject beyond saying it was confidential.

Well, that was something. She had a date that might land the unholy three in jail, and she'd made it over a phone that had extensions in Edie's and Jasper's suites, as well as half a dozen other places in that impossible palace. Which answers the question of why now, why one of them picked this particular time to kill her. The next question was who.

Remember what I said last night, Pam, that if they all had the same motive and opportunity, you could just about draw lots to see which one? Well, that's exactly what happened, and here's how I found out.

We'd been going through all the trash in the place, looking for something and anything. That's routine. You can pick up a letter or a notation on a pad — anything at all can break a case. Well, I happened to be sitting in the library, I'd just finished up a session with Manch, I'd accused him of the tax rebate scheme, and I had him worried.

"I," he told me in that fine, sanctimonious voice of his, "am a member in good standing of the bar of this state. As an attorney I am an officer of the court, dedicated to the principles of justice and to the maintenance of our Anglo-American system of the Common Law, which is the foundation of our society and of this great country of ours. It is an insult to infer that I would break the law, and I resent it."

I let him go on like that for a while. I like to sling lingo. A serving of good, juicy rhetoric dripping with old-fashioned rodomontade can gladden my heart, but Manch didn't measure up. He was turgid, worse than that, he was trite. And prolix and bombastic, and after the first few sentences I was hardly listening. I kept fiddling with a copy of the annual report of Ware Manufacturing, which happened to be there on a coffee table in front of me. I was turning the pages while I was waiting for his peroration, and I was thinking up a nice phrase or two to cut him down to size, when I happened to notice that three pages of the report had their margins cut off in strips about an inch wide.

When I was ten or eleven years old, any job that us kids didn't want to do, like sweeping the porch or carrying out the slops, or when only one lollypop was in that tin box, we'd draw lots. We'd cut strips of paper and leave them all blank except one, and whoever drew that would be *it*. So it hit me that maybe my unholy trio had drawn lots about something, and why wouldn't that something be which one was going to kill Arabella?

Pam, it kind of got me. I don't shock easy, but the idea of the three of them milking Arabella and then, when they got pushed to the wall and she might really go out and make trouble — then they coldly drew lots to kill her, that was pretty hard to take.

I didn't have much hope of cracking Edie. I'd seen her a little earlier and she'd been laying it on pretty thick. She was dressed in mourning and she went around with a long face and kept telling everybody she hadn't slept all night. "Poor, sad thing," she was saying. "Poor, sad Arabella. What an end!"

When I interrogated her, she burst out crying. "I can't think straight," she said. "I keep wondering what that poor dear thing could have done to push somebody into murder."

"You ought to know," I said. "You had a hand in it."

"That," she said, "is a very poor joke." And after that she wouldn't open her mouth. Any question I asked her, she went mum. She could have been deaf and dumb, and what you do with a *frau* like that, I haven't found out. And nobody else has, either. It takes nerve and will power to shut up like a tombstone, and she managed.

I hadn't gotten very far with Jasper, either. He took the perfectly tenable position that, as her financial adviser, he had unlimited exchequer powers, that he sometimes kept some of her money in his own account, but he always returned it and could prove it. And with his accountant's mind, he would have bamboozled me every time. Pam, if I can't even balance our own bank account, what chance would I have against a mathematical wizard like Jasper?

That left Manch as my boy. He was the weak link, he was the one I had to bust, and I think I did it artistically. First, I called in a uniformed trooper and asked him to take Manch into the next room and keep him there and see that he didn't talk to anybody. Then I went out to the garage where we had all the trash we'd collected yesterday, and Hymie Baer and I went through every single scrap of paper. We found those three slips all right, and they matched the pages of the Ware Manufacturing annual report. No doubt about it. But what threw me was, they all had a mark on them. I was up against a conspiracy.

The lab men were still poking around, and they had their portable iodine-fuming apparatus. What with the slips of paper being crumpled up, there wasn't much hope of picking up a print that would be any good, and even if we did, what would it tell us? Probably that some of the police had handled it. Anyhow, I went through the motions.

We had sample prints of just about everybody in the house; we'd gotten them the day before and photographed them, so I took the picture of Manch's, along with one of those slips of paper, and I went back to the library and called in Manch.

I decided to take a chance on being right, and I dressed it up a little. I had a stenographer with me, and I quoted Miranda and told Manch what his rights were. He knew this was serious and he was plenty nervous, but why wouldn't he be?

I threw it straight at him. I told him that between Edie and Jasper, I now had pretty much the whole story.

"The three of you sat here in this library the night before last," I said. "You knew Arabella was going to see Matthew Mayer, of Hammond, Mayer, Considine, and Higgins. You've heard of them, haven't you?"

He kind of croaked out a yes, because a prestigious firm like this knocked him for a loop. It was like mentioning God.

"The three of you," I said, "must have realized that your handling of Arabella's money would be looked into by both the I.R.S. and a U.S. district attorney, and that larceny and embezzlement charges would probably be brought. And even if you squirmed out of them, Arabella was through with you, and Edie and Jasper would blame you for everything and claim they merely acted on your legal advice. You'd be lucky if you got away with nothing worse than disbarment. You know that, don't you?"

He choked up and stuttered out some kind of mumbo-jumbo. You take a hot-air balloon like Manch, and when you puncture it all you've got left is a hunk of rubber and a broken valve.

"All right," I said. "Tell me what you advised them to do about getting that rebate."

Right then and there I made a mistake, Pam, because he knew I was fishing for information and that he was on solid ground. I gave him the out that he needed.

"I admit," he told me, "that Arabella has given me a great deal of money, perhaps unwisely, and probably given Edie and Jasper substantial amounts also, with the result that an erroneous inference might be drawn. But as the three of us discussed the matter, we knew that our consciences were clear. Arabella had given us money of her own free will."

"That's the story you expect to get away with?" I said.

Manch sputtered as if the very suggestion of dishonesty shocked him. "I," he said, "have nothing to conceal, although it is quite possible that Jasper is not as competent as I had believed. If a man can overpay the I.R.S. by one hundred thousand, one cannot assume his accounting to be of a high order of accuracy. In fact, his errors may well be legion."

I saw the whole scheme then, *Slattery said.* Mix up the books so thoroughly that nobody could straighten them out. A hundred thousand overpayment here, a million disappearing somewhere else — Jasper had been building up to a point where there might be evidence of negligence, but not of criminal intent. That was the idea, and the trio had been relying on it with complete confidence until they found out that the I.R.S. was investigating and that Arabella had an appointment with an outside lawyer. They had to stop that appointment, because they needed time — to stave off the investigation, maybe abort it, but certainly to prepare a better cover-up.

At that point, Slattery told his wife, he accused Manch of the lot business, and Manch drew himself up and said he'd never countenance so nefarious a conspiracy.

The word *nefarious* cued me, *Slattery said.* When Manch got to using big words, that meant he had his confidence back. A couple of minutes ago he'd thought he was sunk, but he'd come up with the excuse of sloppy bookkeeping and he thought he'd gotten by with it, and now he latched on to an explanation of those three slips of paper, and do you know what? He claimed it was a joke, that they were sitting there in the living room and they got hungry and drew lots to see who'd go to the kitchen and scrounge up some food.

Pam, I kept at him for two hours without a break, *Slattery said.* He sweated and stammered and almost gave up, but not quite. I showed him his fingerprints on the marked slip, and he said all the slips were marked, Edie had marked them just for the fun of it. I told him there'd been only one mark at the time of the draw and that the other marks were put on later, which proved conspiracy, but we had a way of knowing which was there first. And we weren't buying Manch's explanation. We knew better.

He didn't fall for it. He managed to cling to that one statement, that the lot-drawing was a joke and that was all he knew.

I tackled Edie next, and she sat there the same as she had in the morning, and never opened her mouth. She tried to look sweet and she had tears in her eyes and she let me talk until I got hoarse. Which is why I let somebody else handle Jasper. And they got nowhere with him. Nowhere at all. Just the excuse that maybe his bookkeeping had gotten out of hand. So what do you think, Pam?

"I'm just wondering," Pamela said, "whether Arabella would have stayed quietly in bed, watching TV and not moving or screaming, when a man came into her room."

"Which man?" Slattery asked.

"I don't know. Either one. If they came into her room late at night, she'd have pulled up the sheets and cringed, or else she would have yelled or struggled or tried to run away. She was scared of men, wasn't she?"

"You mean that Edie must have killed her?" Slattery said.

"Exactly. Anyone but Edie, she would have screamed her head off and made a fuss."

"And how do you prove that?"

"I don't," Pam said. "You do."

Slattery got home a little after six the next evening, and he told her the news.

We made the arrest, *he said,* and in a way it was thanks to you. Because I got to thinking of what you said about the scream, and I figured you were probably right. The only question was, if Arabella screamed, did anybody hear her? The servants couldn't, they were off in a separate wing of the house. And the others, they were in on the crime.

Still, you had a good idea there. That tape was the answer to the case, and I did a lot of thinking about it and I came up with something you could have told me in the first place — namely that only one of the three knew the details of what had happened and could tell the genuine tape from a fake.

From yesterday's investigation I knew where Arabella had been and how much money she'd spent on the day she'd been killed. It was easy to reconstruct her tape, and it was easy to get an actress to imitate her voice. If I played the imitation but told the trio it was the real thing, two of them wouldn't know the difference, but the third one would, because he'd been there.

I told them I'd found Arabella's tape and I wanted them to listen to it. I had Hymie and Felix Brown in the room with me and I had a scream on that tape that little Arabella would have been proud of. Hymie's job was to watch feet, and Felix's was to watch hands, because when the killer heard that scream, he was going to tense up. His fists would clench or his feet would tighten or he'd jerk up on his toes. Some kind of reaction would be automatic, and between Hymie and Felix and myself, we'd spot it. One of our unholy trio would give himself away, while the other two would just be wondering what this was all about.

It was quite a performance, Pam. The dead woman's voice going on and on about how much she'd spent and what her bank account was and how much more the groceries were and what inflation was doing. Stuff like that. Then it stopped. After the break there was a sentence or two that was kind of garbled up, and then the scream. And you know what? It scared the hell out of all three of them. Scared the hell out of me, too.

Well, it just goes to show. A bright idea like that, and it flops. If I got any brains, they weren't much help. Give me a dumb cop every time, one that just slogs along and waits for something to happen. Still, I knew one thing because of that scream.

I knew that whoever really had that tape would hotfoot it back to make sure the thing was still where he'd put it, and that's exactly what happened. We each of us followed one of the three, but Hymie hit the jackpot. He heard Jasper rummaging around in his room, so Hymie walked in and there was Jasper with the tape. After that he broke, and we got a confession out of him. No sweat, either.

"But," Pam said, "I don't understand his keeping the tape. What for? Why didn't he throw it away? Why didn't he destroy it?"

"A good question," Slattery said. "But — why didn't Nixon?"

The Last Party

by B M J D F E P S P U I Z T B M J T C V S Z E B W J T

The beautiful people! Those fun-filled gay individuals who toil not, neither do they spin, but whose lives are a happy round of parties in houses filled with space and art and hobbies and drinks and food and sex. How is it possible not to envy them and not to view our own humdrum lives with sharp dissatisfaction? Well, the beautiful people are mortals, with passions and pettiness and circumstances that leave them, after all, no better off in the long run than the plain people. Witness the descent from merriment to murder . . .

The Winthrops had a tremendous collection of Big Band records — Miller, Lombardo, Harry James . . . But then, the Winthrops had a tremendous collection of almost everything, and when they gave a party, Tom Winthrop's measure of its success was the variety of his possessions to which his guests found their way. His hospitality was excessive: champagne, the best of liquors; the dining-room buffet — replenished throughout the evening, with monster prawns, half-lobsters, mounds of succulent beef, crisp vegetables, mousses, and soufflés, melons, cheeses, and the most delicate of pastries.

The trouble with the Winthrops' parties was that nothing

ever happened at them; paradoxically, too much was going on. There was a billiard room in the basement for those not drawn to the dance. Next to the billiard room was the gun room, with its trophies of ancestral hunts. Tom liked to tell that it was part of Sally's inheritance. Her great-grandfather was supposed to have gone big-game hunting with Teddy Roosevelt. The younger residents of Maiden's End had a modest reverence for *that* Roosevelt, but their politics, for the most part, were in the tradition of his cousin Franklin. Nor did they have much taste for guns or the hunt. It was generally by accident that a guest found himself — or herself — in the gun room. Or he might pass through it on his way to a room Winthrop called "The Double Entendre," where he housed his collection of pornographic art.

It remains to be said of Winthrop — or perhaps of Maiden's End — that since he had built Woodside, a neo-Tudor mansion that dwarfed the sedate, more modest houses, some of which were historically significant, no one in the community had ever asked him if he was related to other Winthrops of their acquaintance.

◆　◆　◆

On the afternoon of what became known as the last Winthrop party, Jan Swift stopped by the Adams house to see what Nancy was going to wear. Jan, a plump, self-conscious woman, didn't like parties, but she went to them. She'd have liked it less not to be asked, and if you didn't go to one, you might not be asked to the next. Or so Jan feared. What it amounted to was that when the invitation came she was so relieved to have been asked — for Fred's sake mostly, she told herself — that there was never any doubt of their accepting.

"Hello?" she called up the stairs. The Adamses still left their door unlocked in the daytime. "Nancy, it's me."

"Hello, you," Nancy called down, a greeting that always gave Jan pleasure, something about the intimacy of it. Jan had never heard her say it to anyone else. "Come up if you like. Or I'll be down in a minute. I'm doing a bed in the guest room."

Jan climbed the stairs, a little aware of her weight, and wondered what she could wear and be comfortable to dance in that wouldn't look like a tent. She loved to dance when she got high enough and someone besides Fred asked her. Fred danced much as he did most things, determined to succeed. She stood at the guest-room door and watched Nancy turn down one of the twin beds.

"A comforter should do him," Nancy said. It was going to be one of those warm summer nights when people would want to go swimming after the party. Or sailing on the river.

Jan thought about the word *comforter,* the coziness of it. "Who's coming?"

"Eddie Dorfman. He was Dick's roommate in college. He shows up now and then on his way somewhere — generally broke, but with great expectations. Is it hot in here? I was going to put him in Ellen's room, but I don't like to do that." Ellen was the oldest of the Adamses' three daughters.

"It'll cool off by bedtime," Jan said. She was thinking how nice it was for Nancy, the girls of an age to take care of themselves. Her own two had to be picked up at the Swim Club any time now. Nancy was ten years older than Jan, well up in her forties, but with a finely boned face and dark, deepset eyes that made her look more striking the older she got. She played tennis and swam and wrote poetry that Jan did her best to understand. Jan nodded at the open bed. "Is he a bachelor?"

"To all intents and purposes. He's a charming rogue, if you want to know."

"I don't particularly. What are you going to wear tonight?"

"Oh, God. Something I won't have to hang up afterward." She gave a last look around the room. Following her eyes, Jan noticed the published volume of Nancy's poems on the bedside table. Nancy gave Jan a nudge into the hall ahead of her. "Eddie tried to seduce me the night Dick and I announced our engagement. Whenever I see him, he pretends regrets at not having succeeded." She hooked her arm through Jan's. "Don't hold it against him, you puritan. He thinks he's being *trés galant.*"

◆   ◆   ◆

Eddie was still at it, Jan judged, by the way he danced with Nancy, cheek to cheek, abdomen to abdomen. Furthermore, Nancy was enjoying it . . . "Moonlight Serenade," "Elmer's Tune," "Black Moonlight" . . . They drew away from one another, took a long look into each other's eyes, laughed, and sailed away to the far end of the deck.

It was pretty much the older crowd that turned on to the music of the Big Bands, and you couldn't say the deck was jammed. The noise would start at midnight with the arrival of a rock group. Jan thought of another drink, which she didn't need but wanted. She didn't even want it. What in hell did she want? Fred and Dick were probably shooting pool in the basement. Billiards: a fine distinction. She did not like Eddie Dorfman. Or did she? Maybe that was the trouble. Baby blue eyes and black hair with a streak of gray, a whispery lower lip. The women kept asking Jan who he was, as though she was Nancy's keeper. It wasn't hard to guess the speculation. Maiden's End (named after a family called Maiden) was by no means famous for marital stability. Jan thought of the switched couples at the party — the Eckstroms and the Bellows. What a mix-up for the kids. And there were at least three grass widows, as her mother called them. She'd have been willing to bet that Liz Toomey would make a play for Eddie Dorfman before the night was over. She emptied her glass and thought of shifting to champagne rather than having to go back to the bar again alone.

Tom Winthrop came up and took the glass from her hand and dropped it over the deck. "Come one, Jan. They're playing our song."

Our song indeed. Neither in nor out of step, he took her with him on a cruise of his guests, wanting to know if everyone was happy and assuming she was, just to be in on the trip. Not a word did he say to her, or she to him, for that matter. When they came alongside Nancy and Dorfman, Jan broke away from Tom and said, "May we cut in?" You could almost say she plucked Eddie out of Nancy's arms.

"What fun!" Dorfman cried, though he cast Nancy a wistful glance. After that he gave Jan his complete attention. He even hummed "Sentimental Journey" in her ear. She had never felt lighter on her feet. He was a good dancer.

"I wonder," she said breathlessly between tunes, "if they have 'Flatfoot Floogie with the Floy Floy.' "

"If they do, I hope it's not contagious."

She laughed too loudly and explained, "My mother used to play all her old records for me on a rainy day and we'd dance up in the attic."

"What fun," he said again. "No wonder you dance so well."

"I do with the right partner." She tossed her head and sang, a bit off tune, but urgently, " 'He danced divinely and I loved him so, but there I go . . .' That was another of my mother's favorites."

The music started again, another set of records. "Glenn Miller," Jan said, "oh, boy."

" 'I saw those harbor lights,' " he crooned, and held her close. He said after a few bars, "I'll be in London this time tomorrow."

"Will you? I wish I were."

He drew back and looked at her.

"I mean just that I love to travel."

He held her close again. "Perhaps we'll meet in some exotic port some day," he said. His cheek, soft, freshly shaven, was scented with lavender. A tango then. They dipped and glided, a backward dip for Jan, something she had never risked before in her life, and then a waltz that dissolved into a seductive whine.

"Salomé," her partner said.

"I forgot my veils," Jan said; she tried to repress the impulse to lead.

"Let's pretend." He disengaged himself and with provocative little gestures coaxed her into letting go. Jan shed veil after imaginary veil, clownish at first, but with a growing feeling that she was actually graceful. Eddie posed as a macho Herod; he demanded more and more letting go. For a few seconds Jan danced with utter abandon, every pound of her a-quiver.

"Help!" she cried finally, and collapsed in self-conscious laughter, sinking to the floor.

Eddie mimed the removal of his own head and brought it to her in cupped hands, which rather thoroughly distorted the story line, to say nothing of de-sanctifying John the Baptist.

Everyone, having given Jan space, now applauded, laughed, and slipped away into the next dance.

She blushed and got to her feet. "I need a drink," she said.

"I'll get it for you."

"I'll go with you," she said and caught his hand. Then: "I'll meet you at the bar. I've got to make some repairs first."

Nancy was waiting for her when she came out of the bathroom, a look of pure disgust on her face.

"Hey," Jan said. "What's the matter?"

"It wasn't funny, kiddo."

"I thought it was fun."

"It was pretty undignified, if you want the truth."

If it was the truth, it was the last thing she wanted. "That wasn't exactly a minuet the two of you were dancing when I pulled you apart," she said. "You wouldn't be jealous, would you?"

"Jan, I care about you and I don't like to see you make a fool of yourself."

"Okay. I get the message." The worst of it was that deep down it hadn't been fun; the make-believe that she had almost bought herself now fell apart.

"Don't sulk over it. For heaven's sake, you're not a little girl anymore."

"I never was a *little* girl."

"Just don't drink so much."

"It's none of your damned business how much I drink. Okay, keep your Don Juan. I'm going to find Fred."

She did not look for Fred right away. She went out to the garden to cool off, to sort out anger from hurt, as though they were divisible at the moment. She took a glass of champagne with her, drank it too fast, and then took another from the tray one of the teen-aged helpers was passing as though his night's wage depended on the score in champagne corks. The feeling of humiliation began to set in, a replay of the exhibition she had made of herself. She did not know whom she disliked more, Nancy, Dorfman, or herself. Herself.

She almost went directly home then, but Fred was always accusing her of disappearing at parties. She spent a lot of time in bathrooms, especially if there was a children's bathroom where the ducks and frogs and floating pigs gave her surcease from the social tensions. Fred was not in the billiard room. No one was. She wandered through the gun room, and wondered vaguely if any of the blunderbusses in the glass cases were loaded. She looked up at the moosehead over the fireplace, its glassy eyes frozen in sadness. "You and me, baby."

THE DOUBLE ENTENDRE: the sign hung above the door. That's me, she thought. I'm a double entendre. She wandered with fascinated distaste from one to another of Tom Winthrop's pornographic objects d'art. He always set out a half-dozen or so for the titillation of his guests. For anyone who appreciated the sampling enough to tell him so, he would come down and show the really important things in the collection. Fred said he'd never seen anything like it. Fred, the connoisseur. It was a strange place to be alone, a strange place to be discovered if anyone came. That was all she needed. She remembered her mother opening the closet door on her, a precocious ten-year-old with a flashlight looking at the illustrations in an anatomy book she had stolen from the locked bookcase. "Wicked girl!" There were no locked bookcases in Fred's and her house. No anatomy books either.

She picked up a picture — in what medium she could not tell — of a unicorn. No larger than three by four inches, in a silver frame, it was exquisite, and she could not imagine what was pornographic about it. Then, when she went to set it down, she saw the trick: a shutter effect where beauty in a different angle of light turned into obscenity. She set it down and turned to flee the room. Dorfman was standing in the doorway.

"Here you are — in the naughty room. What fun!"

She stopped herself from saying that she was looking for her husband. She pushed by him. "Please tell Nancy — if Fred's looking for me, I've gone home."

"Don't leave on my account."

"I'm not," she said.

She found Fred herself. He was in the library where he and Dick and Phil Eckstrom were deep in conversation. Local politics, she gathered. Eckstrom was on the town board. She did not interrupt. The bar wasn't crowded, and she decided on one for the road. The bartender, who worked most parties at Maiden's End, didn't even ask her what she wanted. He knew: Scotch with a splash. Nancy, she observed, was dancing again. With Phil Eckstrom, senior.

Jan finished her drink and went out by way of the garden. From there she cut down along the ravine path that crossed the creek and meandered up near the Adams house, beyond which lay her own. There was a three-quarter moon, but she knew the path from her own childhood. What did Nancy see in him, she wondered. Something. Or she would not have left her poems at his bedside. He certainly wasn't going to understand them if Jan didn't. She often wondered if Dick did, all that symbolism. Not that Nancy cared: It isn't what they say, it's what they show. Simply fireworks? Jan had to believe they were deeper than that. She often imagined Nancy making them up, quite removed, while Dick was telling one of the stories in which he was the hero. It wasn't easy to be a hero in advertising, not and continue to make as much money as Dick did. Pure fantasy. To which all Nancy had to say, in effect, was

"Yes, dear." She'd been flying in a holding pattern for years. But then, who hadn't? After the first child, Jan didn't say, "Yes, dear," to Fred. In Fred's stories he was always the victim; most people found that funny. The trouble was, Fred's stories were true.

Nancy ought not to have spoken to her the way she had. She ought to have understood. Maybe she did. And that was worse, even more humiliating. The hall lights were on in the Adams house, upstairs and down. An unfamiliar car, which had to be Eddie's, sat alongside Nancy's battered V.W. in the driveway. They had taken Dick's Buick. Jan always felt that hall lights made a house look more empty than, say, a light in the living room or an upstairs bedroom. She went round to the kitchen window and got the key from the bird feeder. She returned it after opening the door. There was something she had to know — if there was anything to know: She wanted to see how Nancy had inscribed the book for Eddie Dorfman. In Jan's copy she had written, "Love, toujours."

The stairs creaked beneath her step. It was an old house with a curving banister that many a child's behind had polished over the years. She did not hesitate in turning on the bedside lamp. Somehow it seemed her right to be there. She saw at once that the book had been removed. Dorfman's one large piece of luggage was on the stand, the flap closed but not entirely zipped. So far as she could see, he had not unpacked at all: no hairbrushes or shaving kit, nothing on the dresser. She looked into the bathroom. Not even a toothbrush. And he had been freshly shaved. He reeked of after-shave cologne. The bathroom was still scented with it. It was as though, after dressing, he had repacked.

She went to the suitcase and ran the zipper far enough to lift the flap. Tucked into the corner was *Refraction*, the poems of Nancy Eldridge Adams. There was no inscription. Which brought the shame thundering in her ears. It was more difficult to fit the book back than it had been to take it out and in doing so she disturbed the bathrobe and partially uncovered something in chamois.

Now, Jan had given Nancy a chamois bag of several compartments two Christmases before. Nancy used it, when traveling, to carry such of her jewelry as she took along. She had several nice antique pieces and a valuable pearl necklace. Ordinarily they were kept in an ivory jewel box on Nancy's dressing table. Jan lost no time in discovering that the bag was the same and contained the pearls, a diamond brooch and earrings, and the lovely jade pendant, the only piece of jewelry Jan had ever coveted. Nancy had promised to give it to her some day.

The thought that Dorfman was a thief delighted her after the shock of discovery wore off. The question, however, was what to do about it without placing herself in even deeper disgrace. Her mind grew muddled with the sickening thought of how to explain the discovery; she also wondered then just when the theft had occurred. She had not met him until the party was well on. He could have stayed at the house on some pretext and come along later on his own. But surely he had to expect that Nancy would discover the theft when they came home? Jan understood then why the suitcase was packed: He expected to leave tonight, long before the Winthrop party was over. A rented car, London tomorrow . . .

However humiliating it might be, Jan resolved to bare the truth to Nancy. Replacing everything, she drew the zipper. And changed her resolution even as she put out the light. What was a handful of jewels in comparison to her own pride? She would let the matter run its course and never let on she anticipated the story when Nancy told her of the theft. It did not occur to Jan to wonder why Eddie Dorfman had not put the suitcase in the car before he left for the party. Her main concern was to get out of the house quickly.

But Dorfman was coming up the stairs when she reached the hallway. He quickened his step when he saw her and came round the banister smiling with that nasty lower lip. "I had a feeling we'd meet again before I took off," he said. "Something told me."

Jan gave a little moan of chagrin. She thought of accusing him outright. She had no subtlety, and she was able to defend herself only by striking out in anger. But at the moment she had no anger. Nor could she run: Dorfman stood between her and the stairs, one hand on the railing, the other on the wall.

"Let me guess: You've brought me something. A flower? Something that blooms in the night? Come on, let's have a look." He nodded toward the door. "You're not afraid of me, are you? I'm completely harmless unless stepped on."

Jan made a noise in her throat. No words came.

"I thought that would amuse you," he said. "Light the light and let's see where we are."

Jan turned back into the room and lit the lamp. She would run when the chance came. Simply run.

He leaned in the doorway, seeming to fill it, and looked all around the room before letting his eyes rest on her. "Nothing? Did you put something in my suitcase?"

Jan shook her head.

"I know: Nancy told you I was leaving and you wanted a few minutes alone with me first. If only I had more time . . ."

"You're making fun of me," she said.

"I don't make fun of women, Salomé," he said. He came in and closed the door. He drew the bolt across. There was no key.

"Don't! Leave the door open," Jan said.

He turned, smiling. "Then you shouldn't flirt with a man of my reputation. Didn't Nancy tell you?"

"Just let me go," she pleaded.

"Go." He stepped aside.

But as she tried to pass him, he caught her, pulled her around and kissed her, forcing her back to the closed door.

Jan yielded, as though that might gain her time, or some position of advantage, but with the thrust of his tongue between her lips, its probe of her clenched teeth, she broke away.

A few feet apart, they stood and stared at each other. He took his cigarette case from his pocket, opened it, and closed it again. He put it away without taking a cigarette. "Do you mind telling me what you were doing in my room?"

"I was looking for a book."

He began to laugh, as though at the ridiculousness of the excuse. He stopped. "Nancy's book? Why? Am I not allowed to have it?" Slowly his whole expression changed; he understood. "Salomé, you're jealous! You weren't flirting with *me*. It was an act. And me thinking all the time I was the object of your affections . . . Eddie, my boy, you're slipping. You should have caught that — no vibes, no sparks . . ."

Jan went to the door with as good grace as she could manage. Her main feeling was relief, and at the heart's core, something almost pleasurable. At the sound of the suitcase zipper she glanced back.

"Look here, Salomé. I'm left-handed. You've put the book back in the wrong corner." He plunged his hand into the case and brought out the chamois bag. "Ha! I've found the surprise." He weighed the bag in his hand, opened a compartment, and closed it again after a quick, pretended glimpse at what was in it. "Nancy's jewelry? Surely not." Slowly then in mock wonderment: "By God, I'd never have believed such mischief in a grown woman. You *are* a Salomé. You wanted my head."

Jan felt faint. Her whole body was perspiring. She pulled at the bolt and skinned her knuckles when it gave.

"Wait," he said as she stepped out of the room. "Listen to me for a minute."

Jan paused.

"Why don't you put these back — wherever they came from — and neither of us needs ever to say a word." He brought her the bag.

Jan took it from him and went into the master bedroom

where she put the jewelry, piece by piece, back in the ivory box on Nancy's dressing table. She tucked the chamois bag into the side drawer where Nancy kept it.

He was waiting at the stairs, smiling. He offered her his left hand, as to a child, the suitcase in his right. "No hard feelings. Come on now, give me your hand and no hard feelings."

Jan gave it to him as though it were a bribe.

"I'll bet Nancy doesn't even know," he said. "What fun."

A bribe for what?

With a crack-of-the-whip wrench she whirled him from his feet. He let go of her hand, trying to save himself, but while she fell backward, he hurtled down the stairs, the suitcase clattering after him. She listened for a few seconds and then picked herself up. All she could hear was the pounding of her own heart. The suitcase was lodged between his sprawled legs at the turn in the stairs, the rest of him out of sight from where she stood.

Jan went down carefully. When she stooped and looked into his face Dorfman's lashes fluttered like a wounded butterfly, but the baby blue eyes only stared. His cigarette case had flown out of his pocket, and a lighter. Jan was stepping round them when she blacked out.

Her first awareness was of rock music, the shattering beat of it breaking through what had seemed a silvery stillness. She was walking across the bridge on the ravine path, the moonlight more vivid than seemed natural. Her mind was crystal clear except that she could not understand why she was going in that direction when she had intended to go home. Then everything came back up to the moment of blackout. She sat down on the bridge and said what she knew to be a futile prayer, that it was all a dream.

She got up after a few minutes and returned to the party, going in the way she had come out, through the French doors onto the garden. Fred was standing just indoors, his pipe in hand, watching the disco dancing.

"No," Fred said when she approached.

"No, what?"

"I won't dance."

"Who asked you?" He had not even missed her.

Nancy and Dick were dancing together, very athletic, the best-looking couple among a lot of very chic and handsome people. The Big Band crowd had all gone home.

"Come on," Fred said. "You're pouting. Let's get into the action." He knocked out his pipe and put it in his pocket.

"I don't think so," Jan said after a tremendous effort inside herself. "Why don't you ask Liz Toomey?"

"Why do you always try to make me dance with somebody else?"

"I don't always," Jan said.

"I don't suppose you want to go home yet?"

"Soon," she said.

◆   ◆   ◆

It was after three when Dick and Nancy Adams drove home. They were surprised to see Dorfman's rented car still in the driveway. He had told them at the party he'd been able to get on a delayed flight taking off from Kennedy at two.

By the time the police came, Dick was fairly sure of what had happened, that Eddie had banged his suitcase into the railing and then lost his balance when it caromed into his legs at the top of the stairs. He did not touch anything of course. When the police arrived he went into the study with Nancy.

"Poor, poor man," Nancy kept saying. "Poor restless man. Why couldn't he have waited until morning the way he'd planned?"

Dick sat with his head in his hands.

The police officer in charge came in presently and closed the door behind him. He asked more questions than seemed necessary to Nancy. He did not seem satisfied that Dorfman had left the party alone. She assured him that she had walked to the end of the Winthrop driveway with him.

He turned to Dick and asked him if he could identify the little silver-framed picture which, to all appearances, like the cigarette case and the lighter, had been jarred out of Dorfman's pocket in the fall.

"Yes, I can," Dick said heavily. "It's trick pornography and it belongs to Tom Winthrop."

"Are you saying the deceased stole it, Mr. Adams?"

"I'm not, but I think it's possible."

"Is it valuable? Was it valuable?" the police officer corrected himself.

"Yes."

"And did you notice it when you discovered the body?"

"Yes, sir, I noticed it."

"It looks like somebody ground a heel into it, doesn't it?"

"I only noticed that it was smashed," Dick said.

"A woman's heel, I'd say, but we can't be sure until we get some measurements and pictures." He turned back to Nancy. "I'd like to have the shoes you're wearing, Mrs. Adams, if you don't mind."

"Mine?" Nancy said.

"Well, ma'am, we've got to start somewhere."

Who Killed Father Christmas?

by BTJNPWJTBBDBTQBUSJDJBNPZFT

Here is a Christmas story for you. Every genre has one,
and they're either sentimental or topical wherever you find
one. I must say I prefer them topical, or perhaps I ought
rather to say I detest them sentimental. This one is not
sentimental. After all it takes place in the toy department
of a large store, and where can Christmas possibly be
less sentimental than there? Oh, and if you wonder who
Father Christmas is, we call him "Santa Claus" here in the
Colonies.

Good morning, Mr. Borrowdale. Nippy out, isn't it? You're
in early, I see." Little Miss MacArthur spoke with her usual
brisk brightness, which failed to conceal both envy and dislike.
She was unpacking a consignment of stout teddy bears in the
stockroom behind the toy department at Barnum and Thrums,
the London store. "Smart as ever, Mr. Borrowdale," she added,
jealously.

I laid down my curly-brimmed bowler hat and cane and took
off my British warm overcoat. I don't mind admitting that I do
take pains to dress as well as I can, and for some reason it
seems to infuriate the Miss MacArthurs of the world.

She prattled on. "Nice looking, these teddies, don't you

125

think? Very reasonable, too. Made in Hong Kong, that'll be why. I think I'll take one for my sister's youngest."

The toy department at Barnum's has little to recommend it to anyone over the age of twelve, and normally it is tranquil and little populated. However, at Christmastime it briefly becomes the bustling heart of the great shop, and also provides useful vacation jobs for chaps like me who wish to earn some money during the weeks before the university term begins in January. Gone, I fear, are the days when undergraduates were the gilded youth of England. We all have to work our passages these days, and sometimes it means selling toys.

One advantage of the job is that employees — even Temporaries like me — are allowed to buy goods at a considerable discount, which helps with the Christmas gift problem. As a matter of fact, I had already decided to buy a teddy bear for one of my nephews, and I mentioned as much.

"Well, you'd better take it right away," remarked Miss MacArthur, "because I heard Mr. Harrington say he was taking two, and I think Disaster has her eye on one." Disaster was the unfortunate but inevitable nickname of Miss Aster, who had been with the store for thirty-one years but still made mistakes with her stock book. I felt sorry for the old girl. I had overheard a conversation between Mr. Harrington, the department manager, and Mr. Andrews, the deputy store manager, and so I knew — but Disaster didn't — that she would be getting the sack as soon as the Christmas rush was over.

Meanwhile, Miss MacArthur was arranging the bears on a shelf. They sat there in grinning rows, brown and woolly, with boot-button eyes and red ribbons round their necks.

It was then that Father Christmas came in. He'd been in the cloakroom changing into his costume — white beard, red nose, and all. His name was Bert Denman. He was a cherry soul who got on well with the kids, and he'd had the Father Christmas job at Barnum's each of the three years I'd been selling there. Now, he was carrying his sack, which he filled every morning from the cheap items in the stockroom. A visit to Father

Christmas cost 50 pence, so naturally the gift that was fished out of the sack couldn't be worth more than 20 pence. However, to my surprise, he went straight over to the row of teddy bears and picked one off the shelf: For some reason, he chose the only one with a blue instead of a red ribbon.

Miss MacArthur was on to him in an instant. "What d'you think you're doing, Mr. Denman? Those teddies aren't in your line at all — much too dear. One pound ninety, they are."

Father Christmas did not answer, and suddenly I realized that it was not Bert Denman under the red robe. "Wait a minute," I said. "Who are you? You're not our Father Christmas."

He turned to face me, the teddy bear in his hand. "That's all right," he said. "Charlie Burrows is my name. I live in the same lodging house with Bert Denman. He was taken poorly last night, and I'm standing in for him."

"*Well,*" said Miss MacArthur. "How very odd. Does Mr. Harrington know?"

"Of course he does," said Father Christmas.

As if on cue, Mr. Harrington himself came hurrying into the stockroom. He always hurried everywhere, preceded by his small black moustache. He said, "Ah, there you are, Burrows. Fill up your sack, and I'll explain the job to you. Denman told you about the teddy bear, did he?"

"Yes, Mr. Harrington."

"Father Christmas can't give away an expensive bear like that, Mr. Harrington," Miss MacArthur objected.

"Now, now, Miss MacArthur, it's all arranged," said Harrington, fussily. "A customer came in yesterday and made a special request that Father Christmas should give his small daughter a teddy bear this morning. I knew this consignment was due on the shelves, so I promised him one. It's been paid for. The important thing, Burrows, is to remember the child's name. It's . . . er . . . I have it written down somewhere . . "

"Annabel Whitworth," said Father Christmas. "Four years old, fair hair, will be brought in by her mother."

"I see that Denman briefed you well," said Mr. Harrington,

with an icy smile. "Well, now, I'll collect two bears for myself — one for my son and one for my neighbor's boy — and then I'll show you the booth."

Miss Aster arrived just then, and she and Miss MacArthur finished uncrating the bears and took one out to put on display next to a female doll that, among other endearing traits, actually wet its diaper. Mr. Harrington led our surrogate Father Christmas to his small canvas booth, and the rest of us busied and braced ourselves for the moment when the great glass doors opened and the floodtide was let in. The toy department of a big store on December 23 is no place for weaklings.

It is curious that even such an apparently random stream of humanity as Christmas shoppers displays a pattern of behavior. The earliest arrivals in the toy department are office workers on their way to their jobs. The actual toddlers, bent on an interview with Father Christmas, do not appear until their mothers have had time to wash up breakfast, have a bit of a go around the house, and catch the bus from Kensington or the tube from Uxbridge. On that particular morning, it was just twenty-eight minutes past ten when I saw Disaster, who was sitting in a decorated cash desk labeled "The Elfin Grove," take 50 pence off the first parent to usher her child into Santa's booth. For about two minutes, the mother waited, chatting quietly with Disaster. Then, a loudly wailing infant emerged from the booth.

The mother snatched her up, and — with that sixth sense that mothers everywhere seem to develop — interpreted the incoherent screams. "She says that Father Christmas won't talk to her. She says he's asleep."

It was clearly an emergency, even if a minor one, and Disaster was already showing signs of panic. I excused myself from my customer — a middle-aged gentleman who was playing with an electric train set — and went over to see what I could do. By then, the mother was indignant.

"Fifty pence and the old man sound asleep and drunk as like as not, and at half-past ten in the morning. Disgraceful, I call it.

And here's poor little Poppy what had been looking forward to —"

I rushed into Father Christmas's booth. The man who called himself Charlie Burrows was slumped forward in his chair, looking for all the world as if he were asleep; but when I shook him, his head lolled horribly, and it was obvious that he was more than sleeping. The red robe concealed the blood until it made my hand sticky. Father Christmas had been stabbed in the back, and he was certainly dead.

I acted as fast as I could. First of all, I told Disaster to put up the CLOSED sign outside Santa's booth. Then I smoothed down Poppy's mother by leading her to a counter where I told her she could select any toy up to one pound and have it free. Under pretext of keeping records, I got her name and address. Finally, I cornered Mr. Harrington in his office and told him the news.

I thought he was going to faint. "Dead? Murdered? Are you sure, Mr. Borrowdale?"

"Quite sure, I'm afraid. You'd better telephone the police, Mr. Harrington."

"The police! In Barnum's! What a terrible thing! I'll telephone the deputy store manager first and *then* the police."

As a matter of fact, the police were surprisingly quick and discreet. A plainclothes detective superintendent and his sergeant, a photographer, and the police doctor arrived, not in a posse, but as individuals, unnoticed among the crowd. They assembled in the booth, where the deputy manager — Mr. Andrews — Mr. Harrington, and I were waiting for them.

The superintendent introduced himself — his name was Armitage — and inspected the body with an expression of cold fury on his face that I couldn't quite understand, although the reason became clear later. He said very little. After some tedious formalities, Armitage indicated that the body might be removed.

"What's the least conspicuous way to do it?" he asked.

"You can take him out through the back of the booth," I

said. "The canvas overlaps right behind Santa's chair. The door to the staff quarters and the stockroom is just opposite, and from there you can take the service lift to the goods entrance in the mews."

The doctor and the photographer between them carried off their grim burden on a collapsible stretcher, and Superintendent Armitage began asking questions about the arrangements in the Father Christmas booth. I did the explaining, since Mr. Harrington seemed to be verging on hysteria.

Customers paid their 50 pence to Disaster in the Elfin Grove, and then the child — usually alone — was propelled through the door of the booth and into the presence of Father Christmas, who sat in his canvas-backed director's chair on a small dais facing the entrance, with his sack of toys beside him. The child climbed onto his knee, whispered its Christmas wishes, and was rewarded with a few friendly words and a small gift from Santa's sack. What was not obvious to the clientele was the back entrance to the booth, which enabled Father Christmas to slip in and out unobserved. He usually had his coffee break at about 11:15, unless there was a very heavy rush of business. Disaster would pick a moment when custom seemed slow, put up the CLOSED notice, and inform Bert that he could take a few minutes off. When he returned, he pressed a button by his chair that rang a buzzer in the cashier's booth. Down would come the notice, and Santa was in business again.

Before Superintendent Armitage could comment on my remarks, Mr. Harrington broke into a sort of despairing wail. "It must have been one of the customers!" he cried.

"I don't think so, sir," said Armitage. "This is an inside job. He was stabbed in the back with a long, thin blade of some sort. The murderer must have opened the back flap and stabbed him clean through the canvas back of his chair. That must have been someone who knew the exact arrangements. The murderer then used the back way to enter the booth —"

"I don't see how you can say that!" Harrington's voice was

rising dangerously. "If the man was stabbed from outside, what makes you think anybody came into the booth?"

"I'll explain that in a minute, sir."

Ignoring Armitage, Harrington went on. "In any case, he wasn't our regular Father Christmas! None of us had ever seen him before! Why on earth would anybody kill a man that nobody knew?"

Armitage and the deputy manager exchanged glances. Then Armitage said, "*I* knew him, sir. Very well. Charlie Burrows was one of our finest plainclothes narcotics officers."

Mr. Harrington had gone green. "You mean — he was a policeman?"

"Exactly, sir. I'd better explain. A little time ago we got a tip-off from an informer that an important consignment of high-grade heroin was to be smuggled in from Hong Kong in a consignment of Christmas toys. Teddy bears, in fact. The drug was to be in the Barnum and Thrums carton, hidden inside a particular teddy bear, which would be distinguished by having a blue ribbon around its neck instead of a red one."

"Surely," I said, "you couldn't get what you call an important consignment inside one teddy bear — even a big one."

Armitage sighed. "Shows you aren't familiar with the drug scene, sir," he said. "Why, half a pound of pure, high-grade heroin is worth a fortune on the streets."

With a show of bluster, Harrington said, "If you knew this, Superintendent, why didn't you simply intercept the consignment and confiscate the drug? Look at the trouble that's been —"

Armitage interrupted him. "If you'd just hear me out, sir. What I've told you was the sum total of our information. We didn't know who in Barnum's was going to pick up the heroin, or how or where it was to be disposed of. We're more interested in getting the people — the pushers — than confiscating the cargo. So I had a word with Mr. Andrews here, and he kindly agreed to let Charlie take on the Father Christmas job.

And Charlie set a little trap. Unfortunately, he paid for it with his life." Armitage glared at us all, and there was an awkward silence.

He went on. "Mr. Andrews told us that the consignment had arrived and was to be unpacked today. We know that staff get first pick, as it were, at new stock, and we were naturally interested to see who would select the bear with the blue ribbon. It was Charlie's own idea to concoct a story about a special present for a little girl —"

"You mean, that wasn't true?" Harrington was outraged. "But I spoke to the customer myself!"

"Yes, sir. That's to say, you spoke to another of our people, who was posing as the little girl's father."

"You're very thorough," said Harrington, with a sniff.

"Yes, sir. Thank you, sir. Well, as I was saying, Charlie made a point of selecting the bear with the blue ribbon and taking it off in his sack. He knew that whoever was picking up the drop would have to come and get it — or try to. You see, if we'd just allowed one of the staff to select it, that person could simply have said that it was pure coincidence — blue was such a pretty color. Difficult to prove criminal knowledge. You understand?" Nobody said anything. With quite a sense of dramatic effect, Armitage reached down into Santa's sack and pulled out a teddy bear. It had a blue ribbon round its neck.

In a voice tense with strain, Mr. Andrews said, "So the murderer didn't get away with the heroin. I thought you said —"

Superintendent Armitage produced a knife from his pocket. "We'll see," he said. "With your permission, sir, I'm going to cut this bear open."

"Of course."

The knife ripped through the nobbly brown fabric, and a lot of stuffing fell out. Nothing else. Armitage made a good job of it. By the time he had finished, the bear was in shreds: and nothing had emerged from its interior except kapok.

Armitage surveyed the wreckage with a sort of bleak satisfaction. Suddenly brisk, he said, "Now. Which staff members took bears from the stockroom this morning?"

"I did," I said at once.

"Anybody else?"

There was a silence. I said, "I believe you took two, didn't you, Mr. Harrington?"

"I . . . em . . . yes, now you mention it . . ."

"Miss MacArthur took one," I said. "It was she who unpacked the carton. And she said that Dis — I mean Miss Aster — was going to take one."

"I see." Armitage was making notes. "I presume you each signed for your purchases, and that the bears are now with your things in the staff cloakroom." Without waiting for an answer, he turned to me. "How many of these people saw Burrows select the bear with the blue ribbon?"

"All of us," I said. "Isn't that so, Mr. Harrington?"

Harrington just nodded. He looked sick.

"Well, then," said Armitage, "I shall have to inspect all the bears that you people removed from the stockroom."

There was an element of black humor in the parade of the teddies, with their inane grins and knowing, beady eyes: but as one after the other was dismembered, nothing more sensational was revealed than a growing pile of kapok. The next step was to check the stockbook numbers — and sure enough, one bear was missing.

It was actually Armitage's Sergeant who found it. It had been ripped open and shoved behind a pile of boxes in the stockroom in a hasty attempt at concealment. There was no ribbon round its neck, and it was constructed very differently from the others. The kapok merely served as a thin layer of stuffing between the fabric skin and a spherical womb of pink plastic in the toy's center. This plastic had been cut open and was empty. It was abundantly clear what it must have contained.

"Well," said the Superintendent, "it's obvious what happened. The murderer stabbed Burrows, slipped into the booth and substituted an innocent teddy bear for the loaded one, at the same time changing the neck ribbon. But he — or she — didn't dare try walking out of the store with the bear, not after a murder. So, before Charlie's body was found, the murderer dismembered the bear, took out the heroin and hid it." He sighed again. "I'm afraid this means a body search. I'll call the Yard for a police matron for the ladies."

It was all highly undignified and tedious, and poor old Disaster nearly had a seizure, despite the fact that the police matron seemed a thoroughly nice and kind woman. When it was all over, however, and our persons and clothing had been practically turned inside out, still nothing had been found. The four of us were required to wait in the staff rest room while exhaustive searches were made for both the heroin and the weapon. Disaster was in tears, Miss MacArthur was loudly indignant and threatened to sue the police for false arrest, and Mr. Harrington developed what he called a nervous stomach, on account — he said — of the way the toy department was being left understaffed and unsupervised on one of the busiest days of the year.

At long last, Superintendent Armitage came in. He said, "Nothing. Abso-bloody-lutely nothing. Well, I can't keep you people here indefinitely. I suggest you all go out and get yourselves some lunch." He sounded very tired and cross and almost human.

With considerable relief, we prepared to leave the staffroom. Only Mr. Harrington announced that he felt too ill to eat anything, and that he would remain in the department. The Misses MacArthur and Aster left together. I put on my coat and took the escalator down to the ground floor, among the burdened, chattering crowd of Christmas shoppers.

I was out in the brisk air of the street when I heard Armitage's voice behind me.

"Just one moment, if you please, Mr. Borrowdale."

I turned. "Yes, Superintendent. Can I help you?"

"You're up at the university, aren't you, sir? Just taken a temporary job at Barnum's for the vacation?"

"That's right."

"Do quite a bit of fencing, don't you?"

He had my cane out of my hand before I knew what was happening. The sergeant, an extraordinarily tough and unattractive character, showed surprising dexterity and speed in getting an arm-grip on me. Armitage had unscrewed the top of the cane, and was whistling in a quiet, appreciative manner. "Very nice. Very nice little sword stick. Something like a stiletto. I don't suppose Charlie felt a thing."

"Now, look here," I said. "You can't make insinuations like that. Just because I'm known as a bit of a dandy, and carry a sword stick, that's no reason —"

"A dandy, eh?" said Armitage, thoughtfully. He looked me up and down in a curious manner, as if he thought something was missing.

It was at that moment that Miss MacArthur suddenly appeared round the corner of the building.

"Oh, Mr. Borrowdale, look what I found! Lying down in the mews by the goods entrance! It must have fallen out of the staffroom window! Lucky I've got sharp eyes — it was behind a rubbish bin, I might easily have missed it!" And she handed me my curly-brimmed bowler hat.

That is to say, she would have done if Armitage hadn't intercepted it. It didn't take him more than five seconds to find the packages of white powder hidden between the hard shell of the hat and the oiled-silk lining.

Armitage said, "So you were going to peddle this stuff to young men and women at the university, were you? Charming, I must say. Now you can come back to the Yard and tell us all about your employers — if you want a chance at saving your own neck, that is."

Miss MacArthur was goggling at me. "Oh, Mr. Borrowdale!" she squeaked. "Have I gone and done something wrong?"

I never did like Miss MacArthur.

Widow

by M B V S B O D F B M J D F M B K P F M I F O T M F Z

I wonder how many extremely beautiful girls read mysteries? If any of them do, would they not grow timorous? It is my experience that in mysteries overwhelming feminine perfection and tragedy go hand-in-hand. I wonder what the score is, in that respect, in real life. Will any indescribably gorgeous girl in the audience write and let us know? Or come and tell one of us personally? (Don't bother with Alice.)

She'd called and been sweet right after she filed for divorce. I could come any time that day and pick up my clothes. We could "talk," she said. I parked down the road out of sight and peeped under an improperly drawn shade. I could see her sitting in the shadowed front room of our tiny house. Her attitude was one of patient waiting. She was holding something I couldn't quite identify in her right hand. I rubbed the telephone wire in two.

◆　　◆　　◆

I'm cautious. I've always been. Perhaps it comes out of my Scots ancestry, perhaps it's from seeing my parents burn in the accident where I was thrown clear. After that I lived with my grandparents, who'd as soon waste money as words. There was no one to run to. I was too small for competitive sports. I had some late growth and am of average height and weight now, but I suppose those early years made me more of a thinker and a planner than a doer. It seemed natural to me to want to be a lawyer. Caution has aided, not impeded, my practice.

I met Janice Willingham during my second year in a Bington law firm. I was the "associate" in the office. This meant mostly that when something piddling came up one of the two partners would come to my door and beckon imperiously. I did collections, unimportant damage suits, divorces, and minor criminal stuff. It was a start.

One partner said little to me and smiled condescendingly when I ventured an opinion. To the other, the world was a plural woman. All persons were "she." If Bill Jones came into the office while I was out this partner would dutifully inform me "she'd" been in. Perhaps a result of femlib, perhaps something else. I wondered sometimes how that second partner had lived fifty-odd years without acquiring contusions enough to break the habit. The smiler was named Connell, the gender-confuser was Guyman. My name is Sam Hubbard.

On the day Janice Willingham first came into the office both partners were out, so I got her.

She was something. I think a few like her are born each generation just to make men and women alike recognize true physical perfection. She was a trim blonde, with eyes so deep and green you could fall in them and drown. Her figure made all the figures I'd seen before seem to be totaled wrong. She was wearing a simple little dress. Later, I found out the dress had cost almost three hundred dollars.

Her voice, when it came, was untutored, but soft and feminine. She waited until the awed secretary had gone out.

"I wanted to see you about a divorce," she said.

"Sit down. Sit down." Her voice brought me back to being a lawyer. I opened my third drawer left. There, typed in bold-face and taped to the bottom of the drawer, I kept a list of my state's requirements for obtaining a divorce. I thought I could

now get by without the list, but this was a time of stress and I
didn't trust myself completely.

"What's your name and when and where were you married?"
I asked, to get her started.

Her story was old and trite. She'd married a man named
True Willingham. I instantly recognized the name. The Will-
inghams owned the canning factory and controlled Bington's
largest bank. I'd heard some about True. He was an indolent
member of an industrious family. He'd never worked, factory
or bank. He was much older than Janice, in his far fifties. She
claimed he'd become increasingly jealous. Every glance at another person, every word she uttered was weighed and tested
upon the scales of his colorful imagination.

She showed me bruises on her neck and arms from the night
before. She complained he'd struck her on other occasions.
When she'd threatened him with police he'd laughed at her. I
was properly sympathetic and indignant.

"He told me last night maybe he'd kill me and then commit
suicide," she said. A little tear came in the corner of her eye.
"And he might. He's been drinking heavily. He hasn't been
sober for days. I'm afraid of him."

True Willingham and family didn't worry me much. Our
firm represented neither bank nor factory. I sent her to a photographer to have pictures taken of the bruises. Sometimes
they come in handy in court.

I filed a divorce action for her.

All simple and routine. Except it wasn't. Not for her, and not
for me, for different reasons.

All the time she was in my office I had this tremendous
awareness of her. I thought she recognized it and perhaps used
it. She needed me then.

◆   ◆   ◆

*On that day, after severing the telephone wire, I drove to the sheriff's
office. Things must move. It was going on dusk. I wanted it dark.*

"How about going out with me?" I asked Sheriff Bert Horn. "It'll be

a quiet divorce. She told me to come pick up my clothes. You can be there to see there's no problem."

"Wait a minute," he said. "I'll call little Jannie and tell her we're on our way." He smiled, and I had a sudden bitter taste in my mouth.

He called, but of course there was no answer.

"Phone's probably out again," I said. "Let's take my car."

◆　◆　◆

Two days after I first saw Janice, True Willingham was dead. His death caused a small furor before and after the grand jury finished its work. Poison deaths always do that.

I got the call from the sheriff's office at about three in the morning. I went right on down.

They had Janice in Sheriff Horn's kitchen. Horn was with her. A matron was pouring coffee. Janice sat in one of the straight chairs.

"You represent Mrs. Willingham?" handsome Sheriff Horn asked in the same voice that had helped him win election. I smiled at him. We were acquainted.

"Correct," I said cautiously.

Horn watched me. I could see he was testing the situation out. He said, "There's been some trouble. Did you file a divorce for Mrs. Willingham a few days ago?"

"I did. What kind of trouble?"

He held up a peremptory hand. "Let me ask the questions."

I smiled and shook my head. "Not with me, Sheriff Horn. Until I know what's going on you've gotten your last answer from me or my client if I'm still advising her."

A touch of color came into his face. "All right," he said testily. "True Willingham's dead. Mrs. Willingham tells us he called her to talk reconciliation. She visited his house. She admits they argued. She then says he knocked her around. She does have some bruises. Then he made her drink from a bottle of whiskey laced with strychnine, or thought he made her drink. He then *apparently* drank enough of it himself to kill three people."

I nodded. "They'd been having problems. I'll vouch for that. He threatened suicide."

I watched Janice. She sat carefully in Sheriff Horn's chair. Her voice was low: "He gave up on beating me. I was back in a corner where he'd trapped me, just sort of sitting there. He kept cursing me, calling me unspeakable names, saying I'd be sorry. He had the whiskey bottle, and I knew he had something in it. He poured some in a glass for me and forced me to put it in my mouth, but I spit it out when I could, when he looked away. He drank a lot of it himself and then he fell down and rolled around. After a while he quit moving."

I went to her and held her and, after a while, as if she thought she ought to do it, she put her head on my shoulder and cried.

There were a few new bruises on her neck and arms. I thought I'd seen most of her bruises before, but I didn't say anything. When she'd quit crying I left her with the matron and went into the outer office and talked for a time with Bert Horn about it. He called the circuit judge and talked with him in low tones.

"I'm going to let her go for now," he said to me. He grinned familiarly at me before we went back to the kitchen to announce it. "To convict that lady of a crime she'd have to shoot a police officer or kill a kid, and the law would need the best evidence in the world and half women on the jury."

I never forgot the words.

We were married early the next spring and for a while it was fine. I bought us a handsome little cottage in the country a few miles from town. She wanted then to be away from people. There was some acreage with the cottage and I taught her how to fish and together we learned how to shoot. She became a dead shot.

Although the grand jury had refused to indict her the town still talked. There was money and that didn't aid in stopping the malicious stories. True's will left it to her in trust with his bank as trustee. She couldn't abide that arrangement and so she nagged me into court and I got an order naming myself as trustee. The money wasn't a fortune, but it was enough to keep her comfortable for a long time, carefully used. True had been a member of a family with money, a great deal of it, but most of it was tied up in other trusts where True's interest terminated at death. Janice didn't like that either.

"He left me almost nothing," she said to me shortly before our marriage. She looked at me with those really great eyes. "Oh Sam, what would happen if I lost you?"

I was sentimentalist enough then not to tell her the correct answer. She'd find another man.

I said, "Maybe I could buy some more insurance."

She sniffed. "I've read about insurance."

I smiled. "Remember me? I'm the lawyer. In this state for you to not be paid off on insurance at my death you'd have to be convicted of my murder. True had no insurance. If he had, you'd have gotten it, assuming the policy named you as beneficiary."

She looked a little more enthusiastic.

For a wedding present I gave her a hundred-thousand-dollar term policy and spent a couple of hours with her going over the fine print. I had to dig sometimes to make the payments.

And so we were wed.

◆　◆　◆

It wasn't a long time until she was unfaithful to me, only months from the date of our marriage.

Perhaps it would have worked for us if I'd had plenty of money, but I didn't have money. Young lawyers make a pittance. I was bright enough, but lawyers make money from time spent building a practice, from experience. I was coming along well enough in the office. Small victories had made the smiler begin to ask my opinion and the gender-confuser to nod approvingly. Once the latter even put his arm around my shoulder and announced to the smiler: "She's a good boy." The year we were married they put my name on the stationery and raised my pay.

The trouble was you couldn't buy very many three-hundred-dollar dresses on my salary. She'd come from a marriage with an adoring older man who could pay the bills to a youngster who couldn't. She ran through the trust income at high speed, always behind. She was a wild woman every time she got into a dress shop. I finally called a halt to that when she was spent six months ahead. I made her take something back. It was a cocktail dress, and it had cost more than two hundred dollars. I told her adamantly she'd have to return it and earned a look that contained only hate.

It was a bad marriage for me in many ways. She wasn't very intelligent. She had a kind of inquiring look of brightness that could pass for brains and fool her admirers, but the veneer was thin. She could make a mistake, be corrected, and then make the same mistake again. Other than with clothes she had the attention span of a six-year-old. She was intensely vain. I was something she used. In her mirror there was only a single reflection. She could waste a full day trying on clothes, standing in front of a mirror in rapt, silent contemplation. She was scrupulously neat with her person and her clothes. Other than that living with her was constant cleanup. She left a wake behind her, used glasses and dishes, crumpled, bright cigarettes.

I never stopped wanting her. She was so physically overpowering that I couldn't do that. It was only that I became more fully aware of her. It was like owning a beautiful expensive car. Only after you admired the sleek exterior did you notice that the motor wouldn't start.

As I said, I'm a cautious thinker. I'd pushed hard in school and achieved honors. I'd come to my small town of Bington for many reasons, not the least being an examination of longevity tables.

Marrying Janice was one of the few uncalculated things I'd done in my life. Sometimes I thought a part of me was standing away and shaking a finger at me even as we repeated our marriage vows.

When I was sure she was unfaithful I feigned a cold and moved into the second bedroom and waited and watched. The cerebral me was back in control.

I didn't have to wait long. The very next night she had the bottle out, a pretty party dress on, and wore a smile for me when I came home from the office.

"Cocktails and sin," she said.

I inspected her carefully. On her right arm there was a large, fresh bruise. "You've hurt yourself."

"Fell against a tree while I was outside target shooting." She held out her glass. "I'll fix you one."

"Better not," I said. "Cold's pretty bad and I'm taking pills you're not supposed to mix with liquor."

She looked forlorn and disappointed.

I tried not to look afraid.

I went on back to the second bedroom. I thought about killing her and knew I'd never manage it. I thought about her killing me and thought she probably would manage it. I thought also about the deceased True Willingham and the large insurance policy I'd bought his widow. Would she have the guts to try the same method she'd probably used on True? I remembered her making the same mistakes over and over.

I easily started an argument, then left the house.

Perhaps I could have stopped her desire to kill me by canceling the insurance policy, but I didn't do that.

The new man in her life was Sheriff Horn. I saw his car parked at the house several times.

◆ ◆ ◆

It was full dark when we got to the house. No moon. I parked my car boldly in front. Then I led Horn up the path, staying out of the line of sight from the windows. On the porch I tapped on the door and then stepped quickly away from it.

"It's only me, Janice," I called, before Horn could say anything.

He was smiling when she began firing through the door. That *had* been a gun she was holding when I'd peeped through the windows.

I ran down the porch, vaulted the rail, and looked back. Horn was slumped against the door. He was making noises, but no words came. I wasn't sure how badly he was hit. He slid on down, and she put three more shots through the door. After the first one he didn't seem to notice.

I got back into my car and started it and waited. When nothing happened I put the car in gear and blew the horn. The door opened and she stood there looking down at Sheriff Horn. I noticed she was wearing a brand new dress — was it black?

I drove back to town, staying within all the speed laws. Both as a citizen and as an officer of the court it was now my duty to report a shooting.

Almost Perfect

by JTBBDBTJNPWJTBBDSBMBGGFSUZ

There is a whole subclass of genre that deals with the perfect murder with (alas) a flaw, but I think this is the most ingenious I've seen, both in the nature of the perfection and in the nature of the flaw. (Of course, considering the number of unsolved murders in every police file, I should think that the perfect murder in real life is very common — but reality is for the baseborn. Murder fiction is *art*.)

George Grimoire grinned at Donald Dalton, yet there was something a little crooked about it. When a man grins at another as he kills him it would be odd if there were not something a little crooked about the grin.

"This will be perfect, Donald. We talked once about a perfect killing; you said that there could be no such thing. It amuses me to prove you wrong.

"It is known that you are alone with me. And many people high and low will come to look at you dead here in my place, and to talk to me of your death; and we will say how tragic it all is. Yet never will I be suspected of your murder. Do you not find that ironic, Donald? You were always one to appreciate a good joke."

Then he killed him.

◆　◆　◆

Donald Dalton had always been the richest man in town. He had been heir to much of the town's property from the day of his birth, and he inherited fully when he reached his majority. He wasn't a bad man; overbearing, it's true, and vain to the point of offense; mule-headed and smug. Yet he was a cheerful man with a clattering laugh. It was just that he had the strange facility of souring those about him.

He had four sons: three and a half really — Harold wasn't much of a son. Then there were Eugene, Carl J., and Donny, counting down by ages. Harold outraged what moral sense Donald had, and he did have a little. Eugene was a good man, and yet good for nothing; which is to say that he wasn't too competent. He was the only one who tended to business, and yet he wasn't good at it. Carl J. was a dude. And Donny was a wanderer.

"I have four boys," Donald said once, "a leecher, a nincompoop, a peacock, and a rolling stone. Yet it's mostly my fault. I am a little bit of all four myself. I haven't had the opportunity to leech or roll as much as I'd have liked. I conquered an early tendency toward stupidity, though it was quite a struggle. And I am somewhat proud of my appearance — why shouldn't I be?"

For Donald Dalton had some talent toward self-criticism, but he didn't overdo it. Really the only one in the family worth a second look was Betty Jo, the daughter of Eugene and granddaughter of Donald Dalton. We always did like that girl.

◆　◆　◆

Among the buildings that Dalton owned was a large frame structure on the corner of Main and Missouri streets. This housed a furniture store, an appliance store, a plumbing and electric shop, a shoe shop, an undertaking establishment, and a termite-exterminator business. The peculiarity of these firms was that they all interconnected; and they had but one proprietor, George Grimoire. For it was a small town and none of those businesses could of itself support a man. Sometimes, particularly in the summer, George had a boy to help him. More often not.

George would sell you a sofa, new or used, bottom a chair, fix a radio or a faucet, half-sole your shoes, bury your grand-mother, or exterminate your pests. He was a busy man, but he remained a poor one. All he made went for rent to Donald Dalton; for cigars, whiskey, chops, and ribs, a new suit on the even-numbered years; and interest (again to Donald Dalton) on a loan that was a consolidation of several earlier loans. He lost a dollar a week shooting pool, a dollar a week playing dominoes, and anywhere from one-eighty-five to two-fifty a week playing poker. He ate well, dressed well, and enjoyed his cronies. Being a careful man with no vices he was able to make out. A less careful man would not have been able to make it in that town.

It is true that he did not pay his bills to the plumbing sup-pliers or the furniture wholesalers; but nearly every year there are salesmen through there for new firms, and it is fair game to clip them all once.

◆   ◆   ◆

Doctor Land, Donald Dalton, and George Grimoire sat one night and talked over the whiskey. It was not Dalton's whiskey. He had learned one thing: that a rich man can remain rich only by doing his talking over a poor man's whiskey.

"The doctor gives me a month to live, George," said Donald Dalton.

"The doctor has it not to give," said George Grimoire hol-lowly. He had developed his hollow voice; it was his under-taker's voice. He had also his salesman's voice, his tradesman's voice, his cobbler's voice, his termite-exterminator's voice, and his upholsterer's voice like old velvet. But privately he himself liked his somberly echoing undertaker's voice best, and this he used with his cronies over the whiskey.

"No, I don't have it to give, George," said Doctor Land, "but I am a canny man with an estimate. I will bet a quart of the present that I do not miss by three days the time till you have Donald stretched on this very table." For it was the laying-out table on which they drank.

"Done," said George Grimoire. It sounded like the croak of a sepulchral frog when he said it.

"I wish that there were some way I could enter the bet," said Donald Dalton. "I hate to be excluded from my own death bet. If the doctor wins I will have little chance of sharing it. But if he loses by too much and I outlive the month by three days, I will be here to drink half of it, Grimoire, though it is the last I ever go or drink. And if he loses by too little, and I do not even last the month less three days, I ask you to broach the bottle here in my dead presence, Grimoire. Who knows but I may raise up a hand for that last drink? I believe that a man dies last in his drinking hand and esophagus."

"You may be right," said Doctor Land. "Have you made a will?"

"Four of them. Four undated holographic wills, each one giving all to one of the sons. As you see I play no favorites. And they are in the possession of the only honest member of the family, my granddaughter Betty Jo, so none of them will be prematurely destroyed. There will be hell to pay when they try to settle things." And he gave his clattering laugh so that both of the other men winced.

"I had hoped that you would do a little for me," said Doctor Land. "I have attended you faithfully for many years."

"Yet I've suffered years of pain for my youthful follies, and you have not been able to alleviate them. Nor can you now give me even an extra day of life. Were one to start lavishing bounty on doctors, the whole roots of the world would be upturned."

"I also have hoped," said George Grimoire, "though it is true that I hope without hope, that you might help me. I have paid a burdensome rent to you for many years. A hundred dollars a month for a row of stores is quite steep. Should I not take my bond and quickly write fifty? Who knows, we may gain you a little merit along the way by the act."

"If I am an unjust steward (and I am) I at least have the virtue of consistency. The rents will not be abated one jot. And it pleases me to prove one proverb wrong. I have squeezed quite a bit of blood out of turnips in my day. And George, old turnip, you must still bleed for my quarreling sons after I am gone."

Then he gave that clattering laugh again. When it hit you the wrong way it was really quite an offensive sound.

◆　◆　◆

Well, as it happened, George Grimoire the undertaker won the bet from Doctor Land. Donald Dalton died in twenty-seven days, and it was a thirty-one day month. So that was that.

Grimoire collected the quart of whiskey from Doctor Land, and the body of Donald Dalton from his heirs. He placed both on the laying-out table with a sheet over the one and an old hat over the other. He had other things to do.

He had that day to re-wicker an old chair. He was one of the last of the really good wicker men. He had to go and put in an outlet in the kitchen of Mrs. Thorndyke whose son had sent her an electric coffee pot. He had a radio to fix before a twilight program, and shoes to cobble. He had a rat-killing job and a lock-smithing job. He had a picture to frame and a small chest to refinish, both of which he had promised to have ready the first thing in the morning. So it was quite late at night when he returned to Dalton and the whiskey.

He stripped the corpse, and he uncorked the bottle. He made one small incision, and had one small shot. Then he began to assemble all the tools of his trade.

A long time ago he had learned the undertaker's trade (as well as the saddler's trade which he now seldom used) from an old Switzer. Now he remembered oddly as he took his second shot a caution that his old master had given him.

"If you follow the trade, once in your life it will happen to you. When it happens, if you have enough years in and are rich enough, the wisest thing is to give it up. And if you aren't rich enough, the wisest thing is to put it out of your mind completely and not to live with it. Of course, there are those it doesn't bother."

It was a chilly old thirty-one day month, and the town that was hardly a town faded away at night; and the old building stood up and trembled in a storm-tossed wilderness.

"It's not worth a hundred dollars a month, big as it is," said Grimoire. "It's a badly made and noisy building. And as sure as my name is George Grimoire there is one noise here that I don't like. But how can I be sure unless I look? And if I look, the few remaining hairs that I have are likely to raise out of my head. I can't chance a look till I've had another shot, and the blasted whiskey is with him."

He reached behind him and got the bottle. He had a drink and it calmed him a little.

" 'If you follow the trade, once in your life it will happen to you,' he told me. Well, so it is happening. What then?"

For he knew that the dead man on the table had stirred.

"After all, I am an undertaker. No man should fear the simple hazards of his own trade. I say, Donald, don't overdo it!"

He faced around to the quasi-dead man. Yes, he had writhed and moved.

But that was nothing to what happened now. There can be nothing more unnerving than to watch a dead man sit up; and this Dalton did, though with some difficulty. It was chilling.

"We all but traded places there, Donald," said George Grimoire, "and at the moment I am not sure which of us is the deadest. I will acknowledge that I have never been so frightened in my life. Yet there is no way you can hurt me, and there is every way I can hurt you."

Dalton was breathing with a sort of trembling wheeze. His eyes were opened, though dull; and in that moment it might still have been possible to save his life. He even reached out a stark shaking hand, though blindly.

"Do you know something, Dalton, Doctor Land really won the bet. For it's after midnight and you're still alive. But he's a poor doctor to have certified a live man dead. I feel myself under no compulsion of returning the whiskey to him. I shall not tell him about it, and I doubt if you will. Now I remember that you said a man's drinking hand and esophagus die last. You said also that you might raise up a dead hand for a last drink. Here, I will give it to you and see if you can take it."

But it was Grimoire who was quite incapable of lifting or passing the bottle. There was something the matter with his own hand. He was trembling in pitiful fashion. He talked aimlessly to the once-dead man to work up his courage. But he was as frightened as a man can be.

"I have always believed that you mistreated me, Dalton. I have, in fact, always been afraid of you, as are the poor of those with money. But I will have you for all that. I can let you die. Possibly I can save you. Or I can kill you. And for the full irony of it I have to kill you. I hope you can hear me."

Dalton may have heard him. He moaned, and his eyes (though still dull) had now some sort of recognition in them.

"This will be a perfect murder, Donald. Who could ever suspect an undertaker of killing a man already dead? I will bleed you to death and eviscerate you. And what is wrong with that? Is that not the way you should end up? Do not all leave my table so? I will pump fluid into you, but not too much. For I'll tell you a secret now: I have always been a penny-pinching undertaker.

"There is absolutely no way on earth that your murder could be suspected, traced, or proved. I will have performed the impossible, the perfect murder. Ah, now I see that you begin to understand me. You even plead a little with your eyes. I would be disappointed if you did not. And you are quite horrified, are you not, old bat? The esophagus is not quite dead — but do you call that little croak a scream? Surely you can make more noise than that? No? Well, so much the better."

Grimoire said other things to Dalton then as he recovered his own courage. And, after he had bantered him a while, he opened his veins and killed him.

He worked rapidly over the dead man then, for it was late at night, and he was tired and anxious to get it over with. He was a little disturbed by the look of horror on the finally dead Dalton's face. From inside the mouth he cut into the cheek tendons and made them relax. And he loosened the taut throat with several small incisions.

"What have I forgotten? Nothing. What is there to forget? Not even a medical detective could find anything wrong, outside of my usual sloppy work. He could in no way discern murder here."

But Grimoire was wrong on that. A good medical detective *would* have been able to discern murder; if only he had examined the right man.

Well, they buried Dalton in the morning. There was no question about anything except one odd one that Betty Jo asked.

"Mr. Grimoire, he was so serene appearing after he had just died. Now he looks frightened. How? Why?"

"Miss Dalton, the dead never really look serene. They have put on the mask."

"Yes, he was serene then. He is not now."

She gazed at the card on the wall: "In the sight of the unwise they seemed to die, but they are in peace." George Grimoire had many pious quotations on the wall.

"His face has changed, Mr. Grimoire. How could it have changed?" insisted Betty Jo.

"I am sure you are wrong."

"I am not wrong. How could it have happened?"

"Well, there are such things as spasms post mortem that can affect the appearance. And then there is a general stiffness of face as well as body that sets in and seems to give a harsher expression."

"Spasms? You mean after he was dead? You mean he came back to life?"

"Good God, no! It is purely a mechanical reaction induced

mostly by gas. With death the body becomes a broken machine; but sometimes it creaks a little as it settles."

"I see."

But it may be that she did not see completely. Or it may be that she saw too much.

"Is it possible that it was not perfect after all?" asked Grimoire of himself. "Could I myself be giving it away?"

But anyhow he was relieved when Donald Dalton was covered up for good.

Grimoire did not work that day. Instead he locked up his enterprises and went to bed to rest. And late in the afternoon when he rose and washed and shaved, he discovered a thing about himself: One hand had lost its cunning (he had suspected this the night before), and his face appeared in the mirror to be asymmetrical. One side was drawn and dull.

"I am not a doctor, though I may be as good as Doctor Land. This is easily read. I suffered a slight stroke in the excitement of last night and it has left its mark on me. I will never be quite the same."

He felt bad. He thought of calling Dalton to come and have a drink with him, as he often did when he was low. Then he remembered that Dalton would not be coming anymore.

"The stroke may also have touched my brain a little. I am addled."

Grimoire did not work that day. Instead he locked up his enterprises and went to bed to rest. And late in the afternoon

It was three days later that Eugene Dalton came to see him: Eugene who was a good man, and yet good for nothing. But he soon revealed that he had been misjudged: He was not a good man at all.

"I will come to the point at once, Mr. Grimoire. I am a blunt man."

"No, you are only a dull man, Eugene. There is a difference."

"My father left me everything in a clear will."

"Why tell me?"

"But there are complications."

"Yes, your father left three other wills, one for each son. He was a remarkably impartial man."

"He must have been a remarkably forgetful man, though I hadn't thought so."

"No, he was not forgetful. It was quite intentional."

"But why?"

"A legacy of chaos. Perhaps he did not want you quickly to forget his unique personality, so he left a bit of it with you."

"Well, I am the most deserving son. I should have it, and I mean to get it by fair ways or cloudy. On this matter I approached Dr. Land with a reasonable bargain. He rejected it. I was amazed to find that he is an honest man. With you I trust that I will not be so amazed."

"What is the bargain?"

"My father always treated you badly and overcharged you for years on the rent."

"Never mind the palaver. What is the bargain?"

"I believe that in simple justice the building should go to you."

"What is the bargain?"

"If I inherit, I will immediately deed it to you."

"What is the bargain?"

"That you help me inherit."

"How?"

"Dr. Land refused a simple suggestion and so lost a part of the inheritance by his stubbornness. His loss can be your gain."

"Avarice and doubt have started a little war in me, son. Pull the cork out of the proposition and let it bubble. We are alone."

"Dr. Land was alone with my father when he died, and had been so on and off for several hours. What more easy than a simple sworn statement by the doctor that my father in one of his last rational moments had wished to clarify the confusion of a multiplicity of wills, and name that which was to be authentic?"

"What more easy? And the doctor refused a simple thing like that for a consideration? I would not have refused had I had his opportunity."

"You have it. We will change the roles. We will make you the man who was with my father when he really died. And to you he made the avowal."

"I am an old man, Eugene, and I cannot smell a trap as I once did. And I have always wondered one thing about you: Are you a little smarter or a little stupider than you appear?"

"A little smarter, Mr. Grimoire, a little smarter. There is such a thing as a man being certified as dead who is in a trance and not dead. It would be possible for him to come briefly conscious in the presence of the undertaker and to talk rationally."

"In half a century in the trade I haven't met such a case."

"Then meet it now. It would be much easier for you to own this building than to pay rent on it."

"Is that a stick you have in your hand behind you?"

"Both my hands are on the table here. Is your eyesight failing? Oh, I see what you mean. Have I a threat that I am holding back? Perhaps."

"Or did I just now hand you the stick for you to grab, and to figure out later what it is?"

"It may be so."

"Is Betty Jo in on this?"

"Naturally not. My daughter would not touch such a thing. She is too honest. I don't know where she gets it. She had all four wills in her possession and could have destroyed three of them to my advantage, and did not. A perfidious offspring if ever there was one."

"I will need a little time to think about this."

"Too much time is what creates indecision. You have eight hours. The clan gathers at four this afternoon at the old house.

It will be a formal show with lawyer, clerk, and notary present. You be there."

"Yes, in any case I will be there."

◆ ◆ ◆

After Eugene Dalton had left, George Grimoire sat in his chair for a long while. Then he arose to cross the room.

And in the middle of that, curiously, he lay on the floor for a long while. He knew then that he had suffered another stroke. But he knew also that this one was not yet the killer.

He arose after an hour or so and walked. But one foot dragged slightly, and he understood that it would do so till the end. He thought about the false testimony that he should give to own the building, testimony that would be in one circumstance dangerously true. Then he went to have a talk with Doctor Land.

◆ ◆ ◆

The formalities that afternoon were very formal, and George Grimoire was a tired man. He even slept through part, but he slept with one ear cocked. Eugene Dalton was setting the stage with a few little speeches, setting it so that Grimoire would either have to give the testimony, or stutter painfully backward out of it. Eugene was counting on the tiredness and confusion of the recently grown-old man.

And there was a certain resentment and contempt in the whole bunch of them. They knew that something raw was being pulled, but they could not guess it yet.

"Mr. Grimoire," said Mr. Banks, "please do us the favor of remaining awake. Mr. Eugene Dalton has made some rather amazing introductory remarks on testimony you are to give. You should be listening."

"No need. I know what he is saying."

Mr. Banks was a lawyer. Not *the* lawyer. There were several present.

"I think we should go directly into your testimony then, Mr. Grimoire."

"Beginning where?"

"Beginning with the answer to the question: Did Donald Dalton come alive on your embalming table?"

"Oh yes."

"But that is impossible," said Betty Jo.

"Why, you yourself were the only one who noticed the evidence, girl."

"What?"

"That his expression had changed. That he had been serene before, and was not so after."

"But you explained that. You said that there were sometimes mechanical spasms."

"In this case a spasm in which he sat up and opened his eyes and was conscious."

"I do not believe you," said Lawyer Banks. "I believe rather that Eugene Dalton came to you with a dishonest proposition."

"That's true. He did come to me with a dishonest proposition. And yet unknowingly he put the saw in the kerf. Part of what he wished me to swear to as happening did happen."

"This really does occur outside of macabre stories?"

"The man from whom I learned the trade (as also the saddler's trade) told me that it would happen once in my lifetime. And it has happened once to me as it happened once to him."

"And did Dalton speak? Did he speak of the wills?"

"He spoke not a word. I believe that he wished to speak. I believe that if not prevented he would have spoken. But I prevented him."

"Why? How?"

"I had suddenly the vision of the perfect murder, one absolutely not to be suspected and not to be traced, a work of art. Who would ever get wind of an undertaker killing a man already dead? How could it possibly be proved? How possibly? Was this not perfection? That which had never been achieved before? No clue, no whisper, no inkling. How could there conceivably be a weak link in that chain? Yet there was a weak link that I overlooked.

"Well, briefly, I opened his veins and killed him. And then I prepared him according to the details of the trade. But he did not speak."

The good people among them recoiled with real horror, and the evil of them with simulated horror; and there was a harsh and angry grumbling. Only Lawyer Banks, who was neither one nor the other, did not recoil at all. But he was quite interested.

"But what was the weak link?" he asked. "I confess I can't see it. It looks to me as though it were foolproof, almost sublime in its perfection. It was a perfect murder if I ever heard of one. What was the weak link?"

"It was myself. Some men are just not cut out to be murderers."

"And why do you tell us this," asked Carl J. angrily, "since you seem to have been in the clear and no suspicion attached to you?"

"It is just that Doctor Land gives me a month to live," said Grimoire.

"Want to bet?" asked Carl J. in a fury.

"The doctor would bet," said Grimoire. "The doctor will always bet. He will bet that he does not miss it by three days."

But the doctor would have lost. For they hanged George Grimoire after twenty-seven days, and it was another thirty-one day month.

The Legend of Dirty Dick

by B M J D F M B V S B O D F B M S P C F S U C M P D I

It does the heart good sometimes to get away from today's
emphasis on moral degradation and the corrosion of all
decent values and to return to the basics that made our
country great. Here we have a paean to the virtues of hard
work, devotion to one's line of expertise, orderly proce-
dure, the love of family, and the careful recycling of
wastes. If you find yourself smiling as you read this story it
will be with pleasure at the contemplation of the good old
ways.

Cesspool was a lovely place.

We never did lay claim to being the biggest town in the terri-
tory. Time I speak of we didn't have horsecars or telephones or
any of them newfangled electric streetlights. Matter of fact we
didn't even have a regular sewer system, which is how the town
come by its name.

But what we *did* have was the best, the finest, the absolutely
jim-dandiest little whorehouse this side of Kansas City.

Don't take my word for it. Just ask anybody who was around
in those days. Ask your father.

Miss Fanny's, that was the name of the place. Genuine two-
story red brick mansion, almost as nice as the undertaking par-

159

lor. Very convenient location, too — across from the railroad freight yard and right next door to the livery stable. Didn't pay to keep the windows open, specially during hot weather; but everybody knows location is important when it comes to doing business.

And Miss Fanny's place did business. Any time of night there'd be horses lined up at the hitching post out front and some had brands from spreads fifty–sixty miles away. Heap of city folks were customers, too, but they mostly come by train so's not to be conspicuous.

However they got there it was worth the trip. Everything about Miss Fanny's place was tiptop. Two cast-iron dogs on the front lawn just for the artistic touch, red velvet curtains over the downstairs windows for a homey look. Front door had a brass knocker shaped like a heart with a arrow stuck clean through it, for sentiment.

First thing you'd notice when you come in was a hand-blown glass spittoon, must of been two foot high, set right inside the front door. Thing looked so elegant you'd almost be afraid to park your butt in it.

Talk about elegance — that front parlor had the works. Turkey-red carpet, horsehair sofas, genuine artist paintings showing females in a state of Nature. Don't mistake my meaning — weren't nothing you'd call suggestible — their hands was always covering the right places. All they did was help give sort of a refined air to the proceedings.

Right spang in the corner was this baby grand piano with hand-carved legs, painted pink all over. And for extra tone it had a bird cage set on top with a real live canary inside. Used to sing along with the music, though it weren't much for carrying a tune.

Piano player was a little feller name of LeRoy. Hear tell he could play anything, even classical waltz pieces for dancing, but mostly he stuck to ballads. You'd still find a passle of Southrons amongst the customers in those days, but none of them ever tangled with LeRoy. He wasn't one of your uppity niggers and he knew his place. Some say he only played on the black keys, but that could be stretching it a mite.

He was the only non-female in the outfit, because Miss Fanny didn't have a fancy-man, and there was no bartender in the house. Miss Fanny didn't hold with the Demon Rum. "You want to drink, go to a saloon," she said. "You want to eat, go to a restaurant. This establishment offers its own brand of refreshment, and you can't enjoy it with a glass in one hand and a ham sandwich in the other."

Not that anybody was likely to hanker after food or drink once they laid eyes on Miss Fanny's girls.

There was six of them, and every one a real lollapalooza.

Now you take some of your big city riding academies — folks brag on having maybe fifteen–twenty fillies to choose from. But a real judge of horseflesh can see that most of them are spavined, foundered, and past their prime. Not to speak of having saddle-sores, or worse.

But Miss Fanny's stable was always clean, spirited, and hot to trot. Scarcely looked like more than two-year-olds, though they'd been on the turf for years. Purtiest little herd of thoroughbreds you'd ever hope to see. And whichever you picked, once you mounted up and settled into the saddle, you'd savvy why Miss Fanny drew nothing but high-toned easy riders to her corral.

All but Dirty Dick, that is.

He was a drummer out of Omaha, traveling in corsets and ladies' unmentionables, and he hit town two or three times a year to do business with Levy's Emporium. Used to come in on the morning train, spend the afternoon with old Jake Levy, then stash his sample case at the Ideal Hotel and head for the bar. Along about nine o'clock he'd blow into Miss Fanny's place, skunk-drunk and rarin' to go.

Big fat dude, always wore spats and a checkered weskit with a gold watch chain looped over his belly to show the elk's-tooth. Baldheaded galoot with a reddish-complected face and a grin so oily you'd figure he'd hit a gusher every time he used a toothpick. Real handle was Richard Rinderpest, but everybody called him Dirty Dick. Not to his face, understand, because he was a right mean customer when he was in his cups, which was always. Behind his back, though, that was his monicker.

Now I already spoke of how genteel and refined Miss Fanny's place looked, and this weren't just for show. Miss Fanny was what you call a madam of the old school. She was a little-bitty woman with gray hair tucked in a rat, but she dressed real classy in a stylish purple evening gown with ostrich-feather sleeves, and topped it off with a big diamond choker around her neck. When she took the cigar out of her mouth and smiled, she reminded you of your own mother.

Every time Miss Fanny spotted a new customer she sashayed right up and laid down the law. "Howdy, stranger," she'd say. "Set right down and make yourself at home. For starters, just fork over your shooting iron. Might as well park that bowie knife too. Don't want nobody carrying one upstairs and whittling on my nice mahogany bedsteads.

"While we're at it, pardner, here's a few pointers. Cuspidors are for spitting and carpets are for walking, so don't get them confused. And when you're introduced to my young ladies I want you to mind your manners. Remember, my girls aren't magicians, so don't ask for any parlor tricks. Kindly do not handle the merchandise before you buy, and don't unwrap it until you get upstairs. And do aim to keep a civil tongue in your head at all times. Maybe I'm old-fashioned, but I don't like to listen to a lot of goddamned profanity."

Everybody heeded her palaver because they could tell Miss Fanny spoke sincerely. Besides which she had a voice like a buzzsaw, and wore no rings on her fingers — just a big fat pair of brass knuckles. So everybody toed the mark.

Everybody except Dirty Dick.

That's how he come by his nickname. Dirty talk just purely slopped out of his mouth, along with a whiskey breath that would give a horse the blind staggers at thirty paces. He weren't much for washing, either, and when he went upstairs the girls broke the rules and let him keep his boots on because his socks was so noticeable, even with the windows open.

There was other rules he tried to break too, according to hearsay.

Pearl, the carrot-topped girl, complained he had a careless habit of removing her kimono without bothering to unbutton it. Being a seamstress before she took up the life, she usually managed to stitch it up again, but she didn't rightly relish the inconvenience.

Ida, who was a little on the plump side, didn't hold with the way Dirty Dick used his teeth on her. "It's bad enough if he's got them in his mouth," she said. "But when he holds them in his hand, they pinch something awful."

Bessie was on the skinny side, raised up with a homesteader family, and she'd been kind of sheltered. Used to shock her every time Dirty Dick reached into his trousers and pulled out this big long hard leathery thing he called his secret treasure — which was a wallet full of indecent pictures. Some of them was so ripe she couldn't bear to look at them, so she'd hide her head under the covers whilst he sat there and drooled all over her bolster.

Fifi, the little French girl who come here all the way from Paris, France — or Paris, Illinois, some folks said — she got her dander up because Dirty Dick asked her to commit unnatural acts, like ninety-nine or twenty-three skiddoo.

Then there was Bertha, the tall brunette whose hobby was leatherwork; she made fancy mottoes for the bedroom walls, such as IN GOD WE TRUST — ALL OTHERS PAY CASH. According to her, Dirty Dick forgot to park his wad of chewing tobacco before he went upstairs. Bertha said if his shooting was as bad as his spitting aim, she understood why he didn't carry a gun. Claimed he was the only man alive who could miss a thunder-mug at two paces.

And Cora, the only genuine peroxide blonde in the outfit,

had the worst complaint of all. She caught Dirty Dick walking into her bedroom stifflegged; seems like he smuggled something inside his pants leg, which turned out to be a riding crop. Wanted to beat on her with it, too; said it was all the rage in St. Louis this season.

You might reckon Miss Fanny wouldn't hold still for all this hanky-panky, and she didn't.

Very first time Dirty Dick got out of line, she went straight to Sheriff Plunkett and lodged a complaint.

Now Jasper C. Plunkett was an honest man — for a sheriff, that is — but he just heard her out and pulled a long face. "Happens that Dirty Dick is a relative of mine," he said. "Shirt-tail cousin by marriage, twice removed."

"Then remove him a third time," Miss Fanny said. "From my premises."

"Can't," he told her. "I got to protect the honor of the family."

Miss Fanny fiddled and she fretted, but in the end she threw in the sponge. Many's the time she hankered to give Dirty Dick a knuckle sandwich and toss him out on his canasta, but always she thought the better of it. She knew how Sheriff Plunkett felt, and he was right — family is family, after all. Besides, he was a good customer.

So Dirty Dick kept on with his shenanigans, and Miss Fanny let him get away with it.

Until he laid the honor of her family on the line.

One cold morning in November a guest showed up in Miss Fanny's parlor. Not a customer type guest but a real one, maybe all of seventeen years old, pretty as a straight flush over a full house, and fresh out of finishing school up in Wichita.

Her name was Sarah Jane and she was Miss Fanny's favorite niece, come for a visit over the holiday.

Miss Fanny fussed over her, ever so pleased and proud, and she introduced Sarah Jane to the whole shebang. They took to her right off, because Sarah Jane wasn't one of your stuck-up female critters who looked down her nose at a working girl.

She got real sociable with Ida and she asked Bessie questions about life on the farm. She buttered up Pearl on her sewing and admired Bertha's leatherwork, carried on over Cora's natural-looking peroxide hair, and asked Fifi to learn her how to talk French.

By the time supper rolled around Sarah Jane was like family to everybody, just as cute and pert and lovable as a housebroken kittycat.

After supper when things got humming, Sarah Jane kept out of the way, sort of curling up in a corner of the parlor whilst the girls took care of company. For a while they had quite a play. Thoughtful customers tend to come in early on nights before a holiday, so's to get back home to their families and loved ones.

Around about nine o'clock business was really booming; everyone pitched in upstairs, including Miss Fanny herself. That was one of the things the girls admired about her — when push came to shove she was always ready to lend a hand, in a manner of speaking.

So there was no one left in the parlor except LeRoy and Sarah Jane when Dirty Dick moseyed in.

He come straight from the saloon without stopping at the hotel, because he had his sample case with him and he was cussing a blue streak about Jake Levy being out of town.

But he stopped cussing in a hurry when he took a gander at Sarah Jane.

It was a powerful bad combination — she being such an eyeful and him having such a snoot full — and you can guess what happened.

Sarah Jane tried to explain as how she wasn't gainfully employed on the premises, but Dirty Dick paid her no heed. He kept jawing and he kept pawing, and when LeRoy said to stop, he got a wallop that knocked him off the piano stool and clean into the corner.

That's where Miss Fanny found him when she come back downstairs. By the time she brought him around, the other girls had all finished up and were saying their good nights to the customers at the front door.

Everybody was kind of rattled to see LeRoy lying there, but Miss Fanny explained he'd come over with a dizzy spell from whirling around too fast on the piano stool. She shooed the customers out in a jiffy, locking the door behind them. Then she waved her smelling salts under LeRoy's nose, sat him up, and asked what happened.

"Dirty Dick," said LeRoy.

Miss Fanny looked around. "Where's Sarah Jane?" she asked.

"I dunno," said LeRoy. "He was acting so randy-like, I figure he must of dragged her upstairs."

Miss Fanny almost had herself a conniption fit right then and there, but Ida passed the smelling salts under her nose, too, and she bounced back with a whoop.

Then she tore up those stairs two at a time, with her brass knuckles waving in the breeze.

The girls weren't far behind, but when they caught up with her it was all over.

Sarah Jane was on the bed in the spare room where Miss Fanny found her, bawling like a baby with her drawers at half-mast. Dirty Dick lay sprawled out on the floor, crowned with a thundermug cracked into a hundred pieces.

"I'm sorry I busted it," Sarah Jane kept sobbing. "But it was him or me. If you knew what he was trying to bust —"

"Think nothing of it," said Miss Fanny. "He's just knocked out, is all. Ida, you take Sarah Jane to my room and tuck her into bed. Give her some of that Lydia Pinkham Syrup to calm her nerves and put her to sleep. Pearl, you go downstairs and tell LeRoy to close up. He can sleep under the piano like always, if he wants. The rest of you girls stay here and help me clear away this mess."

After Ida and Sarah Jane and Pearl had left, Miss Fanny squinted down at Dirty Dick. The look on her face was so fierce that the girls just stood there with their jaws hanging open; they'd never seen her like this before.

"Don't you aim we ought to bring him to?" Bertha asked.

Miss Fanny shook her head.

"But he's unconscious," Cora said.

Miss Fanny shook her head again. "Take another squint. He's dead."

Bessie let out a gasp. "Oh no — he can't be!"

"But he is," Miss Fanny told her. "Deader'n a doornail."

"Merde," said Fifi.

Miss Fanny looked mortified. "Don't use that word! Weren't nothing merderous about it — Sarah Jane was acting in self-defense. Just didn't know her own strength, is all."

"We better fetch Sheriff Plunkett," Bertha said.

Miss Fanny gave her a look and she shut up. "We'll do nothing of the sort! I don't calculate to get mixed up in no jury trial and shut down business so's you girls can testify as witnesses. And I plumb refuse to drag poor innocent Sarah Jane into such a to-do. Specially since we all know Dirty Dick is the guilty party and brought it on himself. Far as I'm concerned, justice has been done. Bad enough letting him violate the house rules, but when it comes to violating my own niece —"

"But we can't just leave a stiff lying around like this," Cora said.

"Tote him downstairs," Miss Fanny told her. "I need to think on it a spell."

When Ida and Pearl came back, Miss Fanny was still pondering, but she knocked off to answer questions.

"Where's the thundermug?" Ida asked.

"Swept up all the pieces and put them in the trashbin," Miss Fanny said.

"Didn't Dirty Dick have a sample case with him?" Pearl wanted to know.

"Chucked it into the furnace," Miss Fanny told her. "That takes care of the evidence."

"All but Dirty Dick," said Bertha. "Couldn't we chuck him into the furnace too?"

Miss Fanny gave a shrug. "Furnace won't burn bones. I been

puzzling on that, but it looks like we're stuck with him."

"That's a downright shame," said Cora. "Seeing as how everything else here is in apple-pie order."

"Which reminds me." Miss Fanny looked at the clock. "Here it is, nigh onto midnight. If we want to be ready for tomorrow we got our work cut out for us."

Bessie fetched a frown. "Don't tell me you're still going through with it, after what's happened?"

Miss Fanny gave her a nod. "All the more reason we got to. It's a tradition. And if we call everything off at the last minute they're bound to smell something wrong."

"They'll smell something wrong anyway," said Pearl, "if you leave Dirty Dick lying around on the premises."

All of a sudden Miss Fanny perked up. "Maybe so and maybe not. I have me an idea. But I'll need your help."

"You can count on us," Ida told her. "Right, girls?"

"Then let's go to work," said Miss Fanny.

And they did.

While LeRoy snored under the piano and Sarah Jane slept peaceful in her bed, Miss Fanny and the girls got busy. No telling exactly what they did but it's an easy bet that everybody's know-how come in handy. Bertha's leatherwork made her good at peeling hides, Bessie used to be right sharp with a cleaver on the farm, Pearl's stitching helped for trussing things up, and Fifi knew all about them fancy French herbs and spices.

The other girls made themselves useful too, and by noon they'd all finished up and changed into their best outfits.

When LeRoy and Sarah Jane woke up, they came into the kitchen to say good morning. Miss Fanny and the girls was all smiles.

"Where's Dirty Dick?" LeRoy asked.

"Long gone," Miss Fanny told him. "Don't you trouble your mind about him."

Sarah Jane looked relieved. "Notice you got the dining room

table set for fifteen," she said. "How come so many, when there's only the nine of us?"

"Tradition," said Miss Fanny. "Some of my best customers are bachelors. They got no families to share the holidays with, so I always invite them here for Thanksgiving dinner. Why, there's the doorbell now — would you please go answer it and welcome our guests?"

So Sarah Jane did the honors. She was so sweet and unspoiled that everybody remarked on it, and Sheriff Plunkett himself took her arm and escorted her to the table.

Seeing as how there was such a crowd, Miss Fanny asked permission to do the carving and serve out portions in the kitchen, which she did. By the time Ida passed the plates around and Sarah Jane said grace, everybody was ready to dig in. It was a scrumptious feed with all the trimmings, and whilst the girls and Miss Fanny just sort of pecked at their meal — watching their figures, they said — everyone else came back for seconds and even thirds.

After dinner was over Miss Fanny and the girls relaxed and brightened up considerable. And when Sheriff Plunkett let out a belch they knew everything was a success.

"Bang-up job," he said. "Best cooking I ever et. And in the best company, too."

Miss Fanny started to beam.

Sheriff Plunkett took a pocketknife out of his vest and picked his teeth genteel-like. "Funny thing, though. I hear tell my cousin was in town yesterday. How come you didn't invite him for dinner?"

Miss Fanny stopped beaming.

As for the girls, they looked downright petrified. For a minute nobody said a solitary word.

It was little Miss Sarah Jane who spoke up at last. "If you're referring to Dirty Dick," she said, "I imagine he left town on the midnight train. And after the way he insulted me last night, I doubt if he'll be coming back."

Sheriff Plunkett gave her a big smile. "Insulted you, did he? In that case, good riddance. Far as I'm concerned, I hope I never see that turkey again."

Miss Fanny let out a sigh and then she grinned. "You said a mouthful," said Miss Fanny.

Revelation

by BTJNPWJTBBDSPTFNBSZHBUFOCZ

It's a wise father who knows his own son, they say, which
on the one hand, is an insult to wives, and a reminder that
it is also a wise son who knows his own father. On the
other hand, the saying is a celebration of one great advantage women have. The child who comes out of her womb is
hers. She is certain even though all the candidates for fa-
therhood may be uncertain of his identity.

There was almost a Dickensian flavor to the news when it
broke; certainly the discovery of a nineteen-year-old son — not
simply long lost but actually undreamed of because unheard of,
ever, by the man who was legitimately his father — seemed a
happening more appropriate to the nineteenth century than to
the twentieth, with its shrunken distances, ubiquitous com-
munications, and records kept in triplicate.

The lightning bolt struck with a blinding illumina-
tion — worthy, the Reverend Theodore Kessler felt afterward,
of an apocalypse — late on a May afternoon as Theo's best
friend, John Slawson, was congratulating him on his appointment (temporary at that moment) as president of Mount Hope
College.

They sat in the paneled, leather-chaired study of the sumptuous house John had built when he married for the second time; the host drinking bourbon, and his guest allowing himself a dry sherry.

"No reason, Theo, that they won't make the appointment permanent. You'd be a superlative choice to head the college, and they know it."

Theo Kessler's long, thin face lit up in a smile that showed his buck teeth. "Thanks, John. Actually I'm afraid I covet the job."

His association with the denominational college at the town's edge went back a long way. Though he had his own church here in Plunket, he had been spiritual leader of the college as well, ever since he had come to Ohio. He also sat on the board of trustees, and at President Smith's sudden death the board had turned to him as a handy replacement.

Surely Mount Hope was where he belonged . . . in an *administrative* post. Though he believed it luck, not God's will, as he once would have felt the change in his fortunes to be. It was not that he had lost his faith; rather, he had lost the sense of his calling. It had disintegrated, leaving him stranded in the ministry, feeling like a charlatan in spite of his theological degree.

The phone rang, and John crossed to the fine old desk in the alcove, to answer. "Oh, yes, Hal . . . What obituary?"

Hal Colton, probably — editor of the *Star.* Theo wandered to the window overlooking Amy's rose garden. Rain streamed down the outer surface of the leaded panes. Who had died?

"No, I hadn't heard . . . How did Evelyn —?"

Evelyn! Evelyn Slawson was dead? Chill struck Theo to the heart. Her image, cherished all these years, filled his mind's eye — the small, delicate face with the great brown eyes; the halo of pale blond hair.

Theo turned from the window; watched John's expression shift from measured grief (Evelyn had after all been his wife) to incredulity.

". . . *Grant* Slawson? No, I know nothing about him."

But Theo was not listening now. His whole adult life flashed before him like that of a drowning man . . . The first meeting with Evelyn, soon after he'd realized the disaster his marriage was doomed to be; the friendship extended by the Slawsons — the older man and his beautiful younger wife — to the new minister; the drift of the two of them toward each other, gradual, then accelerating as he and Evelyn were drawn together into what seemed to be a single entity. Then for twenty-one years he'd stood every Sunday in the pulpit aware of the *A* like Hester's that he should be wearing sewn to his vestments; stood unrepentant in God's house, and therefore barred from grace.

She was dead? Gone? Though she'd long been gone from here.

John put down the phone. "Evelyn was killed in a car accident. Killed instantly."

"I'm sorry, John." *And who is there to offer sympathy to me . . . ?*

Surprisingly, John was smiling, an odd, one-sided smile.

"According to the obituary, she's survived by a son, named Grant."

Theo's tongue clove to the roof of his mouth.

A child. And she never told me? Never wrote? Never told — him?

He found his voice. It sounded quite normal. "She must have adopted a child. Perhaps a war orphan?" But twenty years late the logic of Evelyn's departure had assumed an altogether different form.

Within minutes John was speaking with Marybelle Grant, in Pratt City, Montana — the aunt with whom Evelyn had lived before her marriage and after it. Theo watched the look of wonder grow, on John's square-jawed, ruddy face — and turn into a wild sort of joy. When the call was over, he stood with his hand still resting on the phone.

"Grant's nineteen. Evelyn was pregnant when she left me." But the joy had faded. The blunt, undistinguished features darkened.

"I've been a father all these years and never knew it!" He

turned on Theo as though this tragedy were his friend's fault. (*Had he, after all, known about us?* flashed through Theo's mind. But he couldn't have, or they'd not still be friends.) "How could she have done that to me? Knowing I so longed to have a son! How could she have been so cruel?" The last was to himself; almost inaudible.

Cruel? Evelyn? Ah, no!

"Maybe she was afraid you'd find a way to get custody."

What Theo really thought, he didn't say: *The boy may not be your son, John — he may be mine.*

During the week and a half between his reception of the traumatic news and the arrival in town of the Slawson heir apparent, Theo Kessler's days and nights were haunted by the possibility that this son of Evelyn's would turn out to be his spitting image.

The Reverend Kessler was a man you could not easily mistake for another. His very buck teeth and the slanting Mephistophelian brows (so incongruous on the face of a minister of the gospel) set him apart, in appearance, from most other people. His daughter, Peggy, took after her mother in looks. But if Evelyn's child . . .

Though his wife was away, tending her ailing mother in Cleveland, visions of Loretta's fury, her merciless condemnation, should she ever learn of Theo's fall — nay, his leap, as he saw it — from virtue, even though it had been long ago, were all too real.

It would not be the fact that he had broken two of the Lord's Ten Commandments that would trouble Loretta; it would not even be personal anguish at his betrayal of her — the body in the marriage bed — that would set her off. What would unleash her tongue and that other weapon, the mind-shriveling coldness of demeanor she was capable of maintaining for unimaginable lengths of time, was her husband's having exposed her to potential pity and ridicule. She would be right, he felt, and he certainly had been in the wrong.

Unrepentant still (did Adam and Eve repent what they had done? The Bible didn't say so), he worried. Not only was there his wife, there was also his position as acting president of the college to consider, and his hopes of remaining in the post. Not to mention his place in the community as pastor of his church.

One breath of scandal could blight his hopes, end his career.

◆　◆　◆

His daughter's anticipatory chatter on the subject of Grant Slawson did nothing to cheer him.

"At least he'll put a little life into the local social scene; new talent, which we *need,*" Peggy said. And got her brown hair hennaed, making herself disconcertingly brazen and sophisticated in appearance for her eighteen years — or so her father felt. Theo had no control over her, as they both knew.

Before Grant descended on them for better or worse, there was the Mount Hope commencement for Theo to cope with that weekend, including the arrangements for and entertainment of their distinguished commencement speaker — a member of the President's Cabinet.

Through the rest of that hectic week, Theo felt not only bereft but older because of Evelyn's death and the irrevocable loss of a segment of his life, one that had held a rare happiness.

The thought crossed his mind that one person in town must have been aware of Grant Slawson's existence. If Hazel Cummings hadn't known from the first about the baby Evelyn had borne, she would have learned of him when she'd visited her still-dear friend in Montana — some ten years ago, hadn't it been? She'd never said a word.

She'd have said nothing to John in any case; they were not on good terms.

Commencement, that meld of endings and beginnings, was on Sunday; and Theo, taking his place in cap and gown at the front of the procession, for the first time realistically felt himself to be head of the college. An outdoor ceremony had been planned, and thank goodness it didn't rain. All went well: the carefully orchestrated marching and seating of the student and faculty groups, the televising of the Cabinet member receiving an honorary degree, the handing out of the sheepskins — which had been mislaid and were found barely in time.

Only two things, both below the surface, flawed the occasion for Theo: his continued sadness over Evelyn's death, and the apprehension associated with the thought of her son's arrival. But when the day was over and the new graduates had departed, like fledglings from the nest, he experienced a great sense of gratification.

◆　◆　◆

On Monday night Hazel Cummings was killed — though not till Tuesday morning was the tragedy discovered. Her neck had been broken in a fall from the top of the basement stairs. Such a common, everyday sort of accident. It never occurred to anyone — not the doctor, not the coroner, not the police — that Hazel had been pushed. (Because who in Plunket would do a thing like that? Well, no one — it had been done by someone from out of town.)

The Reverend Kessler conducted a nice service, and Hazel, looking like a rosy wax doll, was lowered in her casket and covered over, out at Maple Grove Cemetery. The generally accepted opinion was that she'd tripped because of her new bifocals.

◆　◆　◆

The day after the Cummings funeral Theo, toting along — invisibly, he hoped — the burden of dread that now accompanied him everywhere, came home to the manse to learn from Peggy that Grant had arrived.

"Yesterday? Ah — so he's actually here . . ." If there had

been any sort of explosion, the fallout certainly had not reached him.

"We're invited Sunday night to meet him. Amy called."

"Ah." Well, maybe the boy was a walking likeness of John, demonstrating that the things one worries about seldom come to pass.

"I accepted."

"Didn't you have a date for Sunday evening? You told me —"

"I broke it."

"Oh."

For a moment the unthinkable writhed at the bottom of his thoughts, ugly as the serpent in the garden. Peggy and her half brother?

◆   ◆   ◆

Twice, John Slawson had chosen a wife younger than he. Though John was now fifty-eight, Amy was in her thirties. Theo had always liked her; liking only — no danger of another conflagration.

She welcomed the two Kesslers at the door, the night of the party, and while Peggy made her entrance into the living room — already filling with guests — Theo lingered in the foyer to talk with Amy. A pretty woman, petite, dark-haired, blue-eyed. As they walked toward the living room to join the others, she clung to his arm — almost, he thought, as though her usual self-assurance had deserted her.

Theo at once spotted Grant, the center of attention — tall, nice-looking, emanating a kind of animal energy.

He doesn't look at all like me, he concluded as they came toward him. He searched the tanned features for any trace of Evelyn and found none. Aside from the light hair, streaked from the sun, there seemed to be no physical characteristic he'd inherited from his mother.

Amy introduced him.

"Oh, yes. Reverend Kessler!" There was a special warmth in the young man's greeting.

And special knowledge? Theo could not help wondering as he encountered the eager, speculative gaze.

"May I offer my condolences, Grant, on the death of your mother . . ."

"The Lord giveth, and the Lord taketh away. Right, Reverend?"

Was the boy mocking him? That wasn't a response he would have expected. *That was my line,* he thought — *or he believes it is.*

No, he shouldn't judge. Evelyn's child might be truly pious. A lot of young people nowadays, questioning current values, were turning to the old, time-tested answers.

Theo uttered a few platitudes about the woman he had loved; squirming as those blue eyes scrutinized him.

"Mom often spoke of you."

Often. The knowledge that she had thus thought of him warmed some inner place left untouched in the intervening years — by his wife, by anyone save perhaps Peggy when she had been small.

Could Evelyn have talked about him without a special softness, without a betraying quiver of the voice? Grant may have guessed . . .

He suddenly realized that he was staving off all consideration of Grant Slawson as another human being; as the son of his dear love; as, possibly, flesh of his flesh, sprung from his own seed. He could see the boy only as a threat.

What kind of Christian am I — he wondered — *to be capable of so completely shutting out the human values here . . . ?*

The fact was that he could make no connection between his relationship with Evelyn and this tall youth. If there were one glimmer of some trait the same as hers (or his own) — the set of his head, the shape of his eyes, a gesture. There was nothing. The boy didn't resemble John Slawson, either; he was a total stranger.

An imposter? No. It had been John's call to Evelyn's aunt in

Pratt City that had brought him here. John had spoken, himself, with the boy in a long phone conversation.

Amy left them and he stood alone with Grant. "Now that you're here, you'll be staying on, I expect?"

"Oh, yes." A glance about him. "Wouldn't you?" There was no reason he shouldn't have admired the magnificent establishment in which his father lived — when he himself had no doubt been raised quite modestly; but there was something about his appraisal of the room that jarred. It was as if already he was looking at everything as his, deciding what he would keep and what he'd get rid of.

"You drove, from Montana?"

"Started out to. Only I totaled my car on the way." He shrugged. "So I hitched."

Peggy had materialized at her father's elbow.

"Oh, hi," young Slawson said. "Peggy." Apparently they'd already been introduced.

"Right. I hear, Grant, that your dad's getting you a *Corvette?*"

"Yeah." He grinned.

Why did he dislike this young man so much? . . . As the evening progressed he tried not to worry over indications that Peggy was perhaps smitten with the new arrival. Though other girls had been invited, and Grant, he noted, seemed interested in playing the field.

He should let the past go; stop agonizing over who had fathered Evelyn's child, stop flagellating himself for sins twenty years old.

John had a son at last. Why not let things go at that . . . ?

◆ ◆ ◆

Though the academic year had ended, Theo still had much to do at the college. And most Sundays he preached a sermon at the church — since his temporary replacement had not arrived.

A week or so after the Slawsons' party, Amy came to see him at his office at the church. "I need your advice," she said.

"Certainly. If I have any to give."

She sat in the chair by his desk. "I ought to be happy for John that he has a son. But I find that I wish Grant had never come."

Theo said nothing, so she went on. "I've been sadly disappointed not to have produced a child for John. So I wonder whether I simply resent someone else's having managed to give him what I couldn't."

He shook his head. "I'm sure you could never muster such enmity for a woman who is in her grave. Nor would you take out any such negative feelings on the living. You're not like that."

"Then am I jealous of Grant? Theo, I must be a terrible person." Her hands clenched tight on one another in her lap. "Because I *hate* him!"

He remembered his own unreasoning dislike. It stirred, took shape again as though a reflection of hers. "What seems to be the trouble between you and — John's son?"

"It starts right there. He doesn't seem like John's son at all."

Theo could almost feel the ground giving way beneath him.

But suspicion as to her stepson's bloodlines was no part of Amy's worry. (That was only *his* bugaboo.) "To begin with, I feel unqualified to be the stepmother of someone almost twenty." She gave a jerky little smile. "I'm closer to his age than to my husband's. And Grant seems older than he is. That was the first thing I noticed about him. Though maybe I've just forgotten what it's like to be nineteen."

Yes, there had been something about Grant — as though he'd been around, seen a lot. Of course some kids matured early. Peggy, at eighteen, tried to appear mature, but she was far from the mark.

Amy touched her tongue to her upper lip. "You're a friend, Theo, as well as our minister — so I'll keep nothing back." Yet she hesitated.

"From the moment Grant walked through our door, it was as though there were something *physical* between us. He looks at me and it's as if he's touching me. At first I thought the fault might lie with me; maybe I was subconsciously attracted to him. He *is* good-looking, and he has this sort of — animal vitality? But after I'd studied my own reactions, I concluded that I had no yearnings for him — I disliked him! This uncomfortable physical awareness is something originating with Grant, not me." She paused. "Am I imagining all this?"

"No. You're not imagining anything. That look of his as if he's undressing a woman in his head: I saw him give the same once-over to a couple of girls at your party. It's probably the only way he knows to look at a woman. Since you *are* his step-mother, I'm sure he means nothing by it."

She smiled. "Well, that's reassuring, at least."

But she went on — sober again. "There's more. I worry for fear he's only come here for what he can get out of his father monetarily. I don't see any affection on his part. John adores him — obviously — and if he ends up disappointed in Grant's feeling toward him —"

"Yes, I know how John probably feels. But you realize it's too soon for Grant to have developed a deep love for a parent he never saw till a couple of weeks ago. That will take time."

"Time." Her expression was bleak. "Time will make things worse, not better. Whether he means to or not, Grant's driving a wedge into our marriage. Already John's disappointed in me because I have no motherly feelings. He can't understand it!

"And there's something else . . . John's making a new will." A flush spread over her cheeks and down her neck. "That's fine; Grant's his son and heir. But the way John explained it to me! Believe it or not, Theo, the subject of money has never come up in our marriage. But now — I've been made to feel . . . *mercenary.* I think John's concluded that I begrudge Grant his share. That's not so, but denying it's useless. And if my hus-band thinks all I care about is his money —"

"I've always known, Amy, that what you married John for was something other than his wealth."

A helpless little smile. "Not the kind of thing one can prove. Already our relationship has changed. It can only go downhill now . . ."

"At Grant's age, though, he'll soon be out and gone. If you can hang on till fall, he'll be back at college, won't he? Montana."

"His father wants him to transfer to Mount Hope."

Mount Hope. The news was like word of some unexpected death. *My college. My place. Why did he have to come here?*

"What can I do, Theo?"

He frowned. "You must find the strength to cope, and you must try to be charitable to someone you don't like. Sometimes by trying hard enough, one can, in the end, learn truly to love an enemy."

She nodded her dark head, and the blue eyes came up to meet his. "And if I love him enough he'll make a pass at me."

Theo realized he'd been advising her by rote.

He gave her a lopsided smile. "It won't be easy. The right hue of love. Can't you make it matronly?"

She was looking off into the distance. "If I could be sure he really cares about his father . . ." she said wistfully. "And the other thing, of course — I can't help thinking of him as a changeling.

"Though he couldn't be."

◆　◆　◆

Changeling. Theo turned over the possibility after she'd gone.

A changeling — not at birth, but on the way here? . . .

Grant Slawson had started out in his own car, and someone to whom he had given a ride . . .

Could he possibly be someone other than who he was supposed to be? Hazel Cummings would have known.

For the first time, he connected Hazel's death and Grant's arrival. The young man had gotten to Plunket — with a rucksack, Theo remembered hearing (from John?) — on the day Hazel had been buried. But could he have arrived in town earlier?

Under cover of darkness on the night she died? And pushed her down the stairs?

Certainly Hazel Cummings had been the only person in this part of the country who had ever seen Grant Slawson.

The following day Theo met Amy by chance downtown.

"I was wondering, Amy —" he said. "That remark of yours about changelings. You don't believe he *could* be someone other than —"

"Oh, no. I was only thinking of personality. He's not like John, and from what I've heard about Evelyn, he doesn't resemble her, either. But as to being the real article — oh, he's given us plenty of corroborative detail. Description of Marybelle Grant's big old house where he grew up — porches, cupolas; John's seen the house, he and Evelyn were married in it. Marybelle's going to sell it now that Evelyn's gone. She's moving to a retirement center.

"Then, let's see what else — well, he talks about his freshman year, just past, at the university, and —"

"Has he said anything about Hazel Cummings?"

"Yes, he seemed quite upset to hear she'd died. And surprised — as he said, she wasn't that old. 'Aunt' Hazel, he calls her."

"That all sounds authentic enough."

"I'm afraid so," she said, with a little moue.

Theo smiled. "Forget I asked you about him."

He left her with a feeling of relief that his speculations had been unfounded. It was much too far-fetched a notion that some hitchhiker, stumbling onto the fact that Grant's wealthy father had never seen him, could have killed the boy and taken his place.

At the bottom of his consciousness the fear still lurked, however, that Evelyn's son had somehow ferreted out the secret of her long-ago affair. Yet common sense told him no such danger existed, nor did any prospect of exposure; what was bothering him was that old saw: *There's many a slip 'twixt the cup and the lip.* He cared so deeply about the appointment to be president of the college that any possibility of his losing it loomed unrealistically large in his mind.

He must hang on to his sense of proportion.

◆   ◆   ◆

Peggy Kessler knew her father didn't like Grant; not from anything he'd said, but she'd gotten the message. So she told him nothing about the hours she'd been spending with the new and most talked-about guy in town — at the Gregorys' pool; out dancing with a bunch of her friends who'd gone to the new music place on the road to Dayton; at Sherrill's party.

Though there wasn't anything, really, to keep from her father. Grant hadn't even asked her to go out with him.

◆   ◆   ◆

Only a little over two weeks since Grant had come. Was that possible? It seemed like years.

Amy was making piecrust. Grant sat at the kitchen table, and he'd been watching her till her fingers had all become thumbs.

"You don't like me, do you," he said.

She hesitated. But she knew she was a poor liar. "Not much."

"I can see how you'd feel. Here you had him all to yourself — rich husband; older; crazy about you. Then I came along."

Not for the first time, she viewed herself through Grant's eyes: a younger woman who'd married his father for the money. Could her evaluation of Grant be as far off as his was of her?

She turned to face him. "If you really care about John, we'll get along fine. But if you've come here only for what you can get out of him, then we're very much at odds."

He leaned his chin on his hand. "You been bad-mouthing me to him?"

"No. That would hurt him. I wouldn't do that."

"Good."

He got up and crossed the floor to where she stood, in the

angle between the counters. "We'd better understand each other."

He was so close she had to bend her head back to look up at him.

"You do anything to try to foul me up with my old man — *anything* — and I'll fully disclose to him my embarrassment at the come-on you been givin' me, ever since I got here."

"That's not true!" And yet she was remembering those first few days when she had doubted herself; remembering what she'd said to Theo.

"At *his* age, past his prime . . ." he said, "Dad would find it mighty easy to believe. With you so much younger." He stepped back. Smiled. "Isn't that right?"

"No. And there's been no 'come-on.' You *know* that."

"Be hard for you to prove, wouldn't it?" He sauntered out the kitchen door toward the front of the house.

She was shaking as she went back to fashioning the lattice top for her cherry pie. She'd had doubts about Grant. Only doubts.

Now they were certainties; there was no possible happy outcome.

A wedge in her marriage, she'd said to Theo? Grant had the power to destroy it with no more than a few words. Her husband was utterly confident as a businessman, but his private ego was another matter — the damage it had suffered when Evelyn walked out on him had weakened the structure. Cracks remained. Even though Amy had never given John cause to doubt her, a few words from his son . . . his *embarrassed* son . . . Yes, that was the devilish, believable touch.

◆ ◆ ◆

Marybelle had hoped to have some word from Grant. None came.

Well, he had always been a poor letter writer. If Evelyn were alive, he'd have phoned her by now. He could call *me*, she thought. And since Marybelle herself resorted only in dire emergency to a long-distance call, she did not telephone him.

So she was delighted to receive the letter from Amy Slawson.

According to Amy, Grant's father was dotty about the boy. And why wouldn't he be! Marybelle was glad; there was little she could do for him anymore. In fact, her days were numbered, she suspected.

She went through the photograph album one last time, her small round face with its frame of crisp gray curls bent over the pages filled with pictures. Oh, the happy days they'd had together!

Then she wrapped up the album to send, as the present Mrs. Slawson requested. It was right that John should have it.

Painfully, with her arthritic fingers, Marybelle penned a short note to Grant, and mailed it off at the same time as the package.

◆   ◆   ◆

"It'll be a trust fund, Grant. Even if I drop dead tomorrow, you'll not have access to the money till you're twenty-one. The bank administers it." John enjoyed talking about money; it was a subject he felt at home with. And there was an extra dimension to his pleasure this evening because of the personal element involved: He was doing something concrete to make up for all the things he'd been unable to do for Grant during his childhood.

He sat at dinner with his wife and his son in a corner of the country club porch. *My son.* He didn't know whether the sudden prickle of tears in his eyes — which caused him to lower them momentarily to contemplation of his crabmeat cocktail — was brought on by the sight of his boy sitting, strong and handsome, in the seat beside him, or whether it was caused by the thought of what he was doing for his offspring: giving him all that money.

"In fact," he went on, "you'd not get all of it at twenty-one. Only a third. Another third when you're twenty-five, the rest at thirty."

He thought Grant looked a little uncomfortable; he was embarrassed by the talk of money? A reaction that did him credit.

"I'm not worried about money, Dad. You don't need to do all that, change your will . . ."

John smiled to himself; his son would get used, eventually, to being a wealthy man.

Yet there were things about Grant that didn't please him. His reactions, sometimes, seemed odd; his set of standards — what little John could learn of them — differed unexpectedly from his own. He supposed he could put these vagaries down to the generation gap. He guessed he was a little old to become a father — and the father, at that, of someone whose character was already fully formed, and formed without the shaping he would have given it if he'd had the chance.

He was just thankful that he had a son at all.

Two years? the young man was thinking. Two *years* before he came into any money? He'd never be able to wait it out. *I'm trapped here,* he thought — and looked across at Amy.

On Friday evening of that week Theo drove out through the campus gates, with their archway of ornamental ironwork, and turned toward town. As he looked up at the cluster of Gothic buildings on the rise above him, his heart glowed with love of this place.

The committee appointed by the board of trustees to find a new president was busy, as he knew. But the opinion that their best candidate was already sitting in the president's chair was gaining support. This information had been leaked to him today. A little time in which to see how the Reverend Kessler's administration was shaping up, and the committee felt their job might have been accomplished.

He turned his head for a final glimpse of the college as it passed from sight beyond the trees. Mount Hope. How suitably named.

The image of Evelyn's son crossed his mind. Why had he been so upset over young Slawson's arrival? There'd been nothing to fear. He'd been plagued by his own conscience, that was all . . .

Theo passed his church and turned into the drive of the big old brown-shingled manse, with its massive porch; parked and went in through the side door. No one home.

Loretta's being away was like a vacation for him: no nagging, no sour looks. But for Peggy's sake he wished she'd come home. He had little understanding of teenage girls and knew he was coping poorly with what were supposed to be his parental responsibilities.

There was a note on the refrigerator. GONE TO A PARTY AT KIM'S. HAM AND POT. SALAD IN REFRIG.

She could be anywhere, doing anything.

What would it have been like to have had a son? he wondered as he ate his solitary supper. Would the two of them have gotten on? Or would he still have felt himself, always, a stranger in his own family?

◆   ◆   ◆

The package from Pratt City came on Monday morning — just three and a half weeks after the heir apparent to the Slawson money had shown up. Since the parcel was insured, the postman brought it to the door.

"The wrapping's all tore, there," he said as Amy signed.

"Doesn't look like anything fell out. Thanks, Jacky."

As she closed the door, cutting off her view of the postman's friendly face under his uniform cap and shutting out the summer heat, she glanced at the misshapen letters of the address on the parcel and remembered suddenly that on Friday Grant had had a letter from his great aunt. Had Marybelle told him she was sending this?

What if . . .

Yes, what if Grant wasn't who he was supposed to be? . . . Wasn't that possibility (discounted but not dismissed) the real, if subconscious, reason she'd written to Marybelle Grant?

Why hadn't she stepped outside and closed the door behind

her, talking to Jacky Ogle about something or other, anything, while she ripped off the already torn brown paper and made sure —

Grant was at home. In his room, she thought.

Well, she needn't stay in suspense any longer. She'd make sure little Grant Slawson was the one who was now —

She pried up the already exposed corner of the album, further tearing the wrapping and pushing aside the string; peered between the heavy gray pages at a snapshot pasted near the edge. It was of a half-grown boy, standing with a woman she recognized, from pictures she'd seen, as Evelyn. The boy — scrawny, dark-haired — looked vaguely familiar.

She turned to a later page. And stared.

"Oh!" she said involuntarily. The same boy, but a teenager. He looked hauntingly like Theo Kessler: the same narrow head, the distinctive slanting eyebrows, the buck-toothed smile.

So many things changed shape, during the long moment in which she studied the face.

A sound, or perhaps a sense of someone's being nearby, brought her sharply aware of the present and sent a shiver of fear from head to toe.

"So it came." He stood in the doorway of the hall that led from the foyer to the study, and beyond it to the guest suite that was his.

At least we're not alone in the house, she reminded herself. Florence, her weekday help, was upstairs, vacuuming.

"You've already found out, I see." He raised his hand and she discovered that there was a gun in it.

"No screams," he said. "Cooperate and you won't get hurt. Come on, we're going to the garage."

The garage. What was he doing to do with her there? But she had no choice. Scream and he'd shoot her. Screaming wouldn't help, anyway; either Florence wouldn't hear over the noise of the sweeper, or she'd come running — and be killed.

Amy preceded him down the hall past his room, past the kitchen.

"So Grant's dead. You killed him." It was not bravado that made her say it; it was anger — and she refused, anyhow, to be totally submissive.

"I didn't kill him. He's a friend of mine."

"But he wouldn't let you do this, come here and —"

He shrugged. "Suit yourself." He grinned then, as though it could be a matter of little importance whether Grant was dead or alive. "So I killed him."

She opened the back hall door and stepped into the garage.

◆   ◆   ◆

Theo was in his office at the college when he got the phone call.

"Reverend Kessler?"

"Yes." He didn't recognize the voice.

"Well, listen, Dad, this is Grant."

Theo froze. "I hardly think —"

"Touched a nerve, did I? All I'd have to do is call you 'Dad' just once in public and you'd be finished. Isn't that right?"

"Are you *threatening* me?" The fear, the dread, the stabs of conscience that had earlier tormented him were gone. What he felt was outrage.

"So you're not bothering to deny that you're my father."

"Certainly I deny it!" Every cell in his body denied that there could be any connection between them.

His desire to hang up was exceeded only by the need to know why the call was being made — so that he could set the young man back on his heels.

"Deny what you like. You know what happened — and why she left."

"Why are you calling? If you've any sort of blackmail in mind, forget it! I wouldn't pay to keep you quiet, no matter what you —"

"Not blackmail. Something more — subtle? Yeah, that's a

good word. What I called to tell you, Dad, is that Peggy and I are going away together. Unless you don't want that . . . ?"

◆ ◆ ◆

At a little after four, Theo sat in his car at the road's weedy edge, with a suitcase full of money. John had gotten it for him.

How he'd ever pay John back, he didn't know. A hundred thousand dollars . . . He had told him everything — a revelation from which their friendship would surely never recover.

"He *could* have been mine," John Slawson had said stiffly, looking at Theo while his meaning sank in. "Why are you so sure he's —"

"If he were yours, Evelyn would have told you about him."

"Um. I believe she would've . . . But the young pup came, *knowing?*"

"Must have. The fact that you're a millionaire, or near enough —"

"I'm glad he's *not* mine!" And John arranged about the money.

Theo would have called the police — but Grant had pointed out that this was not a police matter. "She's eighteen — legal age. What law's being broken? You can hardly tell them about the incest angle, can you? But that's why you'll pay."

Indeed that was why he was paying. Fear of scandal would not have made him knuckle under — even though exposure would mean his losing the presidency of Mount Hope, losing his ministry, and would insure a hell on earth with Loretta ever after. But Peggy . . .

He could guess that incest would hold no terrors for Grant.

Theo was not convinced that it was Grant he was dealing with; this person could be an impostor — someone who had discovered there was money to be had for a part well played. A murderer.

"Why has he suddenly given up the pretense that he's *my*

son?" John had asked this morning. "When he was doing so well at it!"

"Something must have gone wrong. And he may not be my son any more than he was yours." He put forth his hypothesis of a substitution's having taken place somewhere between Pratt City and Plunket.

"My God, it's possible!" John said, and got up to pace the floor of his office, where Theo had sought him out with his news and his urgent need for cash. "Theo? If Amy somehow discovered —"

He grabbed up his phone, called home. "Not there," he relayed, and went back to questioning the maid.

"Amy went out," he explained in relief when he'd hung up. "Florence didn't see her go, but she heard the car. Then Grant left a little later — she saw him take off in the Corvette."

"Amy's all right, then — she'd gone while Grant was still at home."

"Yes, I suppose she's all right. She'd better be." John looked at him long and hard. "It's possible he's a killer, isn't it?" His eyes narrowed. "You know, he's talked about someone called Sonny who rode most of the way from Montana with him — till he wrecked his Mustang. If it *was* his Mustang, and not the other way around."

Theo waited, now, in the shade of a tree. A herd of dairy cows cropped grass in the field across the road.

"I haven't been able to locate Amy," John had said, worried, when he'd turned the money over to Theo in the bank's parking lot.

"She's probably out shopping, John," he'd said. And hoped so.

As he waited where he'd been told to wait, he wondered again whether they should have called in the police. Yet on what basis? So far as they knew, no one had been kidnaped. Amy could be lunching with a friend, or playing bridge; and if Peggy wanted to run away and live with Grant, or marry him, her parents had no recourse. Consanguinity? There was no proof that Grant Slawson was his son.

This whole thing could even be a practical joke. Except that no one played that kind of joke. Not with the stakes involved.

No, he was sitting here waiting because of one of two things: Either because incest might be committed — or because murder had been.

◆ ◆ ◆

The Corvette drew up beside him, with the two of them in it. Peggy was all right!

Suitcase in hand, he crossed the dusty roadside to the car.

His daughter was staring at him in stupefaction. "Daddy, what are you doing here?" she said from the other side of the glass.

The transaction took only moments. Grant looked through the windshield at the contents of the opened case, then had it handed through the window. "Peggy," Theo said, "do you know what this is about? You know you can't marry him?"

An odd look crossed her face, and she glanced at Grant. "He didn't ask me."

Grant ignored her. "You haven't called the police?"

"No. Peggy —" Theo tried to open her door, but it was locked.

A wolfish grin parted the young man's lips. "When I'm sure you haven't alerted the fuzz, you'll get your daughter back. Just follow me — if you can." The car took off, the tires throwing dirt and stones out behind them.

Dry-mouthed, feeling foolish, feeling panicked, Theo got into his car and followed. Keep up with a Corvette?

No time to regret that he hadn't first of all made Peggy get out of the car. Now he could only try to keep him in sight and hope Grant wouldn't miss a curve; hope he wouldn't wreck his own car. Zooming around a pickup truck, he narrowly missed an oncoming vehicle at the top of a little hill.

And he lost the Corvette. Had there been any kind of turn-off? He didn't think so; they had simply outdistanced him.

Then he saw her — Peggy, standing by the side of the road, alone.

He stopped and she got in.

◆ ◆ ◆

At one point Theo again wondered whether the whole traumatic episode had after all been a joke. Except for the money, of course, which was gone.

"But all we did," his daughter had said, "was go on a picnic!"

While he'd been suffering the tortures of the damned, she and Grant had been drinking beer and eating cold chicken someplace by the river.

"That's *all?*" But he thought there must have been some physical intimacy involved. All that time, just the two of them . . .

"I don't understand about the money," she said. "Or why he — *dumped* me." Her voice shook with anger. "I've never been treated like that in my life!"

He'd tell her later, maybe — depending on what happened now — why he had given the money to Grant.

She fished something out of her jeans pocket. "Oh, he gave me these. Amy's car keys, I guess — they're for a Thunderbird. He just said, 'Try the park.' Can you tell me what's *happening?*"

◆ ◆ ◆

They found Amy in the trunk of her car, in the parking lot of the Plunket public park, only blocks from the Slawsons' house. She was bound and gagged, and heavily sedated. But whole.

With her was Evelyn's photo album, full of pictures of her son.

Theo called the police. The man who'd been passing himself off as Grant Slawson was at the least an extortionist — and probably a murderer. *He must have killed my son,* Theo reiterated to himself — *my son and Evelyn's* . . .

Chief Merrill Yeo came over to Slawsons'; listened, and looked at the pictures. Fingerprints were taken from the guest suite.

Hazel Cummings's house would now be gone over, also, for fingerprints.

The whole story would break in the morning.

◆   ◆   ◆

Theo sat now in the living room of the manse. Peggy had been bright-eyed, voluble; when she'd at last understood what had happened she had looked at him, he guessed, in a new light — seeing in the long-ago moral transgression a new side of her father, one that made him a sympathetic character for the first time in years. She was ready to be his friend, his champion. "We'll talk in the morning," he'd said, too tired and emotionally drained to cope with his daughter.

She'd gone off to a friend's, Sherrill's. To his relief.

The phone rang, and he went into the front hall to answer.

Chief Yeo. "We've got him — and he's dead. He got rid of the Corvette — too easy to identify. The state police spotted him in a stolen car and gave chase. He skidded off the highway into a stanchion . . . They recovered the money . . ."

"Has he been identified?"

"He had a driver's license issued to Arnold Beavers, some papers belonging to Grant Slawson. But other stuff indicates his real name is Clifford Henry. If he's Henry, he's wanted in California for assaulting his stepfather with a tire iron, also for killing a liquor-store clerk in a holdup."

"Ah."

"Theo — I doubt we'll find young Slawson alive . . . All we really can look for now is his car — we have the plate number from Montana. You gave me that bunch of pictures of the boy, but I can pick the fuzziest of them to hand out to the press. If the car ever does turn up, why, *then* —" Merrill was a friend.

He was trying to save Theo from the scandal, if that was possible.

"Thanks, Merrill. Hand out a nice, clear copy. I'd like to know what happened to him." It would be a relief to assume publicly the responsibility for what he had done in the past. He was weary of pretending to an uprightness he had not possessed.

He put down the phone and looked out the window into the dark.

He couldn't get it out of his head — the vision of his son's car resting undiscovered on some river bottom, its driver dead at the wheel. Or the boy's body lying in a shallow grave in the woods.

The sense of his loss was something unimaginable.

But what would have happened if the real Grant had come here, not knowing he wasn't John's son? Would I have welcomed him? Or would I have been as inimical as I was to the interloper, because I cared more for my job and my reputation than for my own flesh and blood?

Tomorrow Loretta would have to be told. He'd call her early in the morning, before she'd have heard the news or seen a paper.

◆　◆　◆

It was past sunset when the Mustang entered Ohio, crossing the country this time East to West. The driver had been to New York City and seen it, and hadn't found any answers there, either.

He hadn't been thinking at all, Grant realized now. He'd only been reacting — and immaturely — when he had left Sonny Beavers.

Okay, so he'd given away something that wasn't his to claim; but he'd parted with more than that — his own name. Which wouldn't work out.

He had felt so sick, so miserable, when the truth had hit him right in the face; he and his mother had been close — and Sonny's way of putting things hadn't helped.

He and his hitchhiking companion had stopped at the motel only so that Grant could clean up before meeting his family the next day . . . What he'd *thought* was his family. And then there had been the local news on the TV, with the Mount Hope commencement.

"You mean that guy was your mother and father's best *friend?* You got to be blind or stupid or both not to know that's who your ma was in the sack with when her husband was out. Look in the mirror!"

No wonder John Slawson was never told about me, he thought as he watched close-ups of the Reverend Theodore Kessler chatting with some politico from Washington. And he knew he could never go to Plunket.

It had been Sonny's idea to take his place. So that the opportunity would not be lost. It seemed logical at the time. From what Sonny had told him, he'd had a rotten life — tough breaks, mean stepfather. So Grant had thought why not give him a chance to be someone? If John Slawson was so eager to have a son, well, he could have one.

But now . . . It was crazy to have done what he had. He must try to set things right — if that could be done.

He would stop in Plunket on his way back to Montana. He wanted to meet his father — his real father. Though he'd cause him no trouble. And he'd ask Theo Kessler what he should do.

Of course, Sonny's plan mightn't have come off. It would have depended on Hazel Cummings's going along with it — as he'd carefully explained. But since Aunt Hazel and John Slawson heartily disliked each other, she mightn't care one way or the other; especially since Sonny Beavers had become a friend of Grant's . . .

◆　◆　◆

A very late caller. The police, no doubt.

But when Theo opened the front door he found no one waiting on the mat. A figure detached itself from the shadows at the edge of the spirea in front of the porch and came up the steps.

The boy whose picture he'd seen in the album.

"I don't want to — to cause you trouble —" his son said.

Theo couldn't speak. Then his eyes filled with tears, and he couldn't see.

"I shouldn't have come here. I —"

"Come in, come in!" Theo took him by the shoulders. His vision cleared. They came into the house together, and he closed the door behind them. "I thought you were dead."

"If you'd rather I *were* . . ." Diffidently. "You do know who I am? Really am?"

Theo looked at him intently. This time the sense of the connection was there, as it hadn't been with the other one. Flesh of his flesh, bone of his bone. Evelyn's son as well. "I know who you are." He smiled. "There's no mistaking you."

He loved this boy. Everything else dwindled to unimportance beside that fact.

And the load of guilt he'd carried for so long dropped away.

Twenty years. Long enough for the expiation of any sin. All this time he'd simply been seeing himself as his wife would if she knew — but the Lord would have forgiven him long ago.

He examined his son in the light of the old-fashioned glass chandelier in the hall. The unexpected link with Evelyn gave him a shiver of happiness; something restored to him from the past.

"You must tell me now," Theo said, "how all this came about."

And tomorrow they'd face the consequences together.

The Accomplice

by MBVSBODFBMJDKPIOENBDEPOBME

We all have our value in one way or another. We all fit in somewhere and can be used as part of a clever scheme. Make it a game (after all this is intended as a fun-book). What makes *you* invaluable? Why should someone labor to maneuver you in some fashion to play for large stakes?

Garfield kept thinking about Mrs. Ennis whenever he had a chore to do that did not require thought. He had checked the open stock in Section D, the canned fruit juice and fruit, drawn the necessary cases from stores, checked the most recent retail sheet on brands and sizes, and was now razoring the cartons open and banging the top of each can with the purple calligraphy from the self-inking stamp 2/97¢ 2/97¢ 2/97¢ and putting the cans onto the open display. That was when he would think of how, when you saw her pushing a supermarket cart down one of the fluorescent aisles, pale hair long and thick and glossy, and wearing one of those bright beach coats of hers, and sandals, her legs bare and sturdy and a deeper golden brown each day, you could think she was one of the college kids home in Florida for summer vacation.

2/81¢ 2/81¢ 2/81¢ and he would have in his head the very vivid picture of that little trick she had of lowering her chin, tilting her head, looking up at him in a slanty amused way, and with a slow smile like a sharing of secrets when there were none to share, she would lift her head in a way that would snap the fair hair back, and, as the smile faded, give him a blue-eyed look of challenge before turning away.

He was squatting, sitting on his heels, doing the mechanical chore swiftly. There was a round and solid nudge against the back of his left shoulder, so that he had to put a hand quickly against the shelf in front of him. He looked up and saw Mrs. Ennis smiling down at him, and the abrupt intrusion of reality into his thoughts of her made his face and ears feel hot. She had nudged him off balance with her knee.

As he stood up she said, smiling, "So you don't speak to your friends, huh, Jimmy?"

"Good morning, Mrs. Ennis." He had not expected to see her on a Tuesday morning in the supermarket.

"Oh, I don't mean *now!* I mean last night, like."

"Last night?" he asked blankly.

"I didn't know you lived on the beach, too, Jimmy. I took a long walk up the beach all by myself, and there you were on the screened porch of . . . one, two . . . yes, the third of those tiny little blue and gray cottages right beyond where the pink motel is. It was almost sunset, and you looked as if you were studying or something. You didn't even look up at all."

He said, "I took it when the summer rates started, and if I'm still here when the season starts again, I'll find a room over on the mainland again. If I didn't look up, I guess I didn't have much of a chance to say hello."

She gave him the sharing-secrets look and said, "You'll get another chance, Jimmy, yes you will." And she went off before he could answer. He went back to his work. When he rolled the cargo dolly back to get more cased stock he did not see her in the store. He kept wondering about her. He had seen her the first time when he had been filling in at check-out during a Saturday rush for a missing bag boy, three weeks ago, and had rolled her cart out to a blue convertible in the lot. He saw by the license it was a rental car. She had smiled at him, tipped him, asked him his name, and told him that she was Mrs. Ennis and she was on vacation, living on the beach not far away, and she thought the store was very nice. She had a wide pretty face and broad mouth and small tilted nose, and he guessed she would be maybe twenty-five or -six, but you could think she was eighteen from a little distance, or from the back. Somehow in the other times he had seen her and talked to her in those three weeks, it had become a curiously personal thing, in a way which made him uneasy. She seemed to be weighing and appraising him, and approving of him, but at the same time she did not seem to be making a pass. She seemed to want to be friends. He wondered how soon she would give him the chance to say hello . . .

He studied on the little screened porch again that July evening. The problems were all about store location, and his concentration was not good. He kept looking out at the wide slant of white beach beyond the sea oats, but he could not see her among all the people who were using the beach. He was working out one of the intricate formulae on development housing areas and anticipated gross when, over the gentle sound of the surf and the cries of gulls and children on the beach, Mrs. Ennis said, "So hello!"

She stood on the wooden step looking through the screen door at him, the sun behind her. She wore a blue-and-white checked beach jacket over a two-piece blue swimsuit, and she carried a white canvas beach bag. He got up quickly and accidentally kicked one leg of the old card table so that it collapsed and spilled his notebooks and papers across the narrow porch. She gave a little cry of concern and came in and helped him gather them up.

As they stood up together she said, "So you were studying, huh?"

"They call it the ATP. Administrative Trainee Program."

"Well, don't let me interrupt, Jimmy."

He put the study materials on a wicker chair and folded the card table, saying, "I'm better than a month ahead of schedule on the courses as it is. Enough for tonight anyway. Would you like a cold beer maybe, Mrs. Ennis?"

"Love it! Look, it's Julie. Okay?"

"Okay, Julie."

She sat on the ratty old glider. It banged against the wooden wall behind it. He took the course materials inside and when he came out with the beers she was smoking a cigarette, and she laughed and shook her head and said, "I keep thinking how I tipped you two bits that time. I should have known you weren't just a bag boy."

"How could you know?"

"Well, you're older, obviously. Twenty-two?"

"Three."

"And you speak well . . . and you didn't drop the cans into the bag on top of the tomatoes and the eggs."

"I appreciated getting the two bits, Mrs. . . . Julie."

He sat in the wicker chair half facing her, the beach and sunset at his left. There was a red light of sunset on her face. She looked sad for a moment. "It's lovely here, along this beach. I love it. You must think I'm a crazy or something, Jimmy. What it is, I'm lonely. I came down here alone . . . to do some thinking about . . . a lot of things. Where I'm staying, they're all real old people. You know? I can't go into a bar. Boy, that's asking for trouble! If I'm a pest, just tell me to finish my beer and go. Okay? I just liked you when I saw you. That's all. You just looked sort of . . . gentle. But I don't want to be a pest or anything."

"You're not. I'm glad you stopped by."

"Honest? So okay then, we're friends." She leaned forward and held her hand out and they shook hands. "Now tell me about the PTA."

They talked as the sun went down and until the last light in the west was gone, and the sky was full of stars. He told her about the chances he'd had to make more money right away when he got out of college, but how he decided to go with this chain because their program had the reputation of being tough and good and fair. This was the third outlet they had sent him to, the biggest yet, and the newest, and he did not know if he would go to another store after this, or be sent to one of the Regional Control offices. She made it easy to talk.

At last she said, "Jimmy, I have the feeling you won't take anything I say wrong. Here's what I'd really like to do, and if it doesn't hit you right, you just say so, huh? What I want to do is walk back down the beach to my place and do a real fast job of getting all glossed up and come back here in the car and we go over to Tampa to Ybor City and eat Spanish. On me. I got a dozen problems, but thank God money isn't one of them lately. What about it?"

"Well . . ."

"Please? Please, Jimmy?"

He drove her in the blue convertible across the Courtney Campbell Causeway, and they ate well at the Columbia Restaurant in Ybor City. He had never dated anyone quite like her. She had a tough, skeptical confidence, a talent for irony. She told him, saying she hadn't intended to tell him, that she was not exactly on vacation, that she had come down from Detroit to try to sort out her life a little. She said her marriage was sour. She said she and her husband had been convinced the difference in their ages wouldn't mean a thing. But after a while it created funny emotional problems being married to a man who could be your father. It made you act too elfin and girly-girl. It made the old man push himself to go disco when he'd rather put his feet up and watch the late show.

They got back to her place at two in the morning. He was going to walk back up the beach to his cottage. She had a cabaña by a big resort motel pool. All the cabañas were dark. He walked her to the door. She unlocked it, turned to him, pulled him gently into the air-conditioned coolness. The door clicked shut. She was sturdy and resilient and fragrant in his arms. The Spanish wine was singing in his head. She whispered, after the vivid kissings, that she hadn't meant it to be like this at all, honest. Over the top of her shiny head he saw star reflections in the black swimming pool, and he said that things happened the way they had to happen. It felt like a profound thought, as he bent to her mouth once more.

He was with her Wednesday evening and Thursday evening. He had to work Friday evening and Saturday evening. When they were together, and when they were not involved with the miracles of mutual discovery, she liked to have him talk about the work, the behind-the-scenes problems of purchasing, display, cash, pilferage, bad checks, personnel problems.

On Friday he worked from eleven in the morning until midnight, an hour after closing. He made several mistakes during the long day. D. A. Camden, the store manager, took him aside late on Friday afternoon and asked him if anything was the matter. Jim Garfield said there was something on his mind, yes. A personal problem. He would get it worked out. He said he was sorry about the goofs. Camden said that if Garfield could explain the personal problem, maybe he could leave any comment about today off the monthly ATP Rating Report. Garfield asked as a personal favor to let it go until Monday and then he would tell Camden what had been bothering him. Camden shrugged, looked unpleasant, and walked away.

On Saturday morning, having finally made up his mind, Jim Garfield asked for an hour off. Camden granted it gracelessly, and was uglier than necessary when the hour became an hour and a half. But the two men arrived in the late afternoon, and spent some time with Camden in his office, and only one of them left.

At midnight on Saturday, as always, Jim Garfield pulled the private door at the rear of the market shut, and checked to make certain it was locked while the man who was usually D. A. Camden, but on this night was not, stood holding the paper bag that would have contained twenty-two thousand in currency and twelve thousand in checks, but on this night contained only the green canvas deposit bag stuffed with several bundles of Soft-Line Paper Dinner Napkins 2/59¢.

When the two men with sheer nylon stockings over their faces appeared as if they had suddenly grown out of the asphalt, guns in hand, the waiting floodlights went on, freezing everyone like bugs on a kitchen floor, and a hugely amplified and official voice demanded instant surrender. But as Jim Garfield dropped flat, as directed, the man who was not D. A. Camden, but was of about the same size, had to shoot one of the pair, not fatally but seriously. The other one put his hands high. Tires screamed as the waiting car tried to catapult on out of the parking lot to safety, but there were shots from elsewhere, authoritative and heavy, and the sedan swerved, climbed a curbing, bent a steel light pole, and rolled over, throwing the driver out, and then rolling across the driver.

The shots brought the people. The police held them back. *Yes,* thought Jimmy Garfield, *I had to realize I was just not all that attractive, not to that kind of a woman. They could write it up as a study problem. A formula for suspicion of robbery. She wanted to keep me talking about the store, about every part of the routine, knowing I'd cover this part of it.*

D. A. Camden was beside Jimmy, plucking at his arm, saying, "Great job! Great! Marvelous!" Camden's voice was shaky and squeaky. *Yes indeed,* thought Jimmy. *I am a company man, through and through.*

But the bright floods were still on and he could not stop looking where the wounded car had rolled, and at what it had left. If you squinched your eyes a little, and didn't see the details, she still looked young. Like a girl home from college for vacation.

It helped the illusion if you thought of stars reflected in the blackness of an unlighted swimming pool, and the memory filled the squinched eyes with tears. He wished Camden would stop squeaking and go away.

Mama and the Bastard

by JTBBDBTJNPGMPSFODFNBZCFSSZ

It's easy to see the world through a child's eyes — if you happen to be a child. It's not so easy after you grow up and the years have gritted the cornea and dulled the retina and confused the brain. Here, though, we have the child's eyes, seeing everything all wrong, but allowing us to see it blindingly right.

When I was very young, San Francisco was a magical place of elegant ladies suited and gloved, their shoes of real leather smooth as silk, their perfume reaching you like the essence of a lovely dream as you passed them going into the St. Francis Hotel. I knew exactly what kind of handmade lingerie they wore beneath the finely tailored suits, because my Mama was one of them. I would walk beside her, trying to imitate her light, swift walk, the turn of her red-gold head as she looked at the shop windows. I longed desperately to look like Mama and knew I never would. Even at six, after living with Mama all those years, I was sure I had to be beautiful if ever men would love me the way they did my mother.

I was always properly dressed, too, as elegant ladies of means dressed their daughters. Gloves on my hands, a navy blue coat with gold buttons, a hand-smocked dress, white socks, patent leather slippers. But my hair wasn't red-gold; it was pale wheaten. Nor were my eyes green like Mama's, that shimmered like strange jewels; they were plain blue. Grownups always confirmed what I already knew by assuring me I would never be the beauty my mother was. She on her part would loyally object, insisting that my features were more delicate, my eyes larger, my nose more aristocratic, my bones finer. "Wait and see, she'll be the real beauty," she would say. "What you see in me is flair. I'm dramatic, an effect, a stage person who knows how to delude an audience."

After her objections I would slip into my bedroom, pose in front of my vanity mirror to check out my fine bones. Bones, for sure, chicken-thin arms, narrow shoulders, a face all eyes. Obviously Mama was lying so my feelings wouldn't be hurt, and I would remind myself not to cry until after I went to bed. I never cried in front of people. I cried a lot in bed.

Perhaps Mama cried in bed, too, because she never cried in front of people either. What she did was laugh when things were sad. Like the time Harry, my stepfather, slapped her backward, and she fell across the divan. Her mouth hit the carved wood armrest and bled all over the satin cover. We had to have it recovered.

I had heard my stepfather yelling at her, tiptoed down the hall, and reached the doorway just as he struck her. Blood spurted from her mouth, and I ran to Harry, sat on his foot, and bit his leg. He swore, grabbed my shoulder. Mama sprang off the divan like a cat, her voice low and furious, "You hurt her and I'll kill you! I swear I'll kill you!"

"The damn little bastard bit me!"

Mama turned dead white, the blood a vicious streak running across her chin. She picked me up, stalked from the room into my bedroom. "Wash your face and hands, and put on a better dress. We're going to the hotel. I'll send Dacey in to pack your things." Dacey was our maid. We had a cook, too, Lee Wang, but he only cooked; Dacey took care of us.

"Let's take Dacey with us this time," I begged. Dacey had

been with us ever since we married Harry, and I loved her.

I don't think Mama heard me because already she had begun to laugh, laugh and laugh, with her eyes miserable like her insides hurt. As she turned down the hall to her bedroom the laughter kept coming in gasps. Harry left the living room and followed her into the bedroom. "What's so damn funny?" he yelled.

"The fact I married you," Mama answered, the laughter still bubbling up with the words. "A six-foot-two man, head of a corporation, who calls a little child defending her mother a bastard." She stopped, struggling with the laughter, and when she spoke her voice had regained its fury. "You can call me names, I don't care, I may even deserve them. But not my daughter, no cruel names for her."

"She is, isn't she? It's only a fact."

The laughter came again, crackly, harsh. I slammed my door to muffle the sound, went to the mirror, skinned back my lips, showed my teeth, trying to see if I looked cruel. But I just looked silly. Dacey came in, said, "Why you wasting time making faces, we got to pack agin. Now git your britches running, help Dacey."

I guess that was either the third or fourth time Mama had Dacey pack my things.

It was exciting, living in the hotel, and if Harry hadn't hurt Mama, which brought us there, he could have called me a cruel bastard for all I cared. At the hotel we always had our breakfast sent up. The waiter would wheel in a table with heat in its innards to keep the food nice and hot. Roses on the table, shining metal covers over the plates. After breakfast, if it wasn't a school day, Mama and I would explore Chinatown, or go out to the Japanese Tea Garden and Stow Lake in Golden Gate Park, or to the zoo by the beach. Afternoons we might go to a movie or just go shopping. Of course we could do all those things when we lived with Harry, but at the hotel when Mama and I were alone it became special, like a party.

It added to the party effect when the presents began to arrive, after we had been at the hotel for a couple of weeks or so. Beautiful presents, lots of them, from Harry, as he tried to get Mama to make up with him. At first, bouquets for Mama, candy for me. As the days went by, the presents became more and more exciting. After he made Mama's lip bleed we stayed in the hotel almost a month, and I ended up with a doll exactly my size that could walk and talk, and Mama got her sable coat.

Harry apologized to me, too. "Cissy, I'm sorry I called you that bad word. Forget it, will you, kid?"

I nodded yes, but little kids never forget anything they're asked to forget.

When we were home again I asked Dacey what bastard meant but all she said was, "Poor baby, don't you never use that word again, hear?" So she was no help. But on account of having no brothers or sisters to distract me, I had learned to read when I was four and knew what a dictionary was for, so I looked it up. "A person born of parents not married to each other; anything spurious, inferior, or varying from standard; a person regarded with contempt, hatred, pity, resentment, or sometimes with playful affection."

Which was Harry about me? Not playful affection, for sure. Actually Harry wasn't anything about me. It was just that he was everything about Mama.

So was Mr. Francini, who owned a chain of restaurants up and down California. With my own ears I heard him tell Mama she was the most beautiful woman in San Francisco, which, he said twice, made her the most beautiful woman in the world. He told Mama that while we were eating lunch in his downtown restaurant and he stopped being the boss and ate with us. Mama said, "Sh-h-h!" So I kept listening, even though I was entranced with the scrumptious charlotte russe Mr. Francini ordered for me.

After lunch he drove us home. Mama told me to run on inside with Dacey, then she and Mr. Francini drove away.

I never told Harry about the lunch or that Mr. Francini thought Mama was the most beautiful woman in the world and he was crazy about her. But somebody did — maybe one of his friends ate lunch there that day, too. Because it was that night when Harry made Mama's mouth bleed.

Right after I looked up bastard in the dictionary I asked Mama, "Is Mr. Francini my father and you didn't marry him?"

She was making up her face with mascara on one eye and not yet on the other. She whirled around from the mirror, and it made me laugh because with one side dark eyelashes and the other light ones she looked like she was winking at me. "Oh God, Cissy, you're going to be like your crazy mother, laugh when you ought to cry. No, Mr. Francini is not your father. Harry is your father now."

"No, he isn't. I'm a bastard, and you're married to Harry, so he can't be my father."

"Oh no, oh no!" Softly, almost like she was praying. "I forgot you can read."

"Does Harry hate me?"

"Certainly not. He just —" Her voice dropped again. "If he hates anyone, he hates me."

That wasn't true. Harry was crazy about Mama, so crazy about her after our last trip to the hotel, that he couldn't bear to have her out of his sight. So when he had to go to New York on business he insisted she go with him. So she did.

A couple of days after they were gone Dacey answered a telephone call and said, kind of snappy, "No sir, she ain't here. No sir, I don't know where she is." And hung up.

"You do too know," I said. "Who was that?"

"Didn't give no name. Don't trust nobody don't give no name. Besides, he got no business calling your Mama."

But the telephone rang again on another day when Dacey was out buying things for Lee Wang, and I answered. "Is Mrs. Frankl in?" a deep soft voice asked. It sounded exactly like Mr. Francini's eyes looked, dark and velvety.

"This is Cecily. Mama's at the Waldorf Hotel in New York." I added, "Thank you for the charlotte russe, Mr. Francini. It was the first time I ever ate one."

"Well, Cecily, you must have another one sometime . . . By the way, you needn't tell anyone I called."

"I won't. Because if I do, Harry might knock my mother down again."

He gave a quick hard breath like all of a sudden he felt bad some place. So I said, "But her mouth's all right now."

"Good-bye, Cecily. Don't forget our secret." And he hung up.

When Mama returned, she acted so happy to be back in San Francisco again. And why not? The city was so beautiful, especially when you saw it from our apartment up on top of Nob Hill. The Bay below us, the white island of Alcatraz seeming to float on it. Ships heading out to sea, ferries splashing water on their way to Sausalito. Cable cars clanging down the steep hill toward Chinatown. The late afternoon fog rolling in from the sea, softening outlines of buildings and streets, the sea smell making the heart leap. It was so beautiful then, San Francisco. Still beautiful, but now like a lady who has fallen into the gutter too many times, grown dirty-mouthed and hollow cheeked. Oh well —

San Francisco and my mother were made for each other. You should have seen her when she and Harry went to the opera, wearing my favorite dress, a floating sea-green chiffon, her skin like cream against it, sable coat slipped back to show smooth shoulders, red-gold hair shining above her laughing face. Harry dark and heavy beside her, an athlete gone thick in the middle, forming a background for her.

The newspapers even wrote about her. "Looky here, your Mama in today's paper," Dacey told me, her finger pointing at the lines. "The gorgeous Mrs. Harold Frankl as usual was surrounded by a bevy — what's a bevy, Cissy, no, not now, you gonna ruin your eyes with that dictionary — a bevy of admirers, regaling — might look up that too while you're at it — us raw westerners with N'Yawk's latest. How come she ain't told us much 'bout N'Yawk?"

She did, though, when we were alone. The shows, shops, dinners, lunches. "Such fun, Baby, I wish you could have been along. Harry always tied up with some business deal, and I hate being alone."

"I talked to Mr. Francini on the phone while you were gone."

"Did you, Cissy?" Her light, casual voice tossed the whole thing away as not important. Somehow the way she looked and the tone of her voice told me she already knew that. How? Not from Dacey or Lee Wang. I hadn't told them. So who did? Mr. Francini, that's who.

"I told him you were in New York. At the Waldorf. Did Mr. Francini go to New York too? Because you were lonesome?"

"Cissy, why don't we go to the zoo this afternoon? We haven't been anywhere since I came home. Run get your heaviest sweater — it's chilly."

She picked up the telephone as I left her room, and she was still talking on it when I came back. She saw me, said quickly, "All right, then. A little later," and hung up.

At the zoo, as I always did, I headed immediately for my favorite animal, the chimpanzee. He was so funny the way he hated people, made faces at them, threw food through the cage bars. Served us all right; we were always laughing at him, and even if he hated me I loved him. Sure enough he was at his best today, squealing, jumping up and down with his back turned on the crowd. Then he whirled and spat right in the face of a big boy who was making the most noise. I shrieked with delight, turned to see if Mama was enjoying it too. But she wasn't looking at me. She was smiling at Mr. Francini, who was standing close beside her.

It should have been a lovely afternoon. Rides on the merry-go-round. Popcorn. Soda pop. Giraffes, lions, elephants, zebras, everything. Afterward a drive along the beach, across Golden Gate Bridge into Sausalito, up the hill to Mr. Francini's house, where Luis, his man servant, brought me a lemonade. Then Mr. Francini asked Luis to show me the tropical fish and the cockatoo and the games in his game room. I grew tired of that after a while, dropped Luis's hand and ran back into the living room.

They didn't see me at first. Because Mr. Francini was kissing Mama and she was kissing back. They didn't notice me until I was right beside them. "Maybe Harry will hit you again," I said.

They moved apart quickly. Mama tried to laugh, said nervously, "Mr. Francini is an old friend, Cissy, and I was just telling him how nice he's been to us this afternoon. So unless you tell Harry, neither will I."

"I never tell Harry anything." I swallowed hard to keep my stomach in place. "I think I want to go home."

They were very quiet as Mr. Francini drove us back to San Francisco. He stopped the car around the corner from our apartment; Mama didn't say anything to him, just waved good-bye. As we turned the corner she started laughing so hard she had to cover her mouth. Jim, our doorman, said, "Seems like you ladies had a mighty good time today."

That made Mama laugh more than ever. My stomach tickled in sympathy, and even though I didn't feel funny I laughed with her. When we were in the living room she said, "You funny, funny baby! Only you're not the baby. You're a grown-up lady in disguise, and I'm the baby . . . oh Cissy, Cissy, what am I to do with a person like me?"

"Are you sure Mr. Francini's not my father?"

The laughter stuck in her throat, and her eyes became frightened as though she had seen something scary. "I'm sure. That's the last thing — go get your clothes off, Cissy, then I'll help you with your bath."

"Who is my father?"

Just that one time I saw my mother almost cry. She pinched her lips together, and her green eyes shimmered through water that refused to fall. After a moment she asked, "Aren't I enough? Won't just I do?"

I shoved my face against her skirt, said, muffled, "I don't want any father. Not ever, ever."

She hugged me, then impulsively caught my hands, whirled me in a crazy dance, chanting in a choked voice, then loud and

clear, "Cissy and Mama, forever and ever, forever and ever!"
Over and over.

Harry appeared in the doorway, home from the office, demanding, "Why all the noise? Listen, I've got a headache.
You're making that kid as crazy as you are." And the fun was
over.

Harry nagged at dinner, like he did most nights except those
right after we had stayed in the hotel. I suppose he was tired,
doing all that thinking about making money. Maybe that was
why Mama never seemed tired, she never thought about
money. Harry told her that often enough.

He nagged and Mama laughed. He nagged more and Mama
laughed louder, as though she wanted to blot out his voice. Finally he stood up and threw his napkin at her, which only
made her laugh more. It didn't hurt her so I didn't try to bite
him. Instead, I threw up in my plate. Harry swore and
stomped out of the dining room.

Truth was, it wasn't Harry who upset me. I'd had trouble
with my stomach ever since I saw Mr. Francini kissing
Mama.

Soon everything became cozy and secure, with Mama tucking
me in bed, lying beside me, humming and singing in her sweet,
husky voice. The way she sang always made me feel like a
stringed instrument that she strummed and the music came out
of me. I didn't tell you? Before I was born and even after
Mama was a nightclub singer. In big famous clubs in New
York, Chicago, Lake Tahoe, lots of places. It was all in her
clipping book she gave to me when Harry threatened to burn
it. I kept it hidden in my closet.

That night, I awakened suddenly. Sat up in bed, listening to
loud, uneven voices coming from Mama's and Harry's bedroom. I scooted out of bed, stumbled through the dark to the
long inner hallway, too confused to find the light switch. Cracks
of light outlined their door. I hurried to it, heart thumping,
and eased it open. Mama and Harry were rolling on the white
carpet, her hands tangled in his thick, black hair, one of his

hands grasping her neck. On the floor just beyond reach of his other hand lay Lee Wang's slim-bladed boning knife, shining and lethal. They were between me and the knife, and I was afraid to step over them. Dacey and Lee Wang didn't stay with us at night. There was no one to help me.

I ran back down the hall, its blackness snatching at me, to the window seat at the hall's end. I climbed on the seat, tugged open the tall window, shrilled desperately, "Help! Police! Harry's killing Mama! Help! Police!" A cable car rattled past, cars zoomed down the steep hill, a strolling man looked up curiously, moved on. "Help! Help!" I cried, shivering, helpless in a world too big for me.

Abruptly Harry and Mama were behind me, Mama saying, "No, no, Baby, Mama's all right, we were playing! Only playing."

She picked me up, carried me to bed, Harry following. They stood above me, not touching each other, looking at me. It made my eyes hurt to look back, so I shut them. After a while they turned off the light and left.

I didn't go to sleep, but listened to the soft shush-shush of their slippers going down the hall to their room. Listened to hear if the fight renewed. Soon there was another shush-shush, a single pair of slippers. The swinging door of the kitchen creaked, a silence, then the creak again and the shush-shush of the return trip. Harry taking back Le Wang's knife. At last I slept.

For a while after that scary night Mama and Harry were nice to each other. They even went up to Lake Tahoe for a week, for a second honeymoon, Harry said. Up there they ran into some of Mama's old friends who were entertaining at one of the clubs and they pulled Mama up to the microphone and made her sing for old times' sake. Her eyes sparkled when she told me that. "Oh, it was so good, Cissy! Everyone applauding, applauding. I miss singing and the night crowds. I shouldn't but I do. When I sing I feel I'm gathering everyone in my arms, cuddling them, loving them."

"More than just me?"

She squeezed me, said, "No one more than you."

"Not even my father?"

Her face crumpled. Just suddenly. All crumpled. Then it smoothed and she grabbed my hands, wheedling, "Sing with me, Cissy, let's put on a sister act! Pretend we're stars with a big, big audience!"

But I didn't feel like dancing and pulled away. "Did you sing for my father?"

"Yes." Softly adding, "Many times."

"Did he applaud you?"

"Yes."

"Which did my father look like, Harry or Mr. Francini?"

She caught my shoulders, pushed me before her long mirror, held my face between her hands as we looked into it. "There! Like the little girl in the mirror."

Poor father! Pale hair with bangs shadowing blue eyes too big for my face. Speculative eyes, their expression something like Dacey's as she watched butcher-shop scales.

"Your father was beautiful," she said.. "Not handsome, like Mr. Francini. Or big and powerful like Harry. Just beautiful. Strong too, but the strength was inside, not in muscles. Deep blue eyes that knew everything about you, and loved you for it. A quiet, smiling man who drew noisy troubled people to him. Like a magnet. Like that game of yours, Cissy, the one with steel balls that roll to the magnet."

"I'm not strong."

"Yes, you are. With the same kind of strength. Inside of you. Haven't you been taking care of me all your life?"

She said "was beautiful," so I guessed my father was dead, and I was sorry he could never have Mama the way I did. That day I sort of began to love my father.

After the Lake Tahoe trip Mama was more restless. Almost every day when I came home from school she was out someplace. Dacey would say, "Your Mama gone shopping," or "Your Mama ain't back from lunch, she eating out a lot these

days" — your Mama gone here, your Mama gone there. She
never came home before late afternoon, just before Harry did,
and when she did she would be smiling and sparkly, her green
eyes secretive like she knew something wonderful she wouldn't
tell anyone. I thought about that a lot.

One afternoon when I came home from school and Mama
was gone I told Dacey I was going to play with a friend who
lived in the apartment house next door. Instead, I went around
the corner where Mr. Francini had let Mama and me out after
we were in Sausalito and stood behind a column in a doorway.
The fog came rolling in early, wiped out the sun, and its cold
numbed my fingers. Still I waited, shivering, peering through
the mist at the cars that seemed to float by.

At last Mr. Francini's car slid through the gray veil and
stopped at the curb. Mama got out. Mr. Francini poked his
head through the car's window and blew her a kiss. She bub-
bled with laughter, waved, ran around the corner. After a little
while I went home, too.

"You're like ice!" Mama exclaimed as she kissed me. "You
shouldn't play outdoors in this awful fog. If it hadn't been so
cold I would have waited for you, taken you to the Park. Instead I went by myself to a nice warm theater. A grown-up
movie, you wouldn't have liked it."

What do you do when you're only seven going on eight and
your mother lies to you? Except get scared about her. I kept
thinking *Harry will get Lee Wang's knife again, this time he'll
STICK IT IN HER and she'll be dead like my father.*

I kept on thinking that and finally decided I had to do something to keep her from seeing Mr. Francini anymore. It would
do no good to talk to Mama about it; she already knew what
might happen. And Harry must not know. So who did that
leave but Mr. Francini? I decided to talk to him about it.

It worked out fine. My school had a teachers' meeting, sent a
note home that I would be let out at noon, a note that I didn't
show my mother. Instead, on the afternoon of the meeting I
took the cable car down to Mr. Francini's restaurant.

A tall man with a sniffy nose opened the restaurant door for me and slid his eyes up and down me. "Are you looking for someone miss?"

"Yes, please. Mr. Francini."

"Are you a member of his family?"

"He's kind of a friend. Once he gave me a charlotte russe."

He stared hard at me. I didn't have on gloves, or a hat, or a silk dress like before when Mama brought me to the restaurant. Only a navy blue school dress with chalk on its front and a sweater.

"I'm afraid Mr. Francini is very busy."

I swallowed hard but didn't move when he held open the door. "I want to see Mr. Francini." I set my teeth to keep my chin steady.

"Wait here," he finally said and went inside toward the tables.

Suddenly my mother was in the entrance salon, beautiful and perfumey. "Cissy, whatever is the matter? Are you sick? Why didn't you go home to Dacey? How did you know where to find me?"

Mr. Francini was behind her saying, "Why hello, Cissy, come in and have lunch with us. How about another charlotte russe?"

"Tony, she's sick, I'll have to take her home."

"No, I'm not," I said.

"Then why ever —"

"I'm lonesome. Maybe I'm hungry, too."

Mama laughed, said wasn't that adorable, come on in, Baby. So I had another charlotte russe. But I didn't get to tell Mr. Francini to leave my mother alone.

I wish I had been able to tell him.

About a week later Harry knocked down Mr. Francini and blacked Mama's eye. She was at the restaurant again having lunch with Mr. Francini. Harry came in, but not for lunch. He walked straight to their table, hit Mr. Francini so hard he fell off his chair, blacked Mama's eye, and dragged her out. Next day it was in the newspaper in a special column I found Dacey reading. She slapped the paper shut and said, "Go along, you don't want to read this truk, you too young to read papers," folded the paper and put it in the trash. As soon as she left the kitchen I sneaked the paper to my room and read: "What prominent businessman knocked out what other prominent businessman over what prominent and gorgeous lady in what prominent eatery yesterday? 'Tis rumored the lady now has a fascinating pair of eyes, one an exotic green and the other a gloomy black. Tsch, tsch!"

Harry came storming home from the office in midmorning, yelling he would sue the paper and black both eyes of the columnist. But he hushed that fast because Mama was already packing to go to the hotel.

Orchids for Mama, rosebuds for me sent up by the management as a welcome-back gift. No presents from Harry yet; that took a while. And Mama's dark glasses to hide her black eye made her look like a movie star and everyone turned to look at us as we went in and out of the lobby. Fun, lots of fun, just Mama and me.

But there was a special afternoon that changed all that.

I came into the hotel after school, weaving between the grown-ups in the big lobby, the ladies in furs and beautiful hats, the men groomed and tailored. As usual I turned and went up shallow steps to the higher-level lobby where sometimes Mama waited for me.

She was there, a strange man beside her, teapot and cups on a low table in front of them. Mama saw me, called, "Hi, Cissy!" She didn't motion me to her as she usually did, but I went to her anyway. She said, "Mr. Hughes, this is my daughter, Cecily. Cissy, Mr. Hughes is my lawyer, and we're talking important business. So why don't you go up to our room and have room service bring something nice to drink?"

This was disappointing because I would rather have had something nice in the lobby and watch the people. I ambled away slowly and had just reached the steps when there were quick footsteps behind me and Mama's hand gripped my shoulder. I looked up, wondering what was the matter, but she didn't see me. She was staring at a man walking slowly across the main lobby toward the reception desk, a bellman beside him with cases. The man moved his head as though something had touched his cheek, hesitated, turned and looked full at her. He was a plain man, older and shorter than Harry, not slim and handsome like Mr. Francini. That is, he was plain until he smiled, his blue eyes lighting up as though he couldn't believe what he saw. He came up to Mama, took her hands in his, drew her close, with me caught between them, said, "Little Francie! I can't believe it's you."

She didn't answer and they just stood there staring and staring at each other. It was hot trapped between them so I scooted to one side, tipped back my head to look at them. He did have the nicest smile, a comforting smile, as though if you had troubles he would be the right person to help you through them.

Finally he let Mama's hands go, said, "All these years of not seeing you. How many has it been? It seems forever."

"Almost eight," Mama said.

"Are you — have you been all right?"

"Fine, Arne. Just fine."

"I've dreamed this might happen. Again and again. But I never expected it would. It was so sudden, when you left Reno, not even saying good-bye. I heard you went to New York."

"I did. My husband — I met my husband in New York, but after we married he brought me here. His business is here."

He nodded, as though shaking down thoughts into their proper place. He looked down at me, said, "And you have a little girl. How do you do, young lady?" I leaned bashfully against Mama. She said, "This is Cecily."

Mr. Arne put his hand gently under my chin, raised it so we could look straight at each other. "How old are you, Cecily?"

I opened my mouth to say seven going on eight, but Mama said quickly, "Five!" She caught my shoulder and gave it a hard squeeze.

"She's tall for her age. Is her father tall?"

"Yes. Very tall."

Harry was. But Harry wasn't my father.

Mr. Arne looked a little uncomfortable. "Francie, I wish it would be possible for you and your husband and daughter to have dinner with my wife and me tonight. She's here already, came down a few days early to shop. But we're here to attend our son's graduation from the university and he's arranged a special party for tonight. Then we're leaving right after the graduation."

"Oh, we couldn't anyway," Mama said, her voice tight and strange. "We have something on tonight too. What a pity."

Mr. Arne kept patting my head as he looked at Mama, a long, long time. "Yes," he finally said. "It's a pity. A great pity." Then he turned away quickly and like Mama had done, without even saying good-bye.

Mama told me, "Wait here," and went back to Mr. Hughes. They talked a few minutes, Mr. Hughes shrugged, shook Mama's hand, and left through the lobby. Mama watched until he had gone, then led me down to the street and asked the doorman to call a taxi.

"Where are we going, Mama?"

"Back to Harry."

"But he hasn't had time to send presents. You always wait for presents."

"Never mind presents."

"My teddy bear and clothes are in our room."

"I'll send Dacey for them."

The taxi came and we climbed in. "Why did you tell Mr. Arne I was only five? I'm seven going on eight."

She looked out the taxi window as though fascinated by the Powell Street cable car. She didn't care about cable cars — she saw cable cars every day. She just didn't want to look at me.

"Did you forget?"

She didn't answer.

When we were almost home I said, "Please don't let Harry get Lee Wang's knife again. I'm scared about the knife."

The taxi stopped at our apartment house. Mama paid the fare, we got out, and the taxi drove away.

"Please, Mama, hide Lee Wang's knife so Harry can't find it."

She looked up at the sky like she was talking to the clouds. "That's very funny. Very, very funny. Because Harry wasn't the one who took the knife."

Then she began to laugh and laugh as we went inside and took the elevator back to Harry.

It didn't sound funny to me.

Biographical Notes

JOHN BALL was born in Schenectady, New York, but grew up in Milwaukee, Wisconsin. He graduated from Carrol College, where he later received his doctorate. He is a pilot of long experience and a bona fide black belt in the demanding martial art, Aikido. He has a strong interest in the Orient, about which he has written several books. His black detective, Virgil Tibbs of the Pasadena (California) Police Department, is known throughout the world. He is a full-time professional novelist, with some 25 successful books to his credit. He lives with his author-wife Nan Hamilton in Encino, California.

ROBERT BLOCH began his professional writing career at the age of 17. Over the years, he has published 47 books, over 400 short stories and articles, in addition to radio scripts, teleplays, and screenplays. His work includes fantasy, science fiction, and mystery-suspense. Bloch is a past president of the Mystery Writers of America, and he was guest of honor at the first Anthony Boucher Mystery Convention; and the first French Festival of Mystery Films and Fiction at Reims.

DOROTHY SALISBURY DAVIS was born in Chicago and educated at Barat College in Lake Forest, Illinois. She is a past president of the Mystery Writers of America, a member of the

Authors League, and the Writers Guild of America. Her pub-
lished works include *A Death in the Life, The Little Brothers, Shock
Wave, God Speed the Night,* and *A Gentleman Called.* She lives in
Palisades, New York.

ROSEMARY GATENBY grew up in Indiana, graduated from
Wellesley College, studied playwriting at Columbia University,
and went briefly to law school. Her first suspense novel was *Evil
Is as Evil Does,* published in 1967. Her books have been set in
the United States (New York, Connecticut, Pennsylvania, Indiana, the Great Lakes region, Tennessee, and Texas), Mexico,
and Canada. She writes "how to" articles for *The Writer.* Her
most recent novels are *The Nightmare Chrysalis, Whisper of Evil,*
and *The Third Identity.* She lives on a country hilltop in Connecticut with her husband, a dog, and three cats.

MICHAEL GILBERT, who lives in Kent, England, is a partner
with the London firm of Trower Still & Keeling Solicitors. He
was educated at Blundell's School and London University,
earning his Ll.B. in 1937. He served during World War II in
North Africa and Italy and joined Trower Still & Keeling in
1947. He was a founder of the Crime Writers Association and
is a member of the Mystery Writers of America. His novels
include *The Night of the Twelfth, The Etruscan Net, Be Shot for Six-
pence,* and *The Ninety-Second Tiger.* He also writes plays, radio
and TV scripts, and edited *Crime in Good Company.*

ELIZABETH GRESHAM was born in Plainfield, New Jersey,
and was graduated from Vassar College. Until her marriage to
a Virginian, she was connected with the theater as an actress,
director, and teacher. She was one of the University Players,
working with such people as Henry Fonda, Josh Logan, and
Mildred Natwick, and played the lead in the group's first play.
She now lives in Charlottesville, Virginia, dividing her time between writing and the theater. Her books include *Puzzle in
Patchwork, Puzzle in Pewter,* and *Puzzle in Paisley.*

JOE L. HENSLEY, an attorney, is now Judge of the Fifth Judicial Circuit of the State of Indiana. Hensley was educated at Indiana University and is a veteran of World War II and the Korean War. His novels include *Rivertown Risk, Poison Summer, The Color of Hate,* and *Song of Corpus Juris.* He lives in Madison, Indiana, is married, and has one son, who is studying law.

EDWARD D. HOCH won the Edgar Grand Master Award from the Mystery Writers of America for his story "The Oblong Room" in 1968. He's published nearly 500 stories and novelettes, including stories in every issue of *Ellery Queen Mystery Magazine* since May 1973. His stories have been collected in half a dozen books, he's edited several anthologies, and is the author of several novels, including *The Shattered Raven.* He was born in Rochester, New York, and educated at the University of Rochester. He served in the army from 1950 to 1952, and worked for a library, a publisher, and an advertising agency before becoming a full-time writer. He is a member of the Mystery Writers of America, the Authors League, and Science Fiction Writers of America.

R. A. LAFFERTY published his first mystery story in *Ellery Queen Mystery Magazine,* and it was selected as a Hubin "best of the year." A retired electrical engineer, he was born in Iowa and now lives in Tulsa, Oklahoma. While most of his publications are in the science fiction and fantasy fields (*Past Master, Fourth Mansions, The Reefs of Earth,* and *The Devil Is Dead*), he also writes historical fiction (*The Fall of Rome, The Flame Is Green,* and the acclaimed *Okla Hannali*).

JOHN D. MACDONALD divides his time between Piseco, New York, and Sarasota, Florida; many of his works have a Florida setting. He was born in Sharon, Pennsylvania, attended the University of Pennsylvania, and holds degrees from Syracuse University (B.S.) and Harvard University (M.B.A.). He is married and the father of a son. The author of more than 500 pieces of fiction, he is the recipient of the Benjamin Franklin award for the best American short story of 1955, the Pioneer Medal from Syracuse University in 1971, and the "Edgar" from the Mystery Writers of America in 1972. His works include the wonderful Travis McGee series, the award-winning *A Key to the Suite,* and, recently, *Condominium.*

FLORENCE MAYBERRY is an American, born in Missouri, who has resided in Israel with her husband since 1973. She serves there as a member of the Baha'i International Teaching Centre in Haifa. She has been writing since childhood and recalls that her first story was a mystery involving secret passages filled with dastardly characters; the story was submitted to her sixth grade teacher. Her work has been published in Japan, Holland, France, and England, as well as in the United States; and she is a frequent contributor to *Ellery Queen Mystery Magazine.* Some of her short stories have been scripted for radio production in South Africa. She has also published poetry and a children's book. She is the mother of a grown son, a businessman in California.

PATRICIA MOYES, who was born in Ireland and raised in England, got her start writing while serving in the WAAF during World War II; she was assigned as technical advisor to Peter Ustinov on the film *School for Secrets.* The association with Ustinov continued for eight years, and then Ms. Moyes took a job writing for *Vogue,* where she eventually became assistant editor. Her first mystery, *Dead Men Don't Ski,* was begun when she injured her foot on a skiing vacation. Her other books include *Season of Snows and Sins, Murder Fantastical,* and *Falling Star.* She also translated Jean Anouilh's *Leocadia,* which was produced on Broadway as *Time Remembered,* with Helen Hayes, Richard Burton, and Susan Strasberg. She lives in the Virgin Islands with her husband and an assortment of cats.

RACHEL COSGROVE PAYES was born in Maryland, graduated from West Virginia Wesleyan College, and now lives in Shrub Oak, New York, with her husband and two children. She published her first book in 1951 (a sequel to L. Frank Baum's *The Wizard of Oz*) and since has published 30 novels, seven of them mysteries, six science-fiction mysteries, and the remainder romance novels. Her most recent publications are historical romances: *Moment of Desire* and *The Coach to Hell.*

BILL PRONZINI made his first professional short-story sale in 1966 and has been a full-time freelance writer since 1969. He has published 18 suspense novels (three in collaboration with Barry N. Malzberg, and one in collaboration with Collin Wilcox), and more than 200 short stories and articles. He has also edited or co-edited eight anthologies of mystery, fantasy, and science fiction, including two for the Mystery Writers of America. His work has been translated into a dozen languages and has appeared in 22 countries throughout the world.

RUTH RENDELL, a resident of London, is the author of 18 mystery/psychological suspense novels and many short stories. Her novels include *A Sleeping Life, A Judgement in Stone, Shake Hands Forever,* and *A Demon in My View,* which was awarded the Gold Dagger Award by the British Crime Writers Association. Her newest novel, *Make Death Love Me,* was published in 1979.

LAWRENCE TREAT is a graduate of Dartmouth College and Columbia Law School, though he is not a practicing lawyer and never was. He writes novels, short stories, and detective-puzzle books (*Bringing Sherlock Home*). An innovator of the police procedural school, he twice has won "Edgars": in 1965 for a short story, and in 1978 for the *Mystery Writer's Handbook.* A founder and former president of Mystery Writers of America, he is now a director of that organization. He lives on Martha's Vineyard.

JANWILLEM VAN DE WETERING was born in Rotterdam, the son of a businessman. He lived through the German bombing of the city and, at 19, began his travels. He lived for six years in Africa, a year and a half in England, two and a half years in Japan (where he studied Zen Buddhism), then went to South America where he became a successful businessman. He returned to the Netherlands after a stopover in Australia, and joined the police in his spare time, serving as a constable in Amsterdam. His books include *Outsider in Amsterdam, The Blond Baboon, Death of a Hawker,* and *The Maine Massacre.* He now lives in Maine.

To Break the Code

At the beginning of each story, the name of its author appears in a 26-letter code (there are 26 letters in each cipher to prevent instant identification of the name from the number of letters). The code is a simple substitution code; each letter in the code stands for the letter which immediately precedes it in the alphabet (with "a" being substituted for "z"):

standard:

a b c d e f g h i j k l m n o p q r s t u v w x y z

code:

b c d e f g h i j k l m n o p q r s t u v w x y z a

To break the code, begin with the last letter of each cipher and work backward until you have the name of one of the authors in the book. The remaining letters — repeated as necessary to produce 26 letters — will spell out one of the following: "Isaac Asimov," "Alice Laurance," "Asimov, Isaac," or "Laurance, Alice."